COSMINA

CALISTA
GRAYLOCK

"We can't be monsters, Nix. We're the good guys."

Five years before the events of *Cantamen*, Lilac Frazier is convicted of a crime she did not commit. Before she reaches the prison, she's taken by a band of criminals who tell her the reason for her fate: the Council wants to eliminate all witches with dark affinities. They offer protection, and a home, in exchange for her Magic and the darkness within it. With no other options, she's plunged into a new world of codenames, fighting, spying, broken families, and ruined futures. Revolutions are hard-won, and the lines between right and wrong, friend and foe, and even leader and lover soon blur. Someone else decided her name should go down in Cantamen's history, but she's going to make sure she earns more than a mention.

Dedication

This book is for everyone who simply cannot sit back and let the world stay like it is.

Acknowledgments

Thank you to Liz for beta reading for me.

Gracia, I used your name like you asked. I did not tear your character limb from limb, though you offered, but I can't promise she had a good time, either. I hope you enjoy the story!

Author's Note

Cantamen will be a long series with a lot of worldbuilding. For this reason, I've included images that I hope will be helpful and informative in the book.

Though this book is cohesive and complete without them, there are optional, canonical, adult-themed scenes available at CalistaGraylock.com. You can also find more helpful graphics and stay updated on the series.

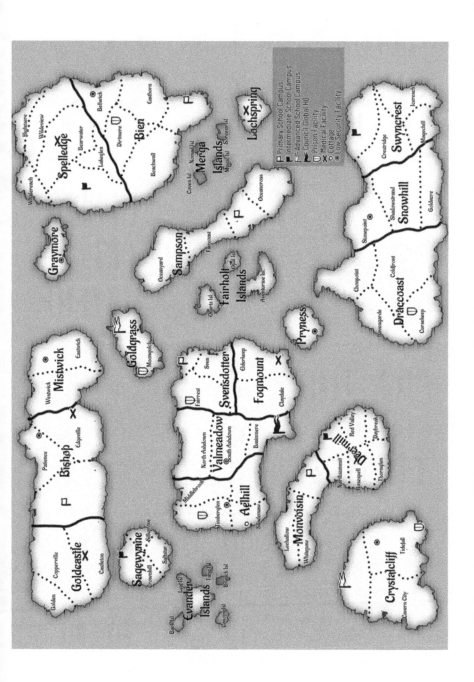

CANIS	1
GEMMA	2
LUNA	3

4	GLADIO
5	DRACO
6	PAPILIO

MURAENA	7
ARMA	8
MILITUS	9

10	FLORA
11	ARBORA
12	AVEM

If the Stories Are True

Luna 315

The Trialmaster was hideous, both in appearance and character.

Until today, Cosmina hadn't believed the stories. Witches weren't corrupt like humans. Multiple people had told her their experiences of false convictions with fabricated evidence, and still she had doubted. She thought they must have done something. They must be downplaying their guilt. The Council was trustworthy.

If the stories were true, what did that mean for the world?

But now it was her, and she finally understood, too late.

Cosmina's legs trembled, but she kept her face blank as the Trialmaster rose to his feet. She resisted the urge to wipe her clammy hands, holding them at her sides, determined to betray no weakness. She refused to give them the satisfaction of seeing her fear.

Though she already knew the verdict, the Trialmaster's words, spoken through a snaggletooth and made more offensive by his bulbous red nose, felt like a slap in the face.

Convicted. Branded. Variant Idealist.

The Hearing Center Chamber, all velvety scarlet chairs, patterned carpet, and gold accents, must have held a dozen people, but Cosmina knew only three of them. They had always had such high hopes for her, and now she had been reduced to this. Her parents believed the verdict and had told her so. Her father's words still rang in her ears: No matter what the court determines, you will not be welcome back in this home, and we will not visit you in prison.

If the stories were true, they would never have the chance anyway.

A guard gestured for Cosmina to turn. Knowing it would be her last, she stole a look at her family. Her parents looked away. They hadn't brought Daisy after all. Cosmina couldn't remember the last time she'd seen her sister. There had been nothing memorable to note; no reason to commit the details to memory. What had been their last words to one another? Did Daisy agree with their parents? Did her sister hate her?

Wrists and ankles bound with cuffs designed to inhibit Magic, Cosmina was escorted down a long, empty hallway to an armored van and a future wasted in prison.

If the stories were true, her future would be worse than wasted.

A pair of wide brown eyes watched from a nearby tree as a black van pulled up to the brick building's side door. The back swung open, releasing three witches in black suits. None were muscular or armed, but the watcher knew these were some of the toughest guards the Witching Council had to offer. They always were, for these cases.

Unaware of their observer, the guards positioned themselves around the van and waited. Like the watcher, who called herself Rinna, they already knew Cosmina would be convicted.

Unlike Rinna, they didn't expect any issues today.

Her muscles tensed as the Hearing Center doors opened and a head of wild blonde curls emerged, flanked by more guards. They handed her off before returning to the building.

Rinna counted the seconds. For one awful moment, she thought they might have to go to Plan B. And then the anticipated cloud of smoke erupted around the van and guards, the bomb whistling as the smoke escaped. Their shouts made her smile.

Time to go.

Rinna swung down from the tree and sprinted the short distance. Her eyes burned with the combination of the smoke and her own energy-seeking vision, allowing her to see through it.

As expected, the guards were quick. They needed a mere moment for comprehension before tightening their grip on their prisoner. Rinna's eyes recognized Magic-binding cuffs and her heart sank. She'd forgotten to account for that.

Cosmina recognized her chance and fought against the guards dragging her to the van, flailing and twisting in their hold. The engine revved, the driver ready to go the moment she was contained.

"Nix!" Rinna shouted, using the code name he'd picked for himself many missions ago. "Cuffs!"

"Van!" he called back.

She should've known he was three steps ahead of her. "Heard!" With a sweep of one foot, Rinna knocked the nearest guard off-balance and drove him to the ground with her elbow. Hopping over him, she tackled the second one from behind, paralyzing him with a touch.

Restricted in her movements, Cosmina could do little, but little she did. She wrenched herself from the final guard and headbutted him in the stomach hard enough to knock the wind from his lungs.

Rinna seized her arm and yanked her back toward the van. "Position?" She shoved Cosmina inside, then kicked hard at the chest of a guard who had resumed pursuit. Yellow ribbons of Magic energy formed in his hands. They needed to get the hell away from those.

"Ready!" Nix said from somewhere. She didn't need to know where. Rinna wrapped an arm around Cosmina's narrow waist and grabbed a pole inside the van with the other.

"GO!"

The van lurched into motion. Rinna clung to her friend and the pole for dear life and watched out the still-open back doors as the smoke dissipated. The guards were left chasing them on foot, flinging Magic, joined by backup that was too late.

They only drove for a mile or so before Nix left the road, driving straight into a wooded area for several hundred yards before he stopped.

Cosmina recognized Nix when he appeared at the back of the van, his black hair pulled into a careless topknot and sharp jaw set. She also recognized Destiny, the short, chubby black woman with intimidating intelligence standing at his side. They'd come with Rinna to Cosmina's house while she awaited her trial and attempted to tell her the gravity of her situation. None of them had any reason to be here now, rescuing her, after she'd ignored their warnings and refused to escape with them.

Destiny placed a hand on each cuff around Cosmina's ankles and murmured a spell. They clinked open. The handcuffs responded to a different enchantment, but she knew that one too.

The moment her binds fell away, Rinna grabbed Cosmina and dragged her deeper into the forest. "We have to move. We didn't travel farther than they can run."

"Why are we leaving the van?" Cosmina's heart pounded in her throat. She stumbled over a log and was caught by the arms by Rinna and Destiny.

"It's a government vehicle," Destiny said. "They can track it."

They sprinted through the woods for a time, until Cosmina was forced to stop, gasping for air.

"Have we gone far enough?" Rinna asked Nix.

"Not quite. Scorpia and Nelson are meeting us at the old well."

Rinna's stomach tightened. "Are we sure they made it out?"

"Positive. I saw them leave, and the guards were chasing us. I don't think they even noticed them."

Nix only allowed them to rest a moment before they walked the remaining mile to the old well. Scorpia and Nelson, two people Cosmina had never met before, were already there. Rinna hugged them both.

"It's too soon to celebrate," Nix said.

Scorpia, a tiny, frail-looking girl with thin black hair and wide-set eyes, removed her backpack and produced a small plastic bag with ten glass vials in it. After taking one for herself, she passed the bag to Nix. "Drink it. It'll mask your scent for six hours."

The bag went around the group. Cosmina's hand trembled as she tipped back the potion, but she did not ask questions. Next they passed around a paste, applying it to their shoes to make them more difficult to track. Then Scorpia used a spray bottle to coat the area around them in a liquid that smelled like feces. Cosmina gagged. Rinna smiled sympathetically. "Alright, let's go."

Nix and Destiny led them on a roundabout hike through the dense forest. Nelson, a tall and gangly brunette in oversized clothes, brought up the rear, using his aerokinesis to blow dirt and leaves over their tracks.

Though exhausted and sore, Cosmina dared not complain. These people had just rescued her from certain torment, even after she'd essentially accused them of lying.

Night had nearly fallen before they reached a bank framed by a thick copse of trees. Several people stood around waiting for them to arrive. They rushed forward, greeting their friends in hushed voices, pushing cups of water and plates of food into their hands. Cosmina felt separated from the scene, watching it play out distantly. No one chastised her for taking her chances with the court, but she felt guilty nonetheless.

After everyone had eaten and the story had been recounted for everyone to hear, Rinna led Cosmina into the copse of trees. It concealed an opening in the rock, just wide enough for three people to stand side by side and tall enough for Cosmina's five feet and ten inches to pass underneath.

Inside the cave, cots and torches lined the walls. It was cold and damp, with the sound of water dripping somewhere deeper inside. Rinna led her to a cot in the back, with many sleeping bodies to pass if she tried to leave. She knew their mistrust was warranted, but it was isolating. She tossed and turned for most of the night.

When she woke, Cosmina had no idea what time it was. It was dark inside the cave, save for the light of a few burning torches, and empty. She considered her new situation, rubbing her eyes roughly as she allowed it to settle over her.

Two weeks ago, she'd been the beloved oldest daughter of a Specialized School professor and a regeneration mentor; two perfectly normal but fantastic people. She was In Excellent Standing at top-tier Swyncrest Intermediate School and an aspiring Primary School magister.

Now, she was an escaped criminal. The rest of her numbered days would be spent alongside these other escaped criminals, merely surviving. Hardly a life at all, but better than the alternative, if the stories were true.

Disentangling herself from her shabby blanket, Cosmina sat up and looked around. There was no one in sight. No guards, no one chatting, no one sleeping.

At the cave's mouth, she found the familiar silhouettes of Destiny and Nix standing guard. They would've looked comical side-by-side if they didn't both possess a ferocity that dissuaded anyone from messing with them. Cosmina, tall herself, had to look up into Nix's face and down into Destiny's. Destiny was fair and sweet and patient, but Cosmina only knew that from their prior meetings. At first glance, she seemed vicious and untouchable and a thousand times smarter than you.

Nix was slender but muscular, with narrow black eyes, shaggy hair, and full lips. He was good-looking, but any potential attraction died soon after being around him. Cosmina had never seen him smile.

Before she could announce herself, Destiny turned to her. "Good, you're awake."

Cosmina wasn't surprised. Everyone at this camp had finely tuned survival skills. It was necessary for them. They were never safe.

And now she was one of them.

"What happens now?"

Nix's voice was emotionless. "Today is your rest day. Everybody gets one."

"And tomorrow?"

"Your guess is as good as ours."

Cosmina huffed in frustration.

Destiny's eyes showed sympathy. "You'll start training tomorrow. You'll learn how to hunt and fish and fight like the rest of us. Then you'll be added to chore rotations."

"Thank you." Cosmina gave Nix a sharp glare he pretended not to notice. "Where's Rinna?"

"Hunting," he grunted.

"When will she be back?"

"When she has something to bring back."

"Am I allowed to leave?"

"Depends on what you mean by 'leave.'"

Cosmina had always disliked Nix, but he was beginning to test the last of her meager patience. "Not the group. Just the cave. Can I walk outside?"

"Of course you can, but stay close." Destiny gave her a reassuring smile. "You're in danger on your own."

Cosmina walked a short distance from the cave's mouth and its protective copse of trees until she felt sufficiently out of sight. Then she paced in circles until her feet ached. She'd escaped with only the clothes on her back, the standard-issue prison uniform of monotone gray pants and short-sleeved shirt. Her white sneakers were filthy and still caked with paste. Her long, mercilessly curly hair was a tangled mess. She did not know most of the other people living inside that cave.

Her insides felt on fire. She'd had such ambition. So much she wanted to accomplish. The opportunity had been stolen from her, and for what reason? She was innocent and they knew it. They'd used fake evidence and character witnesses she had never met in her life, and those things would be published in hearing records and newspapers as fact.

And her parents, who had always been so supportive and loving, were apparently idiots, cruel enough to believe these lies over their own daughter, the woman they raised for twenty years.

They believed she was capable of murder.

She sank onto the dead trunk of a fallen tree and dug the toes of her sneakers into the dirt. There was nothing she could do about it now. She never had to see them again. It didn't matter what they thought.

"Cosmina?" a gentle voice behind her asked. She nearly jumped out of her skin. "Sorry, I didn't mean to startle you." Rinna stepped over the trunk and sat beside her. "Are you alright?"

"I just needed some air."

"I know this is a lot to take in. I'm here if you need to talk."

Cosmina looked into Rinna's pretty face, worn by years of wilderness survival, framed by tangles of chestnut brown hair. She wanted to smile and show gratitude for her rescue but couldn't bring herself to do it. "How was hunting? Nix said you weren't welcome back until you caught something."

Rinna smiled without amusement and opened a worn cloth bag to reveal the raw meat inside. Cosmina struggled not to gag.

"You'll get used to it. You'll get used to everything."

SPRING

Necessary to Fight

Arma 317

Cosmina grunted as she hit the ground, her left hip and elbow taking the brunt of the impact.

"You have to be faster than that! Up! Again!" Nix barked. Scorpia stepped back into a defensive stance as Cosmina leaped to her feet. She'd learned two years ago to ignore the pain in her body. Her lungs burned as she prepared for Scorpia's assault.

This time, she was ready when Scorpia charged. She turned sideways and lifted her knee into the smaller girl's chest. Scorpia, always impossibly quick, slid under Cosmina's leg and aimed her foot at the blonde's, knocking her off-balance and sending her tumbling again. Scorpia rose gracefully as Cosmina fell heavily to her hands and knees. She couldn't believe she'd once felt guilty about sparring with Scorpia. She may be tiny and frail-looking, but she was also quick and ruthless.

"React! Be prepared for anything! You aren't learning a dance routine, you're in active combat! Adapt!"

Cosmina glared up at Nix. She lived her life covered in scrapes, calluses, bruises, and cuts. She'd taken a knife and hacked off all her beautiful curls after only a few days at the camp. She'd come so far from the pretentious, spoiled, self-absorbed girl she'd been. She could kill an animal or gut a fish without flinching, climb a tree in under a minute, scale buildings, run for miles, and do push-ups until he got bored of watching her. And yet, nothing she did was ever good enough for him.

She got to her feet. "I'm done for today."

Nix's jaw tightened, but he knew better than to argue with Rinna's pet. Push her to her limits, yes. Scream and yell at her, sure. But try to make her do something she didn't want to do? Out of the question.

Scorpia came to stand beside him, the top of her head just reaching his bicep. They watched Cosmina's retreating back disappear into the woods. "Don't you think you're a bit hard on her?"

"She has enough help. She doesn't need mine."

"We're all here for the same reason, you know. I think she's done more than enough to prove she's one of us."

Nix turned to Scorpia in disbelief. "That girl has never been to a lab. She hasn't been through what we have."

"She isn't the only witch here who hasn't. Do you think only survivors should be rescued?" Scorpia scratched dried dirt off her cheek. "I think the more witches we prevent from ever seeing the inside of a lab, the better."

"Of course I agree with that. I'm only saying she isn't one of us. She got lucky. She's here for self-preservation, and that's it."

"Aren't we all here for self-preservation? It's not like we're doing more than surviving."

Nix said nothing.

Rinna sat cross-legged on her cot and watched Cosmina's chest rise and fall. She looked peaceful in her sleep. Gentle: a word she would never use for Cosmina otherwise.

Cosmina came to them so clean and pretty and undamaged. It had sparked envy and mistrust in some, but Rinna recognized her potential. Even Nix agreed to rescue her after some initial protesting. And here she lay, her hair cropped close to her head, as filthy and beaten as the rest of them.

Rinna tugged on her own brown ponytail and wondered if she had the bone structure for a pixie cut. Probably not.

A long, low whistle reached her ears from outside the cave. She tensed, waiting to hear it again.

The signal sounded a second time. Her heart leaped into her throat.

"Evacuation!" she shouted, stuffing her feet into her shoes. The others began to stir, gasps and murmurs filling the space.

The group had practiced for this a hundred or more times. Many of them, Rinna included, had abandoned camps before, fleeing in organized terror.

This hideout in particular would be missed. It was a spacious cave, more than big enough for all of them, and well-concealed. It was far enough from the nearest town to avoid detection by hikers, but near enough that a necessary trip wasn't unbearable. It had access to a river for drinking water and baths. Food was abundant enough. They'd all grown comfortable here, feeling safe within this space.

But safety could never last for them. As it had done dozens of times before, Rinna's heart broke for the group as they hurried to vacate a space that had been their home.

They rounded up the youngest and newest and escorted them from the cave first. Scorpia produced a bag of emergency vials, and everyone drank one to mask their scent. Then the first group left, Nelson following to blow away their tracks.

Rinna surveyed the remaining witches. These were her core group, her fighters. Once the signalers joined them, they would leave next, and escape without fighting if possible.

The twelve of them stood at the ready, the seconds ticking by. One of the four witches on signal duty dashed out of the forest and melded into their ranks. The second, a young girl with shoulder-length blonde hair named Josie, barely eighteen, stumbled into the clearing a moment later, gasping for air.

"At least...ten," she panted. "Definitely...Council."

Rinna stared into the dark treeline, willing the others to appear. They couldn't afford to lose anyone, not alive. Every bit of information the Council discovered put them all at greater risk.

The others finally sprinted into the clearing together. "They're close!"

"Go. Now," Rinna ordered.

The group moved as a unit, signalers in the center and surrounded by fighters. The witches bringing up the rear walked backward, eyes peeled for signs of movement.

When they'd been walking for several minutes, Cosmina said, "To the left." Rinna saw it too; a dark figure, fifty feet away, moving parallel to them through the forest. To the right, she identified another.

"We're being tracked."

"Signalers and Rank B keep moving, Rank A fight?" Nix suggested, keeping his voice low.

Rinna's stomach flip-flopped. She knew that was the best plan, but it meant separating from Cosmina. She hesitated.

"We've got some behind us, too," Destiny said.

"Yes. Only fight if necessary. No one gets left behind. We'll regroup once it's safe. Go."

Rinna and six other witches stopped walking abruptly. The remaining five fighters filed into place around the four signalers and quickened their pace. Rinna stared after Cosmina for the briefest of moments, memorizing the sight just in case. Then she turned her attention to the fight.

She kept her voice low. "I'll take the left, Nix to the right. Destiny, try to run ahead and make sure we aren't being herded. The rest of you take the followers."

They responded immediately. Destiny became a blur as she sprinted ahead, Nix faded into the trees. Scorpia and Nino disappeared into the darkness, running back the way they'd come. Xia and Sam stood in place, waiting for a reason to spring into action. Rinna allowed herself a second of pride before following their example.

Locating the Councilwitch tailing them was easy. They weren't known for their subtlety. Rinna grabbed a branch near her head and pulled herself up. The forest was dense here, allowing her to travel discreetly above the Councilwitch.

High above his head, she snapped a thin branch. He froze in place and spun around. She watched him.

The Council employed many witches, and most fieldwork agents failed to impress. An excellent way to determine how much the Council knew about the rogue group was to see which soldiers they sent.

The witch pressed his fingers to his ear. "Anyone see where the rest went? I lost some."

Rinna waited. A couple minutes passed while he did nothing but stand there and look around.

As he turned to keep walking, muttering that now he'd lost all of them, he blew some leaves away from his feet with a blast of air from his hands. Rinna grinned. A useless display of his unique ability meant this guy was a joke. Any good soldier knew the value of surprise.

She dropped onto his back.

Any worry he was smarter than he looked vanished as he shouted and crumpled to the ground. Rinna paralyzed him with a touch and used a vine from a nearby tree to bind his hands and feet. He continued to yell as she dragged him back to the others.

Five-foot-tall Scorpia towered over an unconscious man three times her size, sprinkling sleeping powder in his face. Nino was tying together the feet of two smaller witches.

"Is that necessary?" Rinna arched an eyebrow at the small, brown-skinned boy, a young recruit who was eager to prove himself.

"No, but it's fun."

"Where's everyone else?"

"We're here!" Sam and Xia jogged over with Nix. Sam's dark face sported a fresh cut below the right eye, and Xia held a strip of bloody cloth to her nose, box braids falling from her ponytail. Nix looked the same as always, if a little dirty. "Apparently we got the tough ones, but Nix helped us out."

"Did you take care of them?" Rinna asked.

Sam waggled his fingers at her. "Sure did. Anyone else?"

He made his way around, extrapolating memories from the Council employees' brains. Rinna stared impatiently into the forest where the rest of their little group had gone.

As if reading her mind, Nix said, "Des isn't back."

"I know. We need to catch up to the others fast." Josie had said "at least ten" Councilwitches were approaching their camp, and they'd only taken out seven.

Cosmina did not relish the idea of being separated from Rinna, but she was determined to prove herself. As their divided group moved through the dark, quiet forest, she used every skill she'd honed over the last year. She had heightened senses and lighter steps, and knew how to channel Magic to the forefront of her body to be ready for use at a moment's notice.

A hundred or so feet ahead on their path, a scream pierced the night, freezing them in place. There shouldn't be anyone ahead of them. Not this close.

"Reggie, with me," Maren said. "Everyone else, keep your guard up."

Maren was a short, fierce blonde a little older than Cosmina, and in charge of Rank B in Rinna's absence. She'd been with the group for three years and would soon be Rank A. Everyone was just waiting on Rinna to make it official.

Cosmina always disagreed with Maren, this time included. Frustration flared in her chest. Leaving three witches to guard four was a mistake. Either Reggie or Maren could walk a hundred feet alone and yell for help if necessary.

One minute passed, then two. The forest was still, save for the rustling of leaves in the wind and the occasional hoot of an owl. The quiet was ominous.

A movement to Cosmina's left caught her eye just as black-clad figures stepped out of the trees. They surrounded the group, which pressed together. One signaler whimpered, and another shushed them. Cosmina's heart pounded. They'd been left with few defenses and no leader.

There were seven Councilwitches and seven rogues, but four of the rogues were only trained in basic self-defense. One was fifteen and too young to use Magic at all. The Council never came to kill; they took prisoners. But if the stories were true, being captured would be worse than being killed.

"Time to fight," Cosmina said, just loud enough for the others to hear. "Don't let anyone get taken."

For a long moment, no one moved at all. Then one of the Councilwitches stepped forward, and Cosmina sprang into action. The suddenness caught them off guard, giving her a priceless moment to somersault the distance and land a hard kick in his face.

The other six witches charged the rogues. Brison used their substantial size and brute strength to take out two more, ignoring the flop of brown hair they'd been meaning to cut as it fell over their eyes. Josie used her forcefield to protect the signalers from the Magic attacks flying through the air, but she wasn't very powerful yet. It would help for a little bit, and then she'd be too tired to be of any further use.

Cosmina slid across the ground to sweep a witch's feet from beneath her. She shouted as she fell, and Cosmina grabbed her hair and slammed her head into the ground once, twice, until she stopped struggling. Cosmina didn't stop to check for blood. Rinna never condoned killing, but she was not quite as moralistic.

They'd been joined by others. Destiny and Scorpia fought two witches who had gotten too close to the signalers. Nix dropped from a tree to take out the man holding Brison in a chokehold. Backup had arrived, and now the Council's goons were outnumbered. Cosmina pumped her fist in celebration.

"Look, I found the Frazier girl," said a gravelly voice behind her. Arms snaked around her body, a hand tightening over her throat. "So this is where you've been. We should've known."

No one was looking at her. She was too far away, and it was loud and chaotic with all the fighting. She tried to scream anyway, the noise cut off too soon by his hand over her mouth.

Cosmina relaxed all her muscles, making herself dead weight in his arms. He stumbled forward with a grunt. "Still feisty, I see."

He attempted to adjust his hold on her, and she seized the moment. Uprighting herself, she spun to face him and lifted her knee into his crotch with all the force she could manage in her awkward position. He screamed and folded. She grabbed the back of his head and lifted her knee again, this time into his face.

There was something to be said for hand-to-hand combat. She'd always thought it was a waste of time, but tonight she'd seen firsthand how the undervaluing of it by the Witching Council was precisely what allowed the rogues to maintain their freedom. Witches didn't need to throw punches when most could harm someone without lifting a finger, but it was a mistake to think everyone felt that way.

The man was unconscious now, so she found some vines for his hands and feet. Then she dragged him back to where the fight was winding down, rogues victorious.

After ensuring all Councilwitches were paralyzed and bound with their memories removed, Rinna did a quick headcount and breathed a sigh of relief. They resumed their trek, her energy-seeking vision guiding them toward a huddled mass of Magic energy.

The other group had run into no trouble at all. They walked for an hour, until confident there was no more immediate danger, before stopping to rest. They had several long days of foot travel before they could even consider finding a new camp.

A week and a half after the attack, they stumbled across a wooden house in a small clearing deep in the forest. There were no lights inside despite the late hour. They decided to camp nearby and watch the house for signs of life. Three days passed before an old woman rode a horse out of the forest and dismounted at the front door. Cosmina and Rinna, on watch duty, observed with bated breath as she walked inside and disappeared from view.

"Orid," Rinna swore. "I had so hoped it was abandoned."

They returned to camp to announce the house was occupied, and they would resume their travels the following morning. The woman in the house, however, had other plans.

She approached their camp late that night, escaping the notice of everyone on guard duty and walking right into the circle of sleeping bodies. Gray clouds had moved over the light of Cantamen's two moons, and an eerie chill had settled over the night. Even the bugs and birds were silent. She looked around until she spotted someone awake and said, "I would like to meet whoever is in charge here."

The young boy ran to rouse Rinna, who shooed him away until he told her a stranger was there to meet her. She ordered him to wake the other fighters and approached the woman cautiously, astonished to recognize her as the woman from the cottage.

"We don't want any trouble," she said. "We're only sleeping here for the night. We'll move on in the morning."

The old woman smiled, many leathery layers of wrinkles folding over themselves. "What is your name, dear?"

"Rinna," she said, confused.

"Rinna, I am Tiz Agathe. I am concerned by all the young people sleeping on the hard ground."

Rinna narrowed her eyes. "We're used to it."

"Perhaps I can offer a better option. My home has several beds inside."

"I'm afraid I must refuse. Thank you, though." Rinna glanced sidelong at Nix, who had appeared at her side. Her own confusion was reflected in his eyes.

"Perhaps you will come and sit with me then. We may speak more privately."

Rinna hesitated, consulting Nix. He shrugged. "Maybe we should wake everyone and go now. She could have already called the authorities."

"I assure you I have not," the old woman said. "I know who you are, and I wish to help."

"You cannot possibly know who we are." Rinna crossed her arms.

"Ah, but I do. And I am certain that I could come across your real names with only a bit of scrying. You are lost fledglings, fighting for your survival. And I understand your plight because I, too, hold an affinity for dark Magic."

Rinna took Nix and Cosmina inside the old woman's home with her. She made a few other fighters wait outside. She wanted to see what this woman knew, but their safety was her priority.

The woman's home was dated and simple. Inside, almost everything was made crudely of wood. Spices lined shelves along the kitchen wall, and herbs dangled from the ceiling. The gathering room was furnished with a small floral-print sofa and matching chaise. A hallway to the right led into darkness, and a narrow staircase led to a loft area with two dressers and shelves lining the walls. It was spacious, for an old witch who lived alone.

"Welcome to my humble abode." Tiz Agathe removed her cloak to reveal vibrant silver hair. "The presence of young people is a rare treat. This place could use the youth."

"How do you know about us?" Rinna asked, deciding not to waste time.

"I could sense that amount of dark energy from miles away. And I've heard the stories, of course."

"The stories?" Nix furrowed his brow.

"Yes. The legends, if you prefer. A roving band of witches deemed dangerous to society: escaped Variant Idealists and Magically volatile fledglings. There are rumors that some of you have grouped up for the purposes of survival, but few believe you are such a large and organized group. I am surprised by it myself."

"You said you also have an affinity for dark Magic?" Cosmina asked.

"I do. I was fortunate to be born before this fear of the unknown took over, but that does not mean it has been easy for me. As you can see, I live alone in a forest cottage, isolated from most of the world. I have been forced to support myself by doing illegal Magic for hire most of my adult life."

"You said you wanted to help us," Rinna interrupted. "How?"

Tiz Agathe smiled, revealing the gaps between her remaining teeth. "I can assist with shelter, food, protection, and training in the dark arts."

The rogues looked at one another, stunned.

"But why? Why do so much for us?" Rinna demanded. "And how can we be sure we can trust you? This seems like a trap."

Tiz Agathe took a few steps toward Rinna and pushed the younger woman's tangled brown hair out of her face. "You doubt your intuition right now, but ask your friends. What is your Magic telling you? Can I be trusted?"

Rinna turned to Cosmina and Nix for help.

Cosmina's eyes widened. She didn't want to be responsible for this decision, not even a little bit.

Nix inclined his head. "What shelter are you offering us?"

"My home." Tiz Agathe gestured to the cottage around them.

"There are too many of us to stay here," Cosmina said.

"We can place cots in the loft. I have two private bedrooms aside from my own, you can take turns using them if you would like. And we can certainly build another small shelter for more cots. If I am not mistaken, you do not all sleep at once, correct? It will be crowded, indeed, but not impossible."

"And you want to train us on how to control our dark Magic?" Rinna sounded uneasy.

"I can," Tiz Agathe said. "If you would like. Gods know they do not teach it in those schools you went to. They would rather pretend it does not exist and squash it entirely if they can."

"I need to talk to my friends," Rinna said. The old woman left the room without another word.

"What do you think?" Rinna turned to Nix.

"Obviously, it's risky."

"Obviously."

"And I am notoriously opposed to risky things."

"Yes, of course."

"So this is going to come as a shock to you, but…"

Cosmina raised her eyebrows.

"…I think I trust the old woman."

Rinna blinked, stunned into silence.

As much as she wanted to stay out of the discussion and bear zero responsibility for whatever decision was made here tonight, Cosmina found herself unable to keep quiet. "Don't you feel the dark energy here? I noticed it the moment we arrived. I don't think this place is aligned with the Council. And look at this." She approached a framed plaque on the wall. "The Significant Magical Achievement Award. Look at the name. This woman is *the* Citizen Agathe Thoreau."

Rinna stepped forward to read the plaque. "'This honor is presented to Citizen Agathe Thoreau on this eleventh day of Papilio in the year 187 for the invention of the Kinforte Box.' Those are the little boxes we had in school!"

Cosmina noticed Nix staring at her over Rinna's head and did her best to ignore him. "But after she sold the invention, they went back to treating her like a criminal. I doubt she considers the Council to be any good, and certainly not her allies."

"But what if she's planning to turn us in as a way to get on the Council's good side or something? I really don't know about this."

"It's risky," Nix agreed, "but if she was planning to report us, wouldn't she have done it already? Can we really pass up this opportunity to learn from Tiz Agathe, to ally ourselves with her, even briefly?"

Rinna turned to Cosmina, who nodded. She never had been good at staying out of things.

Rinna sighed. "Fine. We'll stay for a bit. But we leave at the first sign of danger, and we stay ready to move at a moment's notice. And we keep a close eye on the old woman."

The rogue group took only two days to complete a simple wooden shack amongst the trees. Most of them slept on the hard ground or the loft floor since they had little to make beds. The youngest and weakest took turns sharing the two private rooms.

There was one small bathroom with a tiny washbasin, sink, and toilet. The mirror mounted above the sink had a single large crack cutting diagonally up the length of it. As a result of the inadequate facilities, most rogues relieved themselves deep in the woods and bathed in the river, which was a bit of a walk from the cottage and quite cold.

Tiz Agathe taught them to make soap and offered Magic lessons to whoever wished to attend. Cosmina was an eager student. She readily understood that dark Magic was a different force, but not inherently evil. It just needed to be handled differently than regular Magic.

"Dark Magic is more primal and less logical. It will not feel like sunshine and daisies. To use it, you need to tap into your inner feral creature. It will make you feel wild and dark and free, and you must embrace that. It will save you. It already has. That wildness within you is what allowed you to kill animals to survive. It is how you are able to sleep on the ground and override your fear. It is how you can punch, paralyze, and pounce on your enemies without guilt. It makes you strong. Honor that power."

After two weeks, Tiz Agathe explained she must leave for a time to do a job for someone. She urged them to practice their Magic and promised to return in a week.

Nix, who had taken a liking to the horse and prepared it for the journey through the woods, tucked an extra bag of food into the saddlebag as Tiz Agathe approached.

"Thank you, young man."

Nix nodded once. "Safe riding."

"Safe riding?" Cosmina arched an eyebrow at him as the old woman left.

"Well, what do you say to someone who's leaving on horseback? Personally, I've never experienced it."

Cosmina laughed.

Rinna did not like Tiz Agathe's departure. She was convinced the time had come for the woman's betrayal, and she increased guard duty.

On the second day of Tiz Agathe's absence, the hunting party returned from a full day with no food. They were forced to make do with vegetables from the garden and eggs from the old woman's chickens, and several people went to bed hungry.

After the third day of finding little food, everyone was sluggish and grumpy. People started having accidents, cutting themselves, falling out of trees, tripping over their own feet.

On the day of Tiz Agathe's return, Nino stumbled on a wolf den. No sooner had he identified four puppies than the mother returned from her hunt and attacked him. He tried to defend himself, but his Magic failed. Destiny, hunting nearby, heard his screams and rushed to his aid. She subdued the wolf with a small shock from her electrokinesis and dragged Nino back to camp with a lot of effort, one of his legs bleeding and useless. Tiz Agathe was able to heal him, but a heavy fear settled over the camp. It seemed their string of bad luck was only getting worse.

Rinna's anxiety grew as the days passed. She had attended the lessons for a few days before deciding it wasn't for her. She channeled dark energy and hated it. The heat of it, the surge of it, the way it pulsed beneath her skin, barely contained; it frightened her. The last time she lost control of her Magic, someone died. She headed this group and rescued others as a way of honoring the memory of that witch. She could never forgive herself if it happened again, especially as a result of her own recklessness.

Tiz Agathe's secrets resonated with Cosmina, though. She rose long before the sun to meditate. Some days she climbed a tree; others, she floated in the river. Her pores vibrated with untapped Magic energy. She timed herself sprinting distances, climbing trees, and swimming against the current. She worked herself into exhaustion that she never slept enough to combat.

Rinna noticed her friend's odd behavior but kept it to herself.

SUMMER

Let's Get Proactive

Flora 317

The weeks passed, leaving in their wake a growing tension in the group. Rinna's feelings toward her friends who took the Magic lessons grew more volatile until most of them gave up altogether. The food shortage did not improve, and more people's Magic failed them. Rinna was outspoken in her distrust of Tiz Agathe and their dark Magic, creating an uncomfortable environment for everyone. Unwilling to risk their leader's wrath but unable to resist the pull of her dark power, Cosmina took her practice into hiding.

She wasn't sneaky enough. One clear, dark morning, as she slipped out of the cottage to meditate in the river, she was stopped by someone far scarier than Rinna.

"Good morning." Nix materialized from the shadow of a tree on her path.

"Good morning." Cosmina kept walking, choosing not to acknowledge anything was strange about the situation.

"Bit early for a walk."

"I couldn't sleep."

"You haven't slept much lately. You know we have ishtis for that."

Cosmina stopped, swearing to herself. She should've known this would happen. Nothing escaped Nix's notice. "What do you want?"

"I want to go with you to the river. I'd like to have a chat." He gestured for Cosmina to lead the way. She didn't budge. "You don't trust me?"

"I don't."

"If I promise not to hurt you, will you listen? I don't even need you to talk."

Cosmina crossed her arms. If Nix wanted to talk with her, it couldn't be about anything good. Still, something was satisfying about getting under his skin, and this would give her some chances. "If you promise."

Nix rolled his eyes so hard his whole head moved in a circle, which was the only reason Cosmina could tell he did it. She decided to count that as her first success.

"Fine. I promise I won't hurt you."

"Alright." Cosmina led the way through the trees, both of them stepping lightly and avoiding things that might make noise, as they'd been trained. It was warm out, and the scent of a rainstorm long subsided lingered in the air. It was several minutes before either of them spoke again. "Well?"

"I want to tell you a story, but I'm not sure where to begin."

Cosmina raised her eyebrows. "You want to tell me a story?"

"Yeah. Well, my story."

Cosmina paused. She had always wondered how Nix came to be part of the group. She wondered how everyone ended up here. It was a rule that you didn't ask people for their story. If they wanted you to know, they would tell you. Asking might as well be coercion, and Rinna wouldn't stand for it. "Go on."

"I went to Karin Svensdotter's Primary School."

"As did I. I think most of us did. We're Magically volatile."

Nix closed his eyes and took a deep breath. Cosmina counted her second success.

"Yes. I stayed In Excellent Standing, channeled Magic on the first try, summoned my familiar on the second try, performed Magic with him on the second try. I was eleventh in my class to be drafted to an Intermediate School."

"I'm not interested in your stats. I'm not even impressed by them. Mine are very similar." But a little better, if she wanted to brag.

Nix chuckled. "I know what your stats are. I've done a lot of research on you, starting the moment Rinna introduced you to us."

Nix was the suspicious one. Rinna was smart, determined, and decisive, and she made for a great leader. But the higher-ranking rogues, the ones in her circle, knew she wouldn't be as successful without Nix. Rinna wanted to save everyone, inviting everyone she met into their group. Nix vetted new members, ensuring they could be trusted. No one knew how he obtained all his information, but no one doubted it either. He was nothing if not accurate.

Cosmina scowled, the expression disguised by the darkness. "I didn't go walking in the woods with you to hear you brag about yourself."

Nix ignored her. "My parents were so proud of me. I was their golden child, which was awkward, since I had two older brothers. Everything fell apart in Intermediate

School. I was channeling Magic with my familiar, as I had done a hundred times before, when something inside me shifted. My Magic had always been blue. A deep, rich hue, somewhere between the Navy Ocean and the Cobalt Skies. It was beautiful. But on this day, it turned gray. I lost control, and I injured a girl.

"I'll never forget it. I had stopped channeling the Magic, but it just kept coming. She was bleeding while I shouted for help, but no one could hear me over the screaming. No one could find us through the smoke. It was terrifying.

"They took my familiar away. I never saw him again. Each time I used Magic, I lost control. I hurt others; I hurt myself. I was afraid to use it at all. One day, my Councilrep loaded me into a van and said I was being taken to a doctor. I was given an exam. They explained nothing to me, only saying they needed to wait for test results to come back. I was taken and locked in a tiny room. For one week, they brought my meals and made me visit the doctor daily. After that, they put me back in the van and took me to what they called a 'long-term infirmary.'"

Cosmina swallowed. When she'd first been arrested, she'd been confused and frightened. She had fought the guards, punching one of them hard enough to break his nose. He'd touched his fingers to the blood, chuckled, and said, "It won't be long at all before you're at long-term." She'd had no idea what he meant and, in the hubbub of the days afterward, she'd forgotten all about it until now.

"I'll spare you most of the details." Nix's eyes fixed on something in the distance behind Cosmina. She realized they'd stopped walking at some point and were now just standing facing one another. "In the labs, you have no bodily autonomy. No one cares if you're in pain, or if you cry, or who you were before being taken there. No one will tell you anything about your parents or siblings or even acknowledge that you're confused and scared. Most of them won't speak to you at all, unless it's to give you orders.

"Scorpia and I were of similar age and symptoms, and taken into custody around the same time, so we were the perfect candidates for whatever test they were conducting on us. We were together a lot but always monitored, so it took a few seasons to build a rapport that allowed us to communicate privately. One day, all the stars lined up just right, and we were able to escape. A couple seasons later, Rinna found us, and the rest is history."

Cosmina's voice shook. "I'm sorry that happened to you. Both of you."

"My point is," Nix said, bringing his eyes back around to glare into hers, "this is still happening all across Cantamen. When they identify a fledgling with a dark affinity, they find some way to make them disappear so they can use them in their experiments. Most often, it's what they did to you—convicting you of a crime you never committed. They're clever, though, so they know when that won't work and how often they can get away with it. The scale of this conspiracy is amazing."

"But what is the purpose? Everyone knows dark Magic isn't bad."

"It isn't, but in many ways, it's more powerful. A person who can harness and master it, like Tiz Agathe, is a threat to them. They want to find a way to eradicate dark Magic from Cantamen, and they want it so badly that abducting and experimenting on children is a justifiable means to that end."

Cosmina took a breath. She'd heard of the labs, of course, since many members of their group had escaped them. She'd overheard bits and pieces of whispered experiences from others. Still, they'd made it clear that she was an outsider because she had never been a test subject. Keeping close to Rinna, who refused to take part in war stories, had been the only way Cosmina felt welcome. Rinna never believed a person's suffering made them worthy; she thought everyone was worthy of not suffering.

"Why are you telling me this?" Cosmina was under no delusion that Nix liked or even respected her, so his vulnerability was unsettling.

"Because I have an idea that's been on my mind for a while, and I think we're finally in a position where it might be feasible." He paused to scan the woods before continuing. "Although Rinna is amazing, we aren't doing enough to help witches with dark affinities. I think we could, and should, be doing more."

"More? Like what?"

Nix pounced on the question. He'd waited years to answer it. "So far, we've been reactive. When we hear of an abduction, we determine if there's a way for us to save them. If there is, we do it. If there isn't, we don't. Rinna feels our group's safety is more important than risking everything to save one witch at a time, but it's never felt right to me. If I die saving the lives of others, isn't that more honorable than hiding?"

He waited for a response, so Cosmina nodded.

"That's why I think we should be more proactive about this. We have to fight back. We have to rescue more people. We have to expose what the labs are doing. We have to show society what their government is doing. If I die while fighting, I'll die a young hero. But if I die after a life wasted in hiding, I'll die an old coward. I know which I prefer."

Cosmina kicked a rock by her foot, watching as it bounced off a nearby tree and out of sight. She also knew which she preferred, especially after turning on her dark power over the last weeks. This life of survival was suffocating her. "Where do I come in?"

"Obviously, Rinna won't be happy about this. It isn't an option with her as our leader. Choosing to be more proactive would mean leaving and probably cutting all ties with Rinna. We'd have to form our own group. I want you to lead it with me."

Cosmina looked him in the eyes, stunned into silence. He waited as she collected her thoughts. At least he knew it was a shocking proposition.

"Why me? Why not Scorpia? Or Destiny?"

"You've taken to the training well, and you're a born leader. But if you don't want to leave Rinna, I understand. I only ask that you don't tell her."

Cosmina grimaced. The last thing she wanted was for anyone to think she was weak, content to stay cozy in the privilege of being Rinna's favorite.

"Think about it. Let me know."

"Obviously, Tiz Agathe's use of dark Magic is bringing evil to our group. We can't stay here."

Cosmina rubbed the rough bar of homemade soap vigorously against her armpits and stared at the surface of the river.

"I don't know where we'll go, but we have to move on," Rinna continued, oblivious to Cosmina's silence. "I can't keep letting her put us in danger like this."

"I don't think Tiz Agathe is putting us in danger. She's been very generous to us. I'm grateful to her."

"And you think I'm not?"

"Well, you're accusing her of bringing evil to us."

"Cos! Are you blind? We'll be starving before long. What's scaring the animals away and causing the garden to die?"

"The fact we're taking enough to feed thirty people? It's an animal's instinct to avoid danger."

"And what of the wolf?" Rinna cried indignantly.

"Pure coincidence?"

"His Magic failed. Other people have reported feeling their Magic weaken. That can't be a good sign. There's no telling what she's putting in the ishti she brews for us."

"Orid, Rinna, you cannot be serious." Cosmina chucked the soap to the riverbank and plunged into the water to her chin. "This woman has given us shelter, food, clothing. She taught us how to make soap. She offered to train us in using our Magic so we can better defend ourselves. You can't just accuse her of things."

"I didn't get to be in my position by trusting everyone blindly," Rinna snapped. Cosmina wanted to object, but let it go. "I know you've taken to her lessons, but you can't deny that strange things are happening."

Cosmina sighed. "Do you want my honest opinion?"

"You know I always do."

"I think everyone's Magic is getting weaker because you're making them afraid of it."

Rinna blinked slowly. "Excuse me?"

"We all know we're here because we have dark affinities, and you've been nothing if not vocal about how dangerous it is for us to embrace that."

"You think it's my fault these things are happening?"

"All I'm saying is, if people fear their Magic is bad, they'll try to repress it. I believe that's what's happening here." Cosmina walked to the edge of the river.

"And what of your own behavior? You've embraced the darkness within you, and you're becoming someone I don't even like."

Cosmina looked over her shoulder. "My Magic isn't getting weaker."

Cosmina slept fitfully that night and meditated poorly in the pre-dawn hours. Giving up, she returned to the cottage, still and dark, the only sounds of light breathing and the occasional shuffling of skin on sheets. She tore the corner off a notebook page and scribbled, "I'm in." Nix was still asleep in his cot, and she pressed the note into his palm, folding his fingers over it. She stepped over Scorpia, looking peaceful in her sleep, stringy black hair covering most of her face, and left to volunteer for hunting duty.

She had a successful hunt, bringing home more meat than the group had seen in a week. She built a fire and cooked as Rinna avoided her. Once everyone was fed, and many were going to the river, Cosmina caught Nix's eye and left camp in the opposite direction. She walked for ten minutes before scaling a tree. Nix joined her a bit later.

"So, what now?"

"We recruit. I think it's best if we get some people to join us before we tell Rinna what we're doing."

"Who do you have in mind?"

"Scorpia for sure. She's been with me for ages. She won't hesitate to help us."

"Of course."

"On the other end of the spectrum, Nelson absolutely will not come. He's too docile and nonviolent. He only hurts people when Rinna makes him. His loyalty to Rinna trumps all."

"I've noticed that."

"Don't you have any ideas?" Nix raised an eyebrow. Cosmina blinked in surprise. "Yeah, I have a few."

"Then let's hear them."

"Uh. Alright. I went hunting today. It wasn't my assigned day, but I had a theory about why we've had such unsuccessful hunts. There are a few of us who are still finding animals, and it's the same people who stare silently at the ground while Rinna is ranting about our affinities."

"I haven't had any trouble, either."

"Exactly. I have four. I think they're our people."

"Perfect. I have four, too. Scorpia, Sam, Nino, and Reggie. I'm also considering Destiny, but I think she's a solid maybe. She thinks we should be doing more, but her loyalty to Rinna might outweigh her desire to save the world."

"Then we'll let her decide once we're established."

"And we need Tiz Agathe on our side."

"She'll be our strongest ally of all. I have no doubt she'll support us."

"Let's talk to her tonight, and talk to our leads over the next three days. Discreetly. Then we'll meet again to discuss our next steps."

"Deal."

Nix went straight back to the camp, but Cosmina took a roundabout walk so she would return half an hour later and from a different direction. Tiz Agathe waited for her at the edge of the clearing. She placed her hand on Cosmina's forearm and leaned in to disguise her whispering as a grandmotherly kiss on the temple. "He waits in the shed for us."

Despite her shock, Cosmina kept her face straight. Tiz Agathe had made it clear when she'd taken in the rogue group that the tiny shed on the back of the property was off-limits to them. As far as she knew, no one in their group was dumb enough to risk angering her. Still, there had been much speculation about the contents of the tiny wooden structure.

The shed was anticlimactic. It had a single round window at eye-level. Every inch of wall space was dedicated to a cabinet or a shelf. It was designed for one person to stand comfortably, so they struggled to fit inside together. Cosmina leaned back into the counter to avoid physical contact with Nix and knocked into several glass bottles.

"It is all right." Tiz Agathe waved away her apology before she'd opened her mouth to make it. "Tell me what you are doing."

Nix filled her in, keeping his voice low. When he'd finished, the old witch scratched her chin in thought. "I suppose you have made some plans for how you will change things."

Cosmina glanced at Nix. He maintained eye contact with their mentor, but she noticed the set of his jaw.

"I have. But some of it is quite drastic."

A smile spread across Tiz Agathe's face. "I think we're long overdue for drastic action."

Blood Oath

Arbora 317

All eight of their leads agreed. Eric required the most persuasion, but ultimately couldn't resist. They were now a group of ten, plus Tiz Agathe. Cosmina surveyed their little band of troublemakers. Nix with his height and shaggy black hair. Nino, short and brown-skinned, rocking eagerly on his heels. Scorpia, hovering by Nix, her black eyes darting in his direction every few seconds. Reggie, tall and skinny, his kinky-coily hair standing almost straight up on his head. Xia with her ethereal black beauty, shoulders touching Sam's dark bicep, wearing determined expressions. Eric, gangly and tan, with an unruly mop of wavy brown hair. Solara, blonde and brown-eyed and beautiful, pulled her long ponytail over one shoulder and looked over at Hiroto, whose long black hair was pulled into a knot atop his head. He met Cosmina's gaze sidelong with his monolid brown eyes.

"Rinna won't have many fighters left," Cosmina said.

"She won't need them as much as we will." To the rest of the group, Nix said, "We're taking a blood oath, so anyone who isn't committed has one last chance to leave." He scanned their faces, but they each held his gaze. Cosmina's heart swelled with pride. Since Nix's proposition, two weeks ago now, she hadn't stopped thinking about the witches trapped in labs. Her mind had stayed with the fledglings in school right now, oblivious to the existence of these horrors, anxious only to learn what their abilities were. Some would have horrifying futures, and they had no idea.

Tiz Agathe cleared the pine needles and fallen leaves from a patch of forest bed. Cosmina took the bundle of sticks in her hands and framed the cleared patch of ground with them, piling the rest in the middle. Tiz Agathe dumped vials of potions over the sticks, whispering a stream of words in a foreign language as she worked. She added a handful of crushed nasturtium for victory in battle, fresh rosemary for loyalty, sage for long life, thyme for loyalty and strength, and zinnia for remembering lost friends. When she'd finished her spell, she lit fire to the sticks with a wave of her hand and stepped back.

"Now is your last chance to leave if you don't want to be blood-bound." Nix removed a knife from his boot and held it against his heart. "I vow to be proactive about ending the persecution of witches with dark affinities. I vow to be loyal to my comrades, keeping their identities secret. I vow to fight to the best of my ability and dedicate my life to this cause for as long as I am able, or until it becomes unnecessary." With the oath made, he sliced the palm of his left hand and squeezed a trickle of blood into the fire. The flame hissed and flashed blue. He passed the knife to Cosmina.

She forced herself to pause a moment and consider if this was indeed what she wanted. Taking this oath meant leaving Rinna. She would lose most of her new family, possibly never seeing them again. Everything would be more dangerous, more aggressive.

Nix lifted an eyebrow. "Backing out now?"

Cosmina shook her head. There was no question. She made the vow. There was no turning back, and she knew it. Life on the run would be a life wasted, and she was an ambitious woman. She would not settle for anything less than purposeful.

The blade stung as it sliced her skin apart. Her blood felt hot in her hand as she squeezed it into the fire. Its redness deepened. She passed the knife to Scorpia.

The problem with trying to keep a secret from someone who has spent a decade honing their observance is that it's impossible to do.

Rinna noticed the wound on Xia's hand while hunting, when the force of drawing the arrow reopened it. Xia downplayed its severity as Rinna wound a cloth around her hand.

"You need to go back to camp and have Tiz Agathe tend to that. How'd you cut your palm, anyway?"

"I cut it on an arrow this morning," Xia lied quickly.

"Ouch."

A few hours later, she returned to the cottage with her meager haul and went to the kitchen to find Cosmina washing dishes. She plunged her hand into the sudsy water, but not before Rinna spotted the clean red line down her palm.

"What happened to your hand?"

"I broke a glass earlier." Cosmina pulled it from the water and turned to show Rinna. "Took me half an hour to replace all this water and get going again."

"Why didn't you let Tiz Agathe heal it? You're going to have a scar."

"Is she back? She was gone earlier. I think she went into town. I'll ask her to treat it when I'm finished." Cosmina turned back to her task.

"Yeah." Rinna paused. "Do you know where Nix is?"

Cosmina laughed out loud. "Do I know where Nix is? No. The less I see of him, the better."

"Of course. I'll find him." She turned and left the room feeling uneasy.

She found Nix cutting vegetables outside. He nodded at her as he dumped the bowl of chopped veggies into the skillet above the fire and tossed a bit of olive oil on top. They were alone, so Rinna took the seat beside him. "Have you noticed anyone behaving strangely today?"

"Since when are you the suspicious one?"

"So you don't think people are acting weird?" Rinna persisted.

"I haven't noticed anything. What's going on, Rin?"

"Xia and Cosmina both have untreated cuts in the palms of their left hands."

"That is unusual, but maybe not suspicious. This life is rough." Nix inclined his head, his heart beating fast. His own palm rested on his knee, and he resisted the urge to squeeze his fist because he knew Rinna would notice.

"They had explanations for the cuts, yes. But the only reason for leaving a cut untreated is if the blood was used in some sort of sacrifice or blood oath." Poor Rinna's eyes widened in horror. "You don't think they're making sacrifices, do you?"

Guilt weighed in Nix's chest. He hated lying to her, this woman who had been such a fierce friend for years and deserved nothing less than loyalty and honesty. "I couldn't begin to guess what sacrifices they'd be making, especially together. The two of them don't really socialize. But I'll keep an eye on them."

"Thanks." Rinna leaned into him and rested her head on his shoulder. "I can always count on you."

He closed his eyes against the emotions triggered by those words.

Rinna's uneasiness subsided only until the following morning, when she rolled over and looked at the cot across from hers. Nino was asleep with his left hand tucked partially under his face, sporting a familiar red wound on his palm.

She hurried downstairs and out the door without brushing her teeth or even putting on shoes.

Rogues milled about in the front yard, preparing for the day. Some wandered off to their daily meditations, some prepared hunting gear, and the guards changed shifts. Two young witches returned from the river with water buckets for scrubbing laundry. Josie hurried by, bumping into Rinna and apologizing profusely. Rinna shooed her away.

"I want to see everyone's hands," she demanded, her voice trembling. The people closest stopped what they were doing and turned perplexed faces to her.

"I want to see everyone's HANDS!" Rinna screeched this time, getting everyone's attention. "Single file line. Now!"

People lined up before her, but she ignored them. She watched for anyone trying to sneak away without being inspected. She spotted Reggie and Eric ducking behind the cottage and whirled on them. "You two first." They froze for a long minute before shuffling over to display the backs of their hands to her.

"You know I mean your palms."

Reluctantly, they flipped their hands to reveal recent untreated cuts.

"And I suppose you both have explanations for those?"

Rinna inspected the palms of every witch present, ordering the ones with wounds to stand together by the fire pit and sending everyone else to their assigned duties. When she felt confident she'd inspected everyone, she turned to the suspicious group. "Tell me the truth."

Cosmina was the only one who would meet her gaze. Everyone else stared at the ground. No one said a word.

"Now! What are you planning?" Rage flashed in her brown eyes.

Nix, the only person Rinna hadn't bothered to inspect, stepped forward and displayed the cut on his palm for her. She froze, horrorstruck.

"Rinna, I don't know if you recall this or not, but I once suggested we make fighting the system our priority."

"Of course I remember that," Rinna snapped. "It was a stupid idea, especially coming from you. We don't have the resources to rescue dozens of people, and I'm unwilling to put our lives in danger like that."

"Yes, those were the objections you had then as well. And they are sensible." Nix shrugged. "But I've never stopped believing that survival isn't enough. And I've recently learned that quite a few people agree with me."

"As long as I'm alive, it doesn't matter what you believe, because I am the leader of this group. Or is that what the sacrifice was for? Some sort of spell to overthrow me?" Rinna laughed nervously.

"Of course not. But some of us have decided to leave this group and form our own, more proactive group. We're making it our mission to overthrow the system that persecutes us."

Another shocked silence fell over the camp. Adults and older teens shared wide-eyed looks. Children made themselves small, confusion and fear on their faces. For a moment, no one dared to speak.

Finally, Rinna whispered, "The cuts are for a blood oath, then."

"They are," Nix confirmed. Cosmina noted he was the only person in the whole camp, aside from herself, who was unafraid of Rinna. She knew that, from a psychological standpoint, most people were inclined to be followers. Most people found it easy, and even enjoyable, to pledge loyalty to a leader and never question it, never change their mind. There were people in this group who would obey Rinna if she ordered them to kill innocents, and she understood then what Nix saw in her.

She wasn't a follower.

Rinna clenched and unclenched her fists. "Surely this is a joke."

Nix only shook his head.

"You've taken nearly all my fighters!" Rinna sliced through the hypnotized silence by flinging her arm toward the witches with palm wounds. "You'll be leaving us defenseless!"

"No, we won't. We haven't even taken half the group. You'll still have plenty of help."

"I don't believe this." Rinna clutched her chest and turned to the proactive rogue group with wide eyes. "You all really want to do this?" Her gaze fell on Cosmina last, punctuating the question.

"Yes," they all affirmed, but not without sadness.

"This is your fault, isn't it?" Rinna turned to Tiz Agathe with angry tears in her eyes. "This was your plan all along. To create an army out of us."

"I am very supportive of their decision, dear," Tiz Agathe said gently. "I will always be of assistance to both groups however I am able."

"We don't need your help." Rinna straightened her back and lifted her chin. "Everyone in my group, pack your things tonight. We're leaving in the morning."

Nix took a step toward her. "Rinna, don't do this." Her glare sharpened, and he dared not move closer. "Don't deprive them of beds and soap and a kitchen. We're happy to co-exist."

"You'll put us all at risk, and I won't allow it. I have to protect them, and I won't let your stupid hero fantasy put them in danger." She raked her fingers through her tangled hair in frustration, then stalked off into the forest alone. Everyone watched her go, but no one followed.

After a minute, they disbanded. A few went down to the river. Others went inside to pack their meager belongings. Tiz Agathe offered to brew ishtis, and several people followed her inside. There remained a hushed, awkward air over the camp, no one sure what to think or how to feel.

"Are you accepting applicants for your proactive group?" A small voice asked. Nix turned and looked down into the face of Lottie, a pretty young witch with plaited brown hair who had managed to escape from a low-security lab with her cellmate, Meg. Meg stood beside her now, shorter, with shoulder-length blonde hair and a round face, clutching her hand and finishing her thought.

"Survival isn't good enough for us either."

Nix glanced at Cosmina, who shrugged. "Just because we didn't think of them doesn't mean they aren't our people. Are you willing to take a blood oath?"

They both nodded. Cosmina led them to Tiz Agathe to prepare another oath.

Destiny stood on her tiptoes to tap Nix on the shoulder. "You know, I'm a little offended you didn't pitch this to me." He turned, sighing in exhaustion.

"I wanted to ask you, but I was worried you'd be too loyal to Rinna. I was going to wait until we had our little group solidified and then talk to you, but you can see how well that went."

"I want to help, but you're right; I don't want to lose Rinna. Let me see what I can do."

Nix watched her go, hoping she would agree to join them. She had an affinity for Magical technology that would be infinitely more useful to them than it would ever be to Rinna.

Or Die Trying

Canis 318

Every sunset was different on the East side of the world. Tonight, the light filtering through the leaves was lilac and weightless with the sensation of good things to come. A breeze sent pollen dancing through the air, bringing with it a floral scent and a chill that made Cosmina's bare arms prickle.

She adjusted her position on the steel rooftop, her tailbone aching.

She loved the Eastern islands, particularly Lochspring. She had vacationed here with her family twice. The first time, Daisy had been a toddler, wobbling around in the sand with her sunglasses upside down. They returned when Daisy was twelve and angry that Cosmina was leaving for Primary School soon.

There had always been something about the quaint island community that beckoned to Cosmina's soul. She had thought about moving here after school. She wondered if she would ever get the chance. A season ago, she would have said absolutely not. She would have pushed the thoughts from her head, angry for hurting herself. Since they'd created their new group, however, she'd found herself hoping that one day she could still have a normal life.

She would do it or die trying.

In the abandoned warehouse beneath her, Nix sat on the concrete floor, leaning against the cool plaster wall. His jeans wrinkled up to his knees, exposing his white socks. By all appearances he was bored, but his heart and head were full of turmoil.

Telling his story to Cosmina a season ago had stirred memories he'd managed to repress. Every night since, he'd dreamed of his familiar and woken in a cold sweat, sometimes even tears. Logically, he knew they'd probably killed him. It was more fuel for the fire of Nix's rage. He would end the horrifying treatment of witches with dark affinities, or he would die trying.

A figure moved in his peripheral vision, and he whipped his head to face it. Scorpia paused in her tracks. "It's nearly time for the meeting."

Nix took a breath, a display of nerves he would never allow in front of anyone else, and escorted Scorpia into the basement. They walked close, but without touching. Though not conventionally attractive, Scorpia was a staggering presence; powerful, innovative, and captivating. They had a traumatic history together, something that made them closer than he'd ever been with another person. But their circumstances made Nix opposed to romance. They had to work as a team, and the complications of love could only weaken them. As such, they had an agreement to avoid the matter entirely.

The agreement was not as firm as they pretended.

The basement smelled musty. A thick layer of dust coated the clutter left upon abandonment. Several lit candles flickered around the room, which had served as a workspace for Scorpia for the past eight days as she concocted her potions. An old wooden desk with three legs sat near the center of the room, two large boxes replacing the fourth leg. Thirty glass vials were clumped together in groups of three atop the desk. Nix studied the bottles while Scorpia watched him.

She opened her mouth to speak but was interrupted by footsteps pounding down the stairs. Instinctively, they ducked behind the desk. They waited until the footsteps had silenced before Scorpia dared a peek.

She stood so abruptly that the other person screamed and swore.

"It's just you. You scared the life out of me." Destiny smoothed her hair. The tufts around her hairline refused to stay contained in a bun.

Nix rose as well, making Destiny grin. "Ooh, what are you two doing back there?"

"Hiding from you," Nix snapped. "You came down those stairs like a lunatic."

"Well, I didn't want to sneak up on you." She approached the desk, leaning to admire the potions. "Scorpia! These are exuding power! You are incredible."

"Oh, stop." Scorpia beamed as she waved the compliment away. "It took me a full eight days to make these."

"Well, you could've given me eight years to do it, and they still wouldn't be right, so shut up and take my compliment."

The rest of the team trickled in. Cosmina was last, as usual. Once she arrived, Nix cleared his throat and said, "For the sake of efficiency, I'm going to make a series of statements, and I only want you to speak if you disagree with what I've said. Does everyone understand?"

The sound of water dripping from a broken pipe was his only answer.

"Perfect. Everyone in this room can find any of the retreat points on their own, especially the final one."

No one said a word.

"Everyone in this room knows the goal of the mission tonight."

Drip. Drip.

"Everyone in this room knows the part they play tonight, and can play that part without assistance or prompting."

Drip. Drip.

"Everyone knows there's a chance they may die, or meet a fate even worse, tonight."

Drip. Drip. Drip. Drip.

"Everyone understands that if you don't make it to the final meeting point by sunup, we'll be forced to move on without you."

Drip. Drip.

"Everyone is resolved to see this through."

Drip. Drip.

"Alright. Scorpia?"

Scorpia smiled grimly. "I've prepared some potions, but use them as a last resort. They have serious side effects and should not be used frivolously. The green one makes you invisible for around an hour. It'll also make you puke your guts out when it wears off. This yellowish-orange one will stop any bleeding within a few minutes but make you seriously dehydrated for a couple days. If you have to drink this one, you need to leave. And find some water on the way, because you'll need it to avoid passing out. The yellow one is a game-ender.

"And finally, the sparkly purplish-black one. It'll make you immune to physical Magic attacks for somewhere between one and two hours. Afterward, though, you'll experience lapses in memory for an average of two weeks.

"Everyone can remember what these potions do and agrees to use them only if necessary."

Drip. Drip.

"Awesome. Also, I brewed these for your size, so don't drink anyone else's, because I can't guarantee the same results." Scorpia grabbed the first set of vials and passed them to Nix. Then she called the others up one by one to get theirs.

"What happens if we drink two of them?" Destiny turned her yellow vial over and inspected it.

"It depends. But no one should have to drink two."

Nix gave them one more chance to bail. No one took it. Nodding solemnly, he announced the start of the mission.

As he watched everyone leave, his heart swelled with pride. Seeing this group of people, so different, so traumatized, united in pursuit of the same goal, gave him hope. Maybe splitting the group would be a good thing.

Lottie and Meg left the warehouse as they'd entered it: arm-in-arm, giggling like bored schoolgirls who stumbled across a spooky building and decided to explore it.

"It was so creepy in there! I can't believe I let you talk me into that!" Meg squealed, giving Lottie a playful shove.

"Ugh, my nose is still itching from all that dust. Don't pretend you didn't want to go in."

Cosmina watched from the roof, flat on her stomach. Once they were out of sight, she started counting backward from one hundred, scanning the area for anything suspicious. They'd been using this abandoned warehouse for weeks, and though they were sneaky and came and went as little as possible, she was surprised no one had bothered them yet.

As she reached fifteen, she pulled her feet beneath her and rose to a perch. Nothing seemed out of the ordinary. She crawled across the roof and dropped to the ground, crossing the pavement into the yard behind it. She adjusted her brown wig and wrapped her thin shawl around the bottom half of her face.

The man living in this home had made it too easy to use him as a cover. He lived alone but shared custody of his two young sons with his ex-wife, and they met every week in the parking lot of a nearby grocery store to exchange the boys. They must be on good terms because the meetings took around twenty minutes.

He also liked young brunettes. They left his house at all hours of the day and night, hiding their faces behind scarves and hats, glancing around nervously. Tonight Cosmina would play that part, but he would never know she'd been there.

Because Nix needed to complete his assignment before she finished hers, she was taking the long way to the facility, cutting through neighborhoods. On the sidewalk across the street, she paused to get a good look at it. It looked like any other old brick building full of rented offices and even had a sign proclaiming as such, but the people renting them were so fake they were silly. Arnold Palmer, Master Chef. Sabrina, Palm Reader. Melissa Finger, Fine Jewelry Maker. Cosmina scoffed. There it was, a prison dedicated to torturing witches with dark affinities, hidden in plain sight on a busy town street.

Not all prisons were reserved for dark affinities, but this one was. Destiny had managed to hack the Council's digital

systems without raising any alarms and compiled a list of
options for the first raid, recommending this one. None of
the recorded prisoners were older than twenty-two. They
should all be in *school*. The group could feel comfortable
releasing everyone inside without worrying if some of them
deserved to be locked up.

The building loomed behind her as she walked, taunting
her. How close had she come to being inside there herself?
If Rinna hadn't intervened, where would that armored van
have taken her after her trial?

She felt safer once she reached the small wooded area
that separated the wealthy neighborhood behind her from
the town's main road in front of her. Destiny had spent
many hours spying from here, and this was where she'd
stashed Cosmina's backpack for the mission.

She fell on it in mild desperation, already pulling off the
itchy wig. She changed from her jacket and dress and into
her comfortable black clothing and watched as employees
left the building, some getting into cars, some walking.
These people participated in medical torture; collected
paychecks in exchange for the suffering of other witches.
Cosmina wondered how many of them knew.

When the shift change was over, she pulled her pack
onto her back and made her way across the grassy space to
the concrete wall behind the facility. Destiny, with her
technological affinity, had briefed them on the security
measures she'd found. There were Magic sensors, but the
cameras wouldn't activate unless they detected energy use
measured at over a thousand units. If they kept it to a
minimum near the building, they should be fine.

The six-foot wall was smooth and hard, but Cosmina
was tall, and had only to grab the top and pull herself up.
She scanned the play yard, seeing no one and nothing of

interest. She tiptoed along the wall until she reached the building, using the rain gutters to pull herself onto the roof. She'd spent more time on top of buildings than inside them today.

She spotted Nix, already climbing the ladder into the attic, only his head and one arm visible. He gave a quick salute before disappearing. She pressed herself flat and counted backward from a hundred again before descending herself.

As planned, Nix had left the door ajar to minimize creaking. According to the scouts, the top floor wasn't used for much, but they were careful nonetheless.

Cosmina channeled a little of her Magic to see if she could sense anyone nearby. She didn't, so she slipped out of the attic and closed the door, making a right to head deeper down the hallway. Everyone else would be going into the belly of the beast tonight, but she had a different task altogether.

The hallway ended in a left turn, which she took. It dead-ended there, at a black door with a gold plaque that read, "Dr. Frank Egert."

Cosmina felt her stomach turn. It was a name she'd only learned a few seasons ago. The man credited with beginning this persecution of dark witches, mysteriously missing for years now. She shook off the goosebumps and closed her eyes. Magically picking the locks without using a detectable amount of energy was an exercise in patience and self-control, and one they'd all practiced many times in the previous weeks.

She got the door open in under a minute. The office smelled musty. Cosmina closed the door and the blinds on the window, ignoring the showering of dust that fell from them. The lights came on then, dimly, and she got to work rummaging through the office, starting with the desk.

In the top drawer, she found a memo pad with some lazily written notes, which she stole. A day planner from four years prior was stashed in the next drawer down, and she took it as well. The desk contained nothing else of note, not even false bottoms in the drawers. She moved to the filing cabinets on the back wall.

These were more interesting. There were two; the left labeled "Current" and the right labeled "Previous." She opened the top Current drawer and removed a few files. They were skinny, the notes inside brief. They listed names and experiments, all in code. Every page ended with the bolded words, "**See original file for more info.**"

Cosmina stashed the files in her bag, then swiped a few from the Previous cabinet as well. She knew these were not up to date, but they might learn something from them.

Sidestepping to the bookshelf, she skimmed over it but found only a couple of books that seemed like more than decoration. She took them for good measure.

She was surprised when she stooped to open the two small doors at the bottom of the bookshelf and found them locked. Everything else in the office had been easy access.

They were easy to pick open, and worth the effort. Inside the small compartment were a few watches and some expensive-looking jewelry. Cosmina grabbed two handfuls and shoved them in her bag. The group always needed more money, and who better to fund them than their enemies?

Behind the jewelry, she spotted an old-school binder notebook propped against the back wall. Every nerve ending in her body tingled as she reached for it, confirming she'd found something worthwhile. She removed it from the cabinet and rearranged the remaining jewelry to hide the burglary, then closed and locked the little doors again before carrying the binder to the desk.

Giddiness overwhelmed her as she flipped through the pages. Blueprints. This binder contained blueprints to at least a dozen government labs, along with their addresses, security level, and list of directors. Some of the information was outdated, but this was a valuable find even so.

Cosmina slipped the binder inside her pack and zipped it, giving the office a final once-over before opening the blinds. She left, blinking in the harsh light of the hallway.

She walked down the corridor slowly, extending her senses to detect Magical energy around her. Ignoring the pit of negative energy on the lower floors, she ducked into a conference room at the intersection of two hallways and approached the window. It took a moment, but she located Nix's tall frame waiting in the darkness on the other side of the security wall, little more than a shadow in the night. He waved to acknowledge he'd seen her, and she removed her bag and levitated it out the window and across the play yard to him before dropping it. He caught it and disappeared from view.

Someone cleared their throat.

Cosmina whirled to find a man in a black suit blocking the entire doorway with his muscular frame. He folded his arms and raised his eyebrows. "What are you doing out of bed?"

Cosmina didn't speak. A quick sweep of her senses confirmed her fears; there were more guards on their way upstairs. She forced herself to breathe. She had known there was a chance she wouldn't make it out of this building tonight. Nix had the evidence she'd stolen, which was the important part. Still, it would be a shame to get taken out of the game in the first mission.

"Then again." The man unfolded his arms and leaned forward menacingly. "None of our residents would be on the top floor, dressed like a criminal. Who are you, and why are you here?" He was buying time, waiting on his backup to arrive. Cowardice. She was a skinny girl, and he was afraid to grab her on his own?

The man shouted as she flung her body out the open window.

Her hands flailed for something to grab as she slid down the side of the building, the bricks tearing at her clothes and skin. She finally grabbed a window ledge on the second floor, but only for a moment before her fingers slipped and she resumed her fall. The delay had been just enough, and she was able to tuck and roll as she hit the yard, running for the wall before the guards had a chance to switch course and chase her downstairs. Her right foot caught on something, and she lurched to her hands and knees. Sharp pain shot through the heels of her hands to her elbows. She jumped up and continued running.

As she'd hoped, she was over the wall and out of sight before the guards reached the yard. She didn't stop running until she reached the first retreat point, a boarded-up old house scheduled for demolition to make space for something more modern. She once again found herself on a rooftop.

She was startled to descend the attic stairs into the home and find six people already inside.

"Cosmina!" Lottie cried as she and Meg relaxed, having been prepared to fight.

"What are you doing here already?" Cosmina surveyed the scene. Lottie and Meg looked fine, but they stood by a group of children, the three youngest huddled together in the corner while the oldest stood in front of them protectively. Even she couldn't have been more than fourteen. Cosmina sucked in a breath at the sight of them.

"Meg and I got caught before we ever got a chance to enter the building."

"Nino rescued these four kids," Meg added quickly.

Cosmina looked between the two of them as they hung their heads in shame. "Well, I'm glad you're safe." She hoped she hid her disappointment well enough. "Where is Nino?"

"Here," a disembodied voice said from the center of the room.

Cosmina groaned. "You drank the invisibility potion."

"I had to. We barely made it out. Lottie and Meg ran with the kids while I fought off a guard, then I had to drink the potion to escape past a few others."

Cosmina's eyes fell on several droplets of blood on the ground near Nino's voice. "Are you hurt?"

"I'll be fine."

Cosmina nodded, then approached the children slowly. "Hi. My name is Cosmina. What's yours?"

The older girl narrowed her eyes. None of them spoke.

"They don't trust us yet," Nino told her.

"Understandable."

Connor Bellingham lifted his eyes from his report to peer over the top of his glasses at the handsome young stranger who'd just entered his office. Normally, he would be furious with any unexpected visitor. The exception was always a young man with uncommonly good looks and an unbothered attitude.

"Good evening." He waited for the stranger to explain himself.

"Good evening, sir." The young man leaned forward to place a white ceramic mug and saucer on the edge of Connor's desk. "Andrew asked me to bring you this. Said to tell you he's a bit backed up downstairs, but he didn't forget about you."

A smile broke across Connor's face as he admired the steaming cup of honey-gold liquid. "That Andrew." He chuckled, lifting his eyes to let the young man in on his private joke. "Dedicated enough to do the work well, but always behind in it. Hasn't quite learned the quality must sometimes be sacrificed for the quantity."

The young man smiled politely.

"You must be one of the new assistants we hired."

"I am. My name is Eli, sir." He ducked his head in a brief, halfhearted display of deference.

"Eli. Pleasure to meet you." Connor took a long drink of the ishti as he pondered the young man. New employees were nervous around him. Awkward. Big smiles. Eager to please. Eli had an air of indifference, though. Aside from barging into Connor's office, Eli knew the niceties he was expected to perform. But they were skin-deep, and if Connor didn't like him, his life would go on unaffected. This made Connor like him immediately.

"Did you or Andrew make this?" Connor extended the cup to Eli.

"Andrew gave me precise instructions, but I made it." Eli stood calmly near the doorway, ready to leave the moment he was dismissed. He was tall and slender, with defined muscles that were shamefully hidden beneath his suit jacket. He stood with his back straight, shoulders back and legs spread for a strong, wide stance. Connor sighed and drank the rest of his ishti.

"Well, it is wonderful. Perfectly made. Tell Andrew I said to stay on his toes, or I might just replace him."

Eli pretended to be amused. "I will tell him, sir."

"You know, the besst—" Connor stopped, embarrassed by the slur of his words. "Fuhgive me. The bessssst—" Connor stopped again, confused. His tongue felt suddenly very thick.

Eli stepped forward. "Are you alright, sir?"

"I feel thrange." Connor furrowed his brow.

"Is your name Connor Bellingham?" Eli leaned over him, both hands on the desk, his entire demeanor changed as though he'd acquired all the power in the room. There was something fierce in the set of his jaw.

Connor frowned. "Yeth?"

"What is your job here?"

"I am the director." Any assistant should know that. Connor felt a twinge of fear, just a small one, deep inside his belly.

"Right, but what does the director do?"

Connor wanted to laugh. Tell him it was none of his business. Instead, to his own surprise, he answered the question, the slurred words hardly sensible to his own ears. "I do many things. I decide who comes to stay here. I decide which experiments to allow on my rats. I oversee their care, and the safety and cleanliness of the place."

Darkness settled over Eli's face. "Who was the director before you?"

"Frank Egert."

"Why is Frank's office left intact while you use this broom closet down here?"

"Frank is coming back."

Eli started visibly, which Connor found gratifying. "You think Frank Egert is coming back?"

"Of course."

"You don't think Frank Egert is dead?"

"No."

"Do you know where he is?"

"No."

"Do you know what he's doing?"

"No."

"Then what makes you think Frank Egert is alive and coming back?"

"Family bond," Connor said with a dazed smile. "I would feel it if he died."

"How are you related to Frank Egert?"

Connor's face brightened, though his eyes remained glassy. "He is my uncle, but he raised me like a son."

Eli leaned closer, lowering his voice. "What determines the level of security for a lab such as this one?"

"Many things. High or low profile of rats. Age of rats. Level of secrecy of experiments being done. Et cetera."

Eli's anger grew with each callous use of the word "rat." He clenched his fists on the desktop. "What experiments are done in this lab?"

"I don't keep track of those. Not my job."

"You said it's your job to decide which experiments to allow."

"It is. They send me a list of experiments, and I decide which ones to allow, but that doesn't mean they're performed. They just become approved options."

"Who decides which experiments to do?"

"The scientists, of course."

"Of course. And where are the reports kept?"

"The copies are in the basement. Each season, we send the originals to headquarters for review."

"Is that true of every lab?"

"It is a requirement, yes."

Eli straightened and backed toward the door. "Do you know where the records are kept at Council Headquarters?"

"No. I don't even know who knows where they are."

Eli felt for the doorknob behind him. "Do you remember my name?"

"Of course I do. It's Eli." Connor was no longer smiling, the poison's hold on him loosening. His eyes darted to the emergency button beneath his desk.

Eli shoved a hand deep inside his pocket. "Do you remember anyone from your past named Eli?"

Connor thought for a moment before shrugging. "I'm afraid I don't."

"Don't worry. You will soon." He pulled his hand from his pocket and blew a fine white powder at Connor. The Director slumped over his desk, asleep in a second.

The moment the door was closed, Nix started down the hall. He hurried to the staircase, taking them two at a time, reaching the attic without incident, climbing the ladder to the roof and tiptoeing across the play yard wall just as he'd done to get inside.

On the other side, he crouched low and watched the windows in the back of the building for Cosmina. She was behind schedule, but not enough to worry him. He'd taken longer than expected as well. Hopefully it meant she'd found something useful.

A light came on inside the farthest window on the left. Nix's attention snapped to it. Cosmina appeared, pushing open the glass and levitating her bag to him. He caught it from midair and turned to run for the retreat point before the thing was on his back.

Xia's leg cramped in her hiding spot behind the ice machine. She listened with her enhanced hearing as two sets of footsteps passed the break room and faded down the hall. Hearing nothing beyond some muted crying and snoring, she crept out of the employee break room and peered down the hallway in both directions. She was relieved to see Sam, already entering the first room. He paused long enough to give her a quick wave.

She went to the first door on her side of the hall and turned the knob. It opened easily, revealing a tall young man with messy blonde hair slumped against the wall behind his bed. He eyed her with something akin to boredom.

"I'm here to free you," she whispered, gesturing for him to follow her. "We have to hurry."

The man pushed himself off the wall and exited his room calmly.

"Around the corner is a break room. Wait in the dark and keep quiet while I rescue as many as I can. Okay?"

The man nodded and walked around the corner. Xia was both confused by his nonchalance and impressed by the silence of his steps but didn't have time to dwell on either of those things. She listened for any unexpected noise as they worked, but this hallway was silent. Between the two of them, they freed all eight prisoners in these rooms. Once they'd met in the middle, Xia joined her four in the break room.

"We're going to escape through the window, then go around the building to the play yard. Once there, head straight for the farthest corner, and I'll help everyone over the wall. Wait for me on the other side. Understand?"

The prisoners were terrified and confused, but they recognized their only chance out of this hell, and they nodded.

The blonde man dropped to the ground and waited to catch the smaller prisoners. One young girl was heavily drugged, and he carried her over his shoulder. When they reached the play yard wall, Xia gave him a boost, repeating this process.

Sam's prisoners joined her a moment later, without him. Xia glanced over her shoulder and saw him holding a wide-eyed facility employee against his body like a hostage, his hand clamped over her mouth. She was just a caregiver, but they couldn't be too careful. She would alert the guards if they let her go.

Everyone froze at the sound of shouting inside the building, above their heads. Xia tuned in and heard a dozen or so sets of feet pounding the stairs.

Xia hoisted the rescues over and into the arms of the blonde man, then scaled the wall herself. Before dropping to safety, she confirmed Sam was gone. The caregiver was alone on the side of the building, looking as dazed as a person whose memories had just been extracted from their head.

Sam rounded the corner, and they herded their eight escaped prisoners into the wooded area for safer travel to the retreat point. Unfortunately, they missed the show as Cosmina hopped the wall after them and guards flooded the yard, shouting.

Reggie exited the underground tunnel first, Eric close at his heels. The basement didn't smell musty, as one would expect. Dim lights lined the wall, illuminating a path for them to move amongst the tall rows of filing cabinets.

"This must be where the records are kept." Eric tugged at one of the drawers. Neither of them was surprised to find it locked.

"Has to be," Reggie said. "Good to know, I guess?"

Eric scoffed. "You think we'll ever get a chance to break in this place again?"

"Useless information, then." Reggie pointed to the end of their current row. "There's the door."

After picking the lock, they entered the prisoner section of the basement. It was well-lit but deserted. Most of the rooms looked like offices, locked up for the night. Only four contained people, each housed alone and too unharmed to have been in the facility long. Reggie eyed their arms, finding no signs of needle abuse. These prisoners were brand new.

"She jumped out the window! Get her! She has to be injured!"

The boys and their rescues broke into a mad dash for the tunnel.

Above them, Destiny and Scorpia looked at one another in horror. They were caught in an open hallway on the first floor with six escaped prisoners huddled between them. One began to cry. Another clamped their hand over his mouth.

Glancing around, Scorpia spotted an emergency exit door. It faced the front of the building, but desperate times called for desperate measures. "We have to make a break for it."

Destiny nodded. "You lead, I'll follow."

Scorpia flung open the door. Alarms sounded throughout the building. Someone was already caught, but now the guards would know there were other intruders. They needed to move fast.

Destiny slipped out the door after the last of the rescues, leaving it wide open. She hurried the prisoners along, glancing over her shoulder every few steps to ensure they weren't being followed. None stopped until they were concealed by trees.

Cosmina and her group arrived at the final retreat point just before sun-up, true to character. The hushed conversation and muffled crying gave way to gasps of horror as they entered with four young children. Cosmina looked at Nix as he took in the sight, his jaw clenched.

"That's messed up," the blonde rescued man said.

"That's everyone." Destiny rose to her feet. "But we aren't in the clear yet. There's a bus parked behind the building. Board it quickly. All prisoners need to keep their heads down and stay away from the windows. We don't want anyone to be recognized."

Destiny drove for two hours before parking in a carpool lot by the woods and ordering everyone out. Nix led them into the trees, Cosmina bringing up the rear.

"We'll catch up soon." Destiny tilted her head in Scorpia's direction by way of explanation. The five-foot witch was already scrubbing the bus's seats free of any fingerprints, DNA, or Magic residue.

They hiked for three hours, Nix carrying the drugged teen. When they reached a safe place, they stopped to discuss the plan.

Nino's stomach upset from the invisibility potion was awful, so they agreed he should return to the cottage first. All the older prisoners volunteered the youngest to go before them. Cosmina watched as the fourteen-year-old girl suspiciously took Reggie's arm, the other children clinging to her. Eric grabbed Nino's arm in one hand and Reggie's in the other, and they teleported away.

A few minutes later, Reggie and Eric returned alone. They had to make several trips, but they were close enough to the cottage that it was feasible. Cosmina and Nix were the last to go.

When they reached their destination, Tiz Agathe waited in the doorway for them. The only sign of her relief was the slight relaxation of her shoulders. She sent Reggie and Eric straight to bed and put the other rogues to work, fetching potion and salve ingredients so she could tend to the rescued prisoners.

Solara and Hiroto went into town to sell the items Cosmina had stolen and buy shoes and other necessities for the rescued prisoners. Tiz Agathe promised to fetch them in four hours.

Following Rinna's example, they allowed the prisoners a day of rest, providing plenty of food, soap, and whatever ishtis or potions they needed. Most were ill from the medication they'd received during their confinement.

On the second day, Nix announced that they needed to get to work. Destiny took a notebook and pen and sat by the fire pit, crossing one leg over the other. "Who'd like to go first?"

"What are we doing?" the blonde man asked. He rarely spoke, but he always sounded uninterested when he did.

"I need to interview each of you. We need to know who you are, where you come from, and how you came to be held in that facility."

"Why do you need to know that?" He didn't even sound curious. Cosmina turned to look at him. He looked much better now that his matted hair had been cut short and he was no longer dressed in stiff gray pajamas, but his skin was colorless and taut against his face and his blue eyes had dark circles under them. Like most of the others, he was sweaty from detoxing some poison meant to destroy his dark affinity.

"So we can figure out how to help you from here," Destiny answered. They hadn't discussed it yet, but no one knew what to do with the prisoners. They couldn't be turned loose in society with no support, but they also couldn't be integrated into this very niche group the way Rinna did when she rescued people. Not to mention they planned to save many more people. It would be impossible to house and protect everyone. They had to come up with something else.

"I'll go first." The oldest of the children rescued by Nino sat on a stump by Destiny, her face resolute. Cosmina's heart hurt for this poor child. Her black hair was cropped almost to her head, like most of the other prisoners, and her sandy-brown skin had lightened a shade after bathing. She had narrow brown eyes and a subtle scattering of freckles on both cheeks.

"Alright," Destiny said. "What is your real, full name?"

"Amara Mondragon." The young girl kept her eyes fixed on a spot on the ground as she answered questions about her birthday, her most recent home address, her family, and school.

"I'm sorry I have to ask you this," Destiny said finally. Amara did not look at her. "How did you come to be at the facility?"

Amara's eyes darkened, and she turned to face Destiny for the first time. "I told my parents for seasons that people were following me. Watching me. They never believed me. One day, I was babysitting while my parents went on a date, and a little girl knocked on our door. I let her in, and she begged me not to call the police because 'they' would know, and 'they' would kill her. I called my mom instead, but then some people broke into our house. My mom answered, but the line disconnected, and I suddenly couldn't see or move. They put us in a vehicle and drove for a long time. When we stopped, someone opened the door, told the other girl she did a good job, and then I smelled something strong and fainted. I don't know if they took any of my siblings, but I never heard them talking, even though I called their names."

Destiny asked about the experiments conducted on Amara, but she didn't remember. She was unconscious for all of them and drugged for hours afterward. She didn't have many details about the facility because she spent most of her time in a haze.

Destiny thanked her, and Amara went to a bedroom alone. For a while, no one dared break the silence. Then the blonde man said, "I'll go next."

His name was Conley Parrish. His story was more like Nix's: removed from Intermediate School under the premise of secluding him for safety, then convicted and branded a Variant Idealist without even attending his own trial. For the first time since being rescued, he showed emotion, eager to discuss his family and curious what they would do with the information.

Once the interviews were complete, the rogue group met to discuss their options. It was decided that Destiny and Scorpia would visit a few of the prisoners' hometowns and see if they could learn anything about their families. They would also see if there was any news circulating about their facility raid.

In the meantime, Lottie and Meg took the children under their wing, teaching them how to make soap, fish, and garden. Nino and Hiroto began training Conley and the older rescues in self-defense and hunting. Tiz Agathe continued to teach the witches who were old enough to control their dark power.

And everyone waited on word from Destiny and Scorpia.

Missing Persons

Gemma 318

They returned to the cottage after twelve days. Nix watched from a window as they made their way to the door, lost in conversation, smiling wide. Scorpia shoved Destiny and both women laughed, the sound echoing around the clearing.

Cosmina watched the tension in his angular jaw betraying the grit of his teeth, the clench of his fist enough to drain his hand of color. The two scenes contrasted before her, confusing her.

Scorpia and Destiny broke free of the group's enthusiastic greetings after several minutes, escaping through the back door. Cosmina and Nix followed. Tiz Agathe was already waiting amongst the trees for them, just out of earshot from the cottage.

"What did you learn?" Nix asked.

"I think we have good news, but it's risky," Destiny said.

"Everything we do is risky," Cosmina said. "Let's hear it."

Destiny and Scorpia shared a long look, silently consulting on how to begin. Cosmina felt Nix tense beside her, glanced sidelong at him as he folded his arms and leaned against a tree. No one else noticed his mood.

Scorpia tore her eyes from Destiny's to address the rest of them. "Well, we have twenty rescued prisoners."

"And twelve of them are open missing-persons cases," Destiny finished for her.

"The little ones," Cosmina presumed. "They were taken when they were children, so they were too young to paint as criminals."

Destiny nodded. "Exactly. They all disappeared without a trace. Amara was taken from her home. Henry disappeared from the playground at his childcare center. Lilly went to the end of the driveway on trash day and never came back inside. Two of them left school to walk home and were never seen again. Two ran away and never came back. Two disappeared from school field trips. One vanished after a bad car accident, while the rest of their family was unconscious. They all have different family dynamics and lived in different parts of the world. I haven't done a ton of digging, but it doesn't seem like these twelve kids had anything in common."

"Except that the Council wanted to experiment on them," Nix said. "But why? They can't even use Magic. The Council cannot possibly know whether they have dark affinities."

Scorpia looked up at him, her eyes round and sad.

"They must know something we don't," Cosmina said.

"It occurred to me," Destiny went on, "that we could solve twelve missing-persons cases at once, all across the world. Twelve kids returned to their families, all with the same story of being held prisoner and experimented on in government-run facilities. Imagine how impactful that would be."

Silence settled as they each pondered it. Scorpia was the first to speak. "I think it's absolutely brilliant, personally."

Cosmina ruffled her own messy hair. "There's a lot to consider here. I doubt the Council will make this as easy as just dropping these kids off with their families. They probably expect that's the first place they'll go, and they're lying in wait to snatch them back up. We're responsible for their safety now. How can we know they'll be safe at home? Who's to say their families will even believe their stories?"

"That's why it's risky," Destiny said.

"It does solve 60% of our problem of where to put these people now," Scorpia said. "And the others can go stay with Rinna."

Cosmina and Nix jerked their heads in her direction. "What?"

Destiny cringed. "I told you I was going to help both groups, and I have. I got Rinna to agree to take in some of the prisoners we rescue, provided they're willing to integrate. Obviously we can't overwhelm her with helpless people, but it's a short-term solution."

Cosmina couldn't say whether it was pride or reasonable objection, but she did not relish the idea of Rinna helping them. "Let's focus on the twelve right now, because that seems complicated. I think we should take a couple weeks and see what we can learn about their homes. What we're asking them to do is dangerous. We need to make sure they can maintain the same story, even under pressure."

Nix said, "Not to mention they know our faces and where we're staying. Sending them back to their families could be foolish."

"I think it makes a huge statement. If we can get the twelve kids back in their homes and get it noticed by the public, the Council would be stupid to abduct them again." Scorpia stretched to her full five feet and crossed her arms.

"And they're kids. They couldn't find their way back here, especially since we teleported. They have no idea what part of the world they're in."

She had a point there. Tiz Agathe had enchanted that bus to teleport them all across the ocean, back to Aelhill, where the cottage was. All the rescues probably thought they were still on Lochspring, if they even knew where the facility was.

"Or the Council could just tie up their loose ends," Nix said. "Make sure bodies are found."

Cosmina watched Nix's dark, dark eyes as his thoughts traveled someplace far away. "Why don't we start with the oldest? Let's send groups of two to check the families and see how we feel after that."

"We can't just send four teenagers back to their homes and call it a night. Especially because two of them are runaways, everyone will think they just made up some ridiculous story. If we do this, it has to be at least ten of them. A major news story." Scorpia scowled at Cosmina, who grinned in response.

"That isn't what I was suggesting. We should use some of our resources to determine if this plan is possible, but not waste too many, in case we decide this isn't an option."

"I could get behind that," Nix agreed with a single nod. "Exploring our options without committing to anything yet seems like the best course of action. Scorpia, why don't you and I check out Amara's family? Cosmina, find a volunteer to go with you to Henry's. We'll send Lottie and Meg to Celeste's, and Xia and Sam to Devlin's."

"You just eliminated half my volunteer pool," Cosmina said.

"You'll be fine. Find someone tonight. We're leaving tomorrow morning."

The Flanagans had been deeply traumatized by the disappearance of their only son. They had debated for a year if they should have more children, afraid it would feel too much like replacing Henry. When Mrs. Flanagan got pregnant with little Arabelle, they left their cute farmhouse in the country for the safety of an upscale suburban neighborhood. They bought a tiny, two-bedroom house with a half-acre lot surrounded on all sides by occupied homes, which was precisely what they wanted.

Mrs. Flanagan left her job two weeks before Arabelle was born and never returned to work. Henry was taken from a childcare facility, so entrusting their daughter to someone else's care was out of the question. The couple rarely let her out of their sight.

Mr. Flanagan was the head of the neighborhood watch. He took nighttime strolls when he couldn't sleep, to ensure there weren't any troublemakers hanging around. Cosmina and Nino discovered this when he walked up to the car they'd borrowed from a rideshare lot and rapped on the window, scaring the life out of them. They pretended to be teenagers caught fooling around and left in a hurry.

"That was disgusting," Nino said when they'd parked at a grocery store nearby. He pretended to gag. Cosmina ignored him. He had some nerve claiming he was humiliated when she was four inches taller than him, and clearly older.

"Let's go to the library."

Libraries had proven to be a major resource for the rogue group. They always held a ton of well-cataloged information on the local community. They wore masks and snuck in the back door, booting up two laptops and using flashlights to navigate the shelves. As usual, the library gave them what they needed.

The Flanagans were desperate for Henry's safe return, as any parent would be. They took every interview offered, regularly updated the reward money, and made weekly public pleas for their son's safe return. They had lost none of their steam in the three years since his disappearance. Even as the region around them lost interest in the story and gave up hope of Henry ever being found, Alroy and Cara Flanagan refused to quit.

"I think we can return Henry to his parents." Cosmina locked the library door behind them.

Nino nodded. "I think those two would sooner die than let him vanish again. But how do we do it without the Council ambushing us?"

"We have to figure out how the Council is scouting that house. It looked impossible to me." Cosmina walked around the driver's side of the car and gestured for Nino to toss her the keys.

"Nothing is impossible if you're creative enough. And the Council has endless means." He climbed into the car and buckled up. "What now?"

"Let's go for a walk," Cosmina suggested. "Even Alroy Flanagan has to sleep sometime."

The sun was still at least an hour from rising. There was no reason for a stroll at this hour, but they were banking on everyone in the neighborhood being in bed. They both tensed as they passed in front of the Flanagans' house and felt the weight of Magic in the air.

"Did you feel that?" Nino whispered when they'd passed.

"Yeah. On our way back down the street, stop to tie your shoe, and I'll look around."

When they passed the spot the second time, on the opposite side of the street, Cosmina spotted a lone crow perched atop the lamppost in front of the Flanagans' home, watching as they passed. "An enchanted bird."

"How do you know it's enchanted?"

"Crows travel in a murder and are rarely alone."

"That isn't a raven?"

"Ravens have wedge-shaped tails. This one is pointy. I wonder how long it's been here."

They wandered back to the car in silence. When they were driving again, Nino asked, "So how do we get close to the Flanagans? I don't suppose you know how to disenchant a bird?"

Cosmina shook her head. "That's some crazy, over-the-top Magic. I do have an idea, though. The Flanagans accept every interview they're offered, right?"

Cosmina made the call, her voice manipulation enabling her to fake the accent from this region. Cara had given her personal phone number in their most recent press conference. They agreed to have the reporter Dana Irving and her cameraman Wally come into their home that afternoon for a brief interview.

Cosmina and Nino napped in the car until morning, then snuck into a gym locker room to shower and change. Nino went into town to find cheap recording equipment. Cosmina found a thrift store and purchased a suit. At the fifteenth hour of the day, she knocked on the Flanagans' door. Both she and Nino could feel the watchful eyes of the crow on their backs as Cara ushered them inside.

Alroy sat on the sofa, feeding baby Arabelle from a pink bottle. He smiled and nodded. Cosmina's shoulders relaxed. She'd worried he would recognize them from the car, but it must have been too dark to make out their faces.

"Oh, she's so beautiful," Cosmina gushed, admiring the fiery red curls growing on the baby's head. The entire family had this red hair, Henry included. She wanted to hold the baby and smell her but pushed the urge to the back of her mind. She took a seat in the armchair as Cara instructed.

The Flanagans' family room was simple but cozy. They were not flashy people. The furniture was modest but comfortable, with a forest green and black color scheme. The wooden coffee table looked handmade, with a custom monogram carved into the top. Cara explained that Alroy was a woodworker, going so far as to give them a business card. Cosmina struggled to hide her pity for them. They'd been through every parent's worst nightmare, and for years had received no answers or comfort. Arabelle would be raised with overprotective parents, never allowed a normal childhood, always bearing the weight of her older brother's disappearance. Even when Henry returned, nothing would ever be normal.

It was one thing to consider the horrible things the Witching Council did on a broad spectrum. It was easy to see on paper that a government experimentation facility held seventy-five prisoners and say, "Wow, seventy-five wasted lives, what a tragedy." It was another thing entirely to sit inside the home of a family ruined by the Council. The rippling effects of this program had not occurred to her because her own parents had disowned her. But here, in the Flanagans' gathering room, with tears already in the blue eyes of Henry's mother, hope still shining on her face as she waited to talk about her beloved missing son yet again, it was impossible not to think about all the tangential pain caused by the Council.

"As I mentioned over the phone," Cosmina began, forcing a gentle smile, "we're working on an article about the effect that losing a child has on a family."

On the opposite end of the spectrum were the Mondragons, who had stayed put in their cabin-style home in the woods. After a few seasons of police interviews and news reports, the family had gone quiet. They refused publicity and changed their phone numbers often.

They had also gone about their normal lives. All of Amara's siblings were still in school, and both of her parents had kept their jobs. The only differences seemed to be that they always hired an adult babysitter now, and they were all in therapy.

Nix and Scorpia had traveled through the forest to the back of the Mondragons' home. They waited in the rain for half an hour for Amara's mother, Sandra, to leave for work. She was running late and swearing but still checked the locks on every door before she left. A few minutes after her car disappeared down the driveway, Nix and Scorpia approached the screened-in back porch. They didn't need prompting from one another or any verbal plan; they had worked together for years. They shed their muddy boots and raincoats and picked the lock on the back door. There was no time to waste.

The inside of the home was cluttered, with too many photographs decorating the walls and tables. The family photos had continued to be updated each year, but the old ones containing Amara were never moved. A row of seven individual portraits decorated the wall from the first floor to the second; the entire family arranged in order from oldest to youngest. Amara's most recent school portrait, before her abduction, still hung third on the wall. But her little brother's face looked older than hers now.

"I'll take the downstairs; you take the upstairs?" Nix opened the door to a private office. Scorpia went upstairs, studying the photos as she passed them. To a stranger, Amara's photographs would look out-of-place. Even the quality and style of them were slightly outdated.

The first bedroom on the left was Amara's, which Scorpia learned by entering. Amara shared her parents' obsession with photography, the room littered with snapshots of her old life. Either Amara was a neat child, or her parents had tidied the room in her absence. Clothes that would no longer fit still hung in the closet. A black flute case sat atop the dresser without a speck of dust on it. The carpet was vacuumed and the bed was made, pillows fluffed and the comforter smoothed free of wrinkles.

The only feature in the room that probably hadn't been there when Amara was taken was a small table in the center. It was adorned with partially burned candles, flower petals, crushed herbs, and a jar filled with the ashes of prayers written for her and then burned. "MAY SHE BE SAFE; MAY SHE BE RETURNED TO US" was etched into the altar's wooden border. Scorpia's heart tightened.

The room told the story of a happy young lady with many friends and hobbies. A framed photograph on the nightstand showed three smiling girls with their arms around each other. On the wall hung a picture of two girls in black dresses posing with their flutes before a wooden stage. A mathematics team holding their trophy, with Amara front and center. An afterschool sports team's yearbook photo. Amara and another girl behind a table, selling baked goods. Amara and several other fledglings in swimsuits at the beach. Precious memories, frozen in time. Scorpia lifted one from the desk, tracing her thumb over Amara's innocent face.

After escaping from the lab, Scorpia and Nix had argued about where to go. Nix had no ideas but knew they couldn't return to their lives, while Scorpia was insistent they go back to their families and explain what had been done to them. There wasn't a doubt in her mind that her family would believe her and help her. That she could end the torture of innocent witches by just telling her parents. They'd find a way to fix it. That was the kind of safe, innocent upbringing she'd had: worry-free, with her parents taking care of anything she needed. She knew nothing had changed. She just had to convince Nix.

A few weeks after their escape, Nix had decided to humor her. They stole a vehicle and drove to her family's vacation home in Elderkeep, where she'd spent every summer since she could remember. She knew they could hide there until her parents arrived. They'd broken in and found some nonperishable food items and soft beds, more luxury than they'd had in years.

The next morning, Scorpia had wandered through the vacant home, overwhelmed with emotions. She was sitting on her little sister's bed and tearfully hugging a pillow when she noticed it; the family portrait hanging in the hallway. There was a girl in the photo with them that she didn't recognize. She was petite but full-figured, with long wisps of black hair curled down her back. Her hand rested on her hip. She was vibrant, alive. Scorpia had gone to the photo and placed her hand over the girl, needing her to disappear.

It took a long time to reconcile that the girl in the photo was her. Not who she was now, but who she used to be. That girl belonged to this family. Scorpia had gone to the bathroom and looked at herself in the mirror. Her hair was thinner, she was underweight, her skin was dull and lifeless. She forced herself to smile, and it was awkward. It looked a little frightening. She stood and stared at herself for over an hour. That was where Nix had found her, consumed by a battle with herself, realizing slowly that things could never go back to the way they were before. Even if her family did believe her and try to help her, she wasn't the same daughter and sister they'd had. They deserved to keep these memories of her and never have to know what she'd become. They'd left that night, and she never spoke of going home again.

"Excuse me." A feminine voice cut through Scorpia's thoughts and sent her into a defensive position. "Why are you in this room? What do you want?" Sandra Mondragon positioned herself between the intruder and her daughter's altar, eyes burning with rage. "Who are you? Answer me!"

Scorpia opened her mouth, but only air came out. This close, she could see that Amara was the spitting image of her mother.

"We're friends. We mean you no harm," Nix said, entering the room with his large hands in the air. Scorpia's body sagged with relief at the sight of him.

"Friends?" Sandra's voice was shrill now. "What sort of friends break into a person's home? Who are you? Take anything you want, but get out of this room!"

Her eyes fell on the photograph in Scorpia's hand. She stopped yelling with her mouth still open. Scorpia returned the photo to its place on the desk, her hands trembling.

"You know Amara."

Scorpia and Nix turned to one another, unsure what to do.

"Where is she?" Sandra lunged to grab Scorpia by the collar. Nix moved to separate them, but Scorpia shook her head.

"Please. Let me go, and we'll explain everything."

Sandra considered it for a long moment before releasing her. "Not in this room." She pointed to the door. "You need to get out of this room now."

Downstairs, Sandra began to pace. "Tell me what you know about Amara."

Scorpia began hesitantly. "We rescued Amara from the place she was held captive."

Sandra nodded slowly, giving herself a moment to prioritize her questions. "Is she hurt?"

"Physically, she's well," Nix said. Scorpia kept her gaze on him as he continued. Nix was not a gentle person, but he kept his face relaxed and his voice soft. She tried and failed to recall the last time she'd seen him in this light. "But she's been through a lot. The people holding her were not kind. It has impacted her mentally and emotionally. There may be physical effects later, but that remains to be seen."

"Please," Sandra said, her voice hoarse. Scorpia's heart wrenched in her chest. "Please, don't talk in riddles. Just tell me what happened to my little girl."

"We will, I promise." Scorpia felt his body tremble as he took a breath. She couldn't believe how much emotion he was betraying, even in this situation. She'd seen him walk away from the corpses of fallen friends without flinching.

"We want to bring her back to you, but we have to make sure she's going to be safe here."

"How could she not be? Did you break into my home to go through Amara's things and insult her mother?"

"Of course not," Scorpia said. Sandra ignored her, eyes on Nix.

"I trust you love her, but I need you to understand that the people who took her are not happy. They might make things difficult for your family once she's back. And Amara is different now. She isn't the same little girl you remember. There's a hardness to her that you won't recognize, but you can't let her know it makes you uncomfortable. She probably doesn't remember how to play the flute. Her friends got to go on with normal lives while she was tortured. That's going to be hard for her. She's going to need patience. Understanding. Therapy. I can't bring her back here if you don't understand those things. If you aren't willing to do all of that for her, and more."

"You can't tell me you have her, but you'll only bring her back on certain conditions," Sandra said. "I should call law enforcement right now."

"No, you shouldn't." Nix's voice was calm, steady. Scorpia tensed on the couch beside him, and Sandra's eyes cut to her. "As far as your world is concerned, we don't exist. If you call law enforcement, we'll leave, and your chances of getting Amara back will be gone forever. They won't be able to find us, trust me."

"Why should I believe you want to help us?"

"We want Amara to come home. All I'm asking is for you to promise you'll do whatever you must to keep her safe."

There was a long pause as Scorpia braced to run. Nix sat calmly, meeting Sandra's gaze, and Sandra wondered what to believe from these home intruders.

"How soon will I see her again?"

"Within the season," Nix answered. "We rescued a lot of underage kids. We need time to ensure they'll be safe with their families."

Sandra's voice was a whisper; a desperate, heartbroken plea for her daughter. "What child wouldn't be safer with their family than anywhere else? What family wouldn't give anything to see them again?"

Nix grimaced. "You'd be surprised. I know more than one person whose family sold them into torture."

In the woods outside again, Nix rounded on Scorpia. "You showed weakness. You let her know you were afraid when she mentioned law enforcement."

Scorpia stepped back. "Of course I was afraid. We're convicted VIs. They'd return us to a lab."

"No one needs to know that. Now she has a detail on us that she shouldn't have. She knows we're on the run from the law."

"So what? She just wants Amara back. She doesn't know who we are or when we plan to return. That detail won't do her any good."

Nix wasn't sure, but he let it go for now.

Over the next nine days, each family was inspected and approved. Lottie, Meg, Reggie, and Sam worked with the rescued children to get them ready. They needed to have their stories straight and be brave enough to stick to their story under pressure. They needed to understand why they could not betray the rogue group if they wanted to help more people like themselves.

A week before the children were returned, Reggie and Eric teleported the ones who couldn't go home to Rinna. Cosmina had expected to feel relieved when the cramped cottage was free of a few people, but felt strangely glum instead.

The following night, Nix called the rogue group to a meeting in the yard.

"I have bad news, and we don't have much time. Des was able to hack into some government emails awhile back. Yesterday, we learned the smallest facility is slated for closure and demolition. There are ten prisoners inside, all children undergoing very minor experiments. They've each received new assignments and are being shipped out at the end of next week. I want to save them before they have to experience true suffering."

Scorpia glanced around. "Where is Des?"

"She's already on surveillance. I need a team of four volunteers to join her. Find out everything you can about this facility: its schedules, employees, weaknesses, strengths. In five nights, we'll attack."

"That's the night before we return the children," Xia said. "What if something goes wrong?"

"We'll just have to do what we can. I refuse to let this happen without trying to help them."

"I agree." Scorpia hopped to her feet. "I volunteer for surveillance."

"Okay. Who else?"

Nino, Xia, and Eric left with Scorpia an hour later.

Cosmina sat hugging her knees on the riverbank that night, staring into the darkness and letting the rushing of the water fill her ears. She tried not to think about Conley and the others, struggling to find their place in an entirely new group of witches, this one more permanent. She hoped the survival lessons had given them a head start on Rinna's training. She wondered who Rinna had assigned to training these days.

All this talk of returning witches to their homes had brought her own family to the front of her mind, and she couldn't shake it. It had been so long since she'd seen them. Her sister had to be close to Primary School now. She wondered if her little lookalike believed whatever her parents told her, or if she doubted Cosmina's conviction.

"What were they like?" a gentle voice broke through the night. Cosmina didn't flinch. She'd felt his energy approaching for some time now, non-threatening. She half-smiled over her shoulder at Nix.

"They were fun," she answered, her voice low. "And supportive. I spent my childhood laughing, never doubting that anything was possible for me. Even my silliest whims were treated like 'proof of my creativity' or 'evidence of my unique genius.'" She turned back to the river, shaking her head. "I couldn't even tell you all the ridiculous things they indulged for me." She paused for a long time before venturing, "What about yours?"

Nix stood beside her with his hands in his pockets. "My parents divorced when I was young. My father was very no-nonsense—responsible, dependable, workaholic. My mother was a dreamer who longed for adventure. She always felt a kinship with the ancient nomadic covens. She said in the beginning she liked that my father kept her tethered to reality. Then, after a while, it became suffocating. They separated, and a few seasons later she met the man who would become my stepfather. He was loud, fun, and impulsive. They were always exploring new places, trying new things. They made sure I had fulfilling life experiences. He always joked that step-parenting was his greatest adventure of all.

"My father also went on to remarry a man, so I have three dads and a mom. My father's husband, Trenton, was a liaison to Earth's military for a long time but worked as a teacher on Cantamen after meeting my father. So their house was all homework and studying and strict diets and being forced to exercise. My mom's house was all fun vacations, staying up late, and having friends over. I'm sure you can guess which I preferred."

Cosmina smiled. She liked imagining Nix as a little boy. She wondered if he was quiet and cold back then, or if the labs made him that way. "You may have preferred your mom's house, but it sounds like you turned out more like your dad."

Nix settled on the grass beside her. "I really did."

"How did they react to your conviction?" Cosmina was afraid to shatter the camaraderie, but desperate to commiserate with someone.

"I have no idea. I haven't spoken to any of them since I was 'taken to the doctor.' I was deemed too dangerous to attend my own trial. I don't even know if they went. I've never had the guts to find out, either. It would hurt too much to know if they believed it."

Cosmina lifted her eyes to his. "My parents believed mine."

"I know." He smiled sadly. "I attended your trial disguised as a reporter. I also spied on your family. I heard what they said the last time you spoke to them."

Cosmina turned this information over in her head. "And yet it didn't make you feel sorry for me."

"It did. But many of our parents believe we're evil. If they didn't, the Council wouldn't keep getting away with this."

"What if we return these children to their families, and something horrible still happens to them? What if, in a few years, they go off to Primary School and start displaying their dark affinities, and all we've succeeded in doing is delaying their torture?"

"That's a few years away," Nix said, "and by then, we'll have rumors circulating the entire planet. Every time a student hurts someone in class and is convicted two seasons later, the public will notice and raise questions. Every time a healthy fledgling dies unexpectedly, their community will demand more of an investigation. Pressure will build until the weight of this is too heavy, and the system will collapse on itself. We just have to set the wheels in motion and keep fueling it."

Cosmina sighed. She knew she couldn't protect everyone, but releasing those helpless kids back into a world that had already failed them once felt like betraying them.

It's a Trap

Luna 318

The second raid felt nothing like the first. There were no peaceful moments spent watching the sunset, no well-constructed plan. They knew little about this place except that it housed ten fledglings. It was more of a mansion than a prison or hospital. A married couple and their two adult children lived in the home and served as caretakers, and there seemed to be one daytime guard and two at night. The only entrance other than the front door was an underground passage connected to the basement of an empty but well-maintained home a half-mile away. Destiny had already determined there were security cameras at the entrance to the tunnel. They were motion-activated and transferred their recordings to a screen in the security room in real-time. She had not been able to hack or disable them yet.

Their back-up plan was causing a distraction, an idea no one relished.

Fifteen minutes before the mission was to start, Destiny closed her laptop and stashed it away, her irritation apparent. "I can't hack them. Plan B it is."

Scorpia scrambled to her feet and fished in her bag for a couple of vials. "We'd better hurry, then." The two of them left the abandoned home through the back door and sprinted through the dark neighborhood to the facility.

"This is going to draw too much attention. I really hate this," Nix muttered to Cosmina. To everyone else, he said, "Because we're using a distraction, we need to get in and out as fast as possible. Let's just rescue as many as we can and get to safety. Remember to save each other if possible but leave them behind if it's too dangerous." The group nodded their understanding, anxiety buzzing in the room.

Scorpia and Destiny returned after twelve minutes, doubling over and wheezing for air. Everyone waited tensely for a minute and a half until the thunderous explosion shook the ground around them.

"Thirty seconds, then we go," Nix said. Everyone counted silently. Cosmina was so nervous she lost count and decided to just go when everyone else did.

Nix was the first to move. Pulling his hat low over his face, he opened the tunnel door and sprinted through it. Cosmina followed, her face already masked, braced for the worst.

Inside the facility, they paused to listen for activity above them before ascending the stairs. Cosmina hung back to riffle through the filing cabinets and drawers. There were thirty-seven patient files, far more than the ten prisoners they held. She stuffed all of them into her pack before chasing the others.

Xia headed straight for the surveillance room and intercepted the guards at the end of the hallway as they ran to investigate the explosion across the street. She rendered them unconscious before tying their feet and hands together, then moved to inspect each room on the first floor for a prisoner.

On the second floor, Cosmina entered a bedroom and was shocked by the state of it. A young teenager with shoulder-length brown hair slept in a real bed, with an actual pillow, covered by a real blanket. A soft, white pair of cat slippers waited on the floor by her bed. This girl must live a normal life, waking each morning to use her real bathroom and brush her teeth with actual toothpaste. Then she must dress in real clothes before going downstairs to eat a real breakfast.

Cosmina pushed away her shock and tiptoed to the dresser, swiping some clothes before approaching the girl's bed. A bit of sleeping powder ensured she wouldn't wake, and then Cosmina levitated her into the hallway. Sam escorted a drowsy-looking young boy out of one room and down the stairs. Xia, Lottie, and Meg each had a teenager by the arm. Nino and Hiroto levitated a rather large older kid between them. Everyone hurried toward the basement.

They were halfway to the first floor when someone screamed above them. Everyone froze.

"They're coming, they're coming through the tunnel!"

Cosmina hoped she was correct in thinking that was Solara screaming. "Who?"

"Council! Don't go through the tunnel!"

Footsteps and shouting spread throughout the mansion. Meg kicked open the front door. No need for discretion anymore. An older man and woman rushed out of a bedroom, sending balls of Magic energy at the intruders. Cosmina ducked under one and sprinted through the door with her rescued prisoner floating in front of her to Retreat Point B, a closed-down department store being renovated into a new school. She reached it alongside Lottie and Sam, who had taken Meg and Xia's rescues from them. Five prisoners were at the retreat point, and she could see Solara coming at them with one more.

Cosmina dropped her sedated rescue and her bag on the ground. "I'm going back. You two stay here and guard them." Sam started to object, but Cosmina didn't give him time. They had to get all of them. And they all had to make it out alive.

In the time since Cosmina made her escape, the Council had descended upon the facility. Xia and Meg tussled with a group of five Councilguards. Nino had just taken out two of his own and was running to help them. Destiny exited the front dragging a teenager by the arm, two Councilwitches in hot pursuit. Scorpia dropped from the roof onto their backs, knocking them both out with her sedative rag before hurrying after Destiny and the prisoner. Cosmina heard more shouting from inside and braced herself to run in.

The sudden shattering of glass made her stop short. A body soared over her head and slammed to the ground, skidding across the grass. Seven Councilwitches appeared from all directions to surround it.

"*NIX!*" Cosmina screamed, starting in his direction.

"Cosmina, don't!" A hand grabbed her forearm. She looked over her shoulder to find herself restrained by Scorpia. "We need you alive. You have to leave him."

Cosmina looked back at Nix, dragging himself to his feet despite serious injury. He didn't quite make it up. One of the Councilwitches laughed at him. She felt a wave of anger like nothing even her temper had felt before. When another Councilwitch joined the laughter, that sealed their fate.

"Cosmina, let's go," Scorpia said again, her voice strained.

Cosmina tore her arm free. A roar erupted from her chest, her hands burning with unbridled energy. She charged into the group and sent a solid black razor of Magic energy from each hand into the two laughing witches.

The energy carved them cleanly in half. The four halves fell to the ground, muscles spasming, blood dumping into the grass like an overturned bucket.

The entire world seemed to fall silent. Cosmina waited, Magic at the ready, for a Councilwitch to move. They were all frozen in place, most with their mouths agape and their Magic fizzling out.

Cosmina's chest heaved. She honed in on her anger, knowing the gravity of what she'd done would suffocate her if she acknowledged it right now.

"Unless you, too, would like to die," she said, her voice deep and throaty in a way she'd never spoken before, "every single one of you is going to remain completely still while my friend is taken away." No one said anything, but no one moved either. Reggie and Nino hurried into the circle to grab Nix. They rushed off to the retreat point, avoiding Cosmina's gaze.

Cosmina waited until they were out of sight before saying anything else.

"Seven Councilwitches on one injured rogue?" She shook her head. "Cowards."

One Councilwitch—a snotty-looking, pale-haired man with dark eyebrows and a prominent forehead—swore at her in a language that surprised her. Raising her eyebrows, she responded, "*Nekt arfalli iopan?*"

The witch's eyes widened, his hands falling to his sides.

"*Nirfisa optobal?*" Cosmina laughed. Turning to the other witches, she said in Cantaminian, "We can all leave here with our lives tonight."

"Except for Mary and Ray," said a tall, silver-haired witch close to Cosmina.

"Yes, well. The rest of us can."

"Look out!" someone behind her shrieked. Cosmina ducked, narrowly avoiding the buzzing yellow energy that soared over her head. She spun in time to see the homeowner send another at her, and then another.

"NO!" Meg tackled the silver-haired Councilwitch, who was aiming a spell at Cosmina. Cosmina launched a ball of black energy at the homeowner, targeting the center of his chest and sending him backward through a window of his own home. It was quite the opposite of what had happened to Nix.

Another Councilwitch conjured fire to throw at Cosmina, but the pale-haired witch who'd spoken the foreign language redirected it. Cosmina turned to him in surprise, providing the perfect opportunity for someone to nail her in the stomach with their Magic.

Cosmina fell to her knees, the air forced from her lungs. At least a dozen people shouted incoherently, and the smell of smoke was thick in the air. Then a swift blow to the head rendered her unconscious.

The rogues managed to snag a few hours of sleep before returning the twelve missing children.

Four of the families traveled to Red Valley because an anonymous tip had suggested they would find their missing children in a park there. Xia and Sam watched from afar as each found their parents and returned to safety. Lottie and Meg each took a child back to their houses, unseen but nevertheless nearby. Reggie took one to a cafe where his older sister worked, Eric to a grocery store as the boy's mother did her weekly shopping. Destiny escorted a teenager to a bookstore to meet their dad. Solara left one in the lobby of a restaurant owned by her parents.

Scorpia took Amara through the woods to her childhood home, noting with concern that the girl seemed to feel no joy. "Are you alright?"

"I'm fine," Amara said. "I have a job to do." Without further hesitation, she strode inside to face whatever awaited her.

Nino dropped Henry off at the end of his street, then walked parallel through the neighbors' backyards as Henry made his way up the sidewalk. He knocked on the door, and his mother and father fell on him in screams of disbelief and joy. A solitary crow took to the sky. Nino grinned up at it and whispered, "We win this time."

Cosmina woke to a dimly lit concrete room, a dry mouth, and a fierce ache in her entire body. As she sat up, more pains made themselves known. She must have taken quite a beating, but she couldn't remember much.

She pushed through the pain and stood, trying to get a good look around the dismal room. It was lit with only a couple of lanterns. Four bare and dirty twin-sized mattresses had been tossed haphazardly inside.

The Councilwitch who had spoken in Helkesian sat in the corner on one of the mattresses, nursing his right arm. Dried blood had turned his blonde hair and his dirty face brown and crusty. He watched her scan the room and waited until she was finished to speak.

"There's water over here." He gestured to a jug of clean-looking drinking water a few feet from his mattress.

Cosmina went for the jug and chugged for a moment before making herself stop. The last thing she wanted to be in a fight was sick to her stomach. "How'd you manage to get arrested by your own people?"

His eyes were blank and emotionless, like his voice when he answered. "I helped you in the fight. Don't you remember?"

"That's enough to get arrested?"

"And branded." He showed her the skin of his forearm, so puffy and bloody she could only just make out the word "TRAITOR" carved into it. She could not stifle her gasp. He chuckled darkly.

They sat in silence for a moment until Cosmina couldn't bear it any longer and ripped a sizable strip off the bottom of her shirt. It left a jagged tear that bared part of her midriff, but she'd worn less than this in places more public. She soaked the fabric in the clean water and knelt in front of the man, reaching for his arm. He obliged, but in a way that made her think it was mostly because he was too weak to protest. She tried to be gentle, but much of the blood had dried and required scrubbing. He winced as she worked, and her heart sank once she got a good look at the cuts.

"This is becoming infected. It needs to be treated soon."

"There's no way out of here. Trust me."

Cosmina knew no one was coming for her. It was too risky, and they'd all sworn to leave behind fallen comrades. If she had kept that promise, neither she nor this man would be here now. Unable to keep still, she tore another strip of fabric and got to work cleaning his head wound.

"Where did you learn it?"

Cosmina paused. "Learn what?"

"Helkesian."

"Oh." She frowned, then resumed scrubbing the side of his face. Her elbow and shoulder ached, but she ignored it. "I took lessons when I was a child."

The man grunted and flinched as she scrubbed too roughly. "Why?"

Cosmina shrugged. "It sounds silly now, but I always was a headstrong kid with wild ideas. I read a book about a little girl who was Helkesian and single-handedly rescued the rest of her coven after they were taken by an evil king. It was my favorite book, and I wanted to be just like that little girl. Then I did an Origins and Ancestry reveal in school and learned I was actually descended from Helkesians. I wanted to learn everything I could about them, even the language. And my parents always indulged me."

His head and arm as clean as she could get them with mere water, Cosmina sat back on her heels and inspected what she could of the man for other wounds. He studied her face. "Your pronunciation is quite good. Almost like a native speaker."

"There are no native Helkesian speakers. It's a dead language."

"I'm a native Helkesian speaker."

"You're full of shit, too."

He laughed. "What's your name?"

She hesitated. She didn't think she could trust him, but she would probably die soon anyway. "Cosmina. You?"

"Roman."

"What made you try to protect me back at the facility?"

"I thought you might be a member of a Helkesian coven.
There are still a few small ones around, you know. I was
born and raised in one. I learned Helkesian and
Cantaminian simultaneously."

"Why?"

"Why to what?"

"Why to all of it."

"Some people put a lot of importance on ancestral
Magic. They still seek out like-minded people and form
covens. The Helkesians are not unique in that. And if I had
found another Helkesian, my blood ties would override any
job description."

"I see." Cosmina tossed the bloody rags away from the
mattress and settled onto it beside him, leaning back against
the wall. She did not believe in that bloodline bullshit. They
were all too diluted by now for it to matter, though many
would say she only thought that because she had no claim
to any powerful bloodlines. "What I wouldn't do for a
painkilling potion right now. Or even just to know what
happened to everyone else. The children. My friends."

Roman looked at her. "I heard them say all the children
were missing. And we were the only prisoners taken."

Cosmina opened her eyes. "That's good. Very good."

"Is it?"

She looked at him like he was stupid. "Don't play dumb.
You know as well as I do about the experiments, or they
wouldn't have sent you to defend the facility."

"That was a small orphanage. There weren't any
experiments being done on those children."

"Maybe not yet." Cosmina pinched the bridge of her
nose and willed her headache away. "But that 'small
orphanage' was closing, and those children were being

transported to prisons this week. And all ten of them are listed as missing by their very alive families."

"Why would the Council take children with families?"

"For the same reason they would carve 'TRAITOR' in your arm and lock you in a cell without a trial, I suppose."

"I'm not a child, and I did betray my team. You must be mistaken."

Cosmina opened one eye to peer into his face. She knew well the look of someone clinging to their reality as it crumbled around them. She closed her eye.

"There were ten children in that home," she said. "Four girls and six boys. The oldest boy was going to Eastwick Prison. The two older girls, to the Bellwick Detention Center for Juveniles. They were supposed to leave the day after our raid.

"The two youngest were going to Middlebrook Home for Challenging Children. The others were going to Elderkeep Fledgling Facility and Thornglen Home. They were all set to leave two days after the raid."

Roman took time to absorb this information before responding. "So your group...you don't consider yourselves anarchists, freeing prisoners and wreaking havoc to overthrow the Council."

The corners of Cosmina's lips tugged upward. "Is that what they say about us? I've always wondered."

Roman pushed himself off the wall and turned to face her. "Who are you really, then?"

She opened her eyes to look at him. "How do I know you're not a plant to get information out of me?"

"They mutilated me." He held his arm up again. "They would hardly do that to someone helping them."

The puffy cuts in his arm made her nauseated. Such wanton cruelty was unfathomable.

"My group is composed of individuals who escaped from facilities after being wrongly convicted and used as test subjects for government experiments."

"Why should I believe any of you were wrongfully convicted? You sure behave criminally now."

"None of us wanted this." Cosmina rolled her eyes. "Do you know what I would give to just be finishing Advanced School and planning my future like a normal witch? Instead, the Council decided my options were to suffer or fight. And I'm nothing if not feisty," she added, recalling the words of the Councilwitch who'd nearly kidnapped her seasons ago.

"What were you convicted of?"

"Murder."

"Funnily enough, I just witnessed you murder two people."

"First two people I ever killed. And I only did it to protect my friends."

"Why should I believe you?"

"I don't give a damn if you do or don't. Your belief in me isn't going to save my life, and I don't care much about Councilguards' opinions. How badly did you hurt my friend before I stopped you?"

Roman pressed his lips together and didn't answer.

"That's what I thought. Just because the law is on your side doesn't mean your violence is more justified than mine."

Roman continued to say nothing. But the silence did nothing to distract them from their pain, so it wasn't long before he spoke again. "So you really are descended from Helkesians?"

Cosmina kept her eyes closed tight so she didn't roll them. "Yes."

"I think it's interesting that you felt so drawn to your ancestry as a child."

"It was just because of that book. I felt drawn to a lot of stuff as a child. I was always looking for excitement back then."

"But to go to all the trouble to learn the language? To become fluent in it? That's not a common reaction to one's heritage anymore."

Cosmina shrugged, wincing as pain shot through her body. "I wasn't really a typical kid."

"You aren't really a typical adult, either," he said dryly. "Do you have any siblings?"

"A little sister. I miss her terribly."

"I have a younger brother. He looks up to me. He'll only know me as a traitor now."

"You'll be dead. You won't have to deal with it. My parents believe I killed that woman, and I've had to live with that for years now."

"I'm sorry for the pain you've endured."

"Likewise."

Roman settled himself back against the wall. "Are you still fluent in it?"

Cosmina glared at him. "You're really obsessed with this Helkesian stuff."

"It's how I was raised. We put stock in our bloodline. Which of your parents is Helkesian?"

"Both, a little bit. My mother more."

"Then you are truly Helkesian."

"I'm just Cantaminian."

Roman opened his mouth to say something else, but they were startled by the vibrating of the wall behind their heads. Cosmina was on her feet in a defensive stance within a moment. Roman was slower to rise, still babying his arm and ogling the wall.

"They're coming to get us," Cosmina said.

Roman shook his head. "The door is on the opposite wall." Cosmina's gaze followed his gesture, and she realized he was right.

"So... what is that, then?"

"I have no idea."

The shaking of the walls grew stronger. Cosmina held her breath, adrenaline abating much of her pain as she waited for whatever was coming.

A torch rattled out of its holder and toppled onto a mattress. The bed caught fire, creating a thick, bluish smoke that began to fill the room.

Cosmina swore. The smoke was already burning her nose and eyes. Behind her, Roman coughed.

The walls continued to shake.

Cosmina removed her shirt and tore it in half, soaking both pieces in the drinking water and tossing one to Roman. She tied the cloth over her nose and mouth, a futile attempt to block out some of the smoke. An action that might buy them minutes at best. She tried not to panic as she scanned the room again. There was nothing she could use as a weapon other than the torches, so she wrenched the nearest one off the wall and ignored the unbearable heat in the room as she waited.

The wall vibrated so hard it made her dizzy, and then it began to visibly crumble. The concrete between the bricks chipped and fell away, the bricks themselves soon following suit. A small gap formed in the wall, and Cosmina braced herself, torch at the ready, as a young woman stepped through the opening with both hands in the air.

"Lottie!" She dropped the torch and raced to hug her.

Still inside the wall, Meg peered around and hissed, "We need to get out of here, now."

"Go! I'm right behind you." Cosmina ushered Lottie through the gap, close at her heels.

"Cosmina!"

She'd forgotten Roman was there. She turned to face him.

"Take me as your prisoner. Please."

Cosmina hesitated.

"They'll kill me if you don't. But I have information. I can be useful for your group."

Cosmina glanced over her shoulder at Lottie, who shrugged. "Your call. But make it quick."

"Let's go then. But no funny business, or I won't hesitate to kill you."

Roman hurried through the gap ahead of her so she could keep an eye on him.

Their escape route was narrow and low, so they had to duck to stumble through it, but Cosmina was still impressed. Even for two witches with terrakinesis, this was a lot of concrete to manipulate. Lottie and Meg must be exhausted.

Nino was waiting outside for them. He ushered Meg and Lottie into the open air, then froze when he saw Roman.

"Bind his hands," Cosmina ordered. After a moment's hesitation, Nino obliged.

"Can you run?" Nino asked, giving her a concerned once-over.

Cosmina nodded, coughing to clear what she could of the smoke from her lungs. "Slowly."

"Let's go then." They hurried away from the building and down a steep slope, where Cosmina lost her footing and tumbled a dozen feet. Nino sprinted to her rescue. He winced at the new scrapes and fresh blood on her exposed back and torso.

"You okay?"

"I'm fine. Where are we going?"

"Reggie and Eric are waiting in a shop just at the bottom of this hill," Meg said. "They're going to send you, and I suppose the prisoner too, straight to the cottage."

Cosmina looked back at Roman. He was breathing hard and quite pale in the face. "Can you keep going?"

He nodded but did not speak.

The moment they reached the bottom, frantic shouting sounded at the top. "We have to move fast," Lottie said. They stood in an alley behind several tall, skinny buildings. Meg hurried up a small set of steps onto a minuscule back porch and opened a door. It led into a dark and cramped bookstore. Lottie shoved Cosmina inside, and then Roman.

"Reggie," she hissed, and he materialized by the door. "Take these two now. We're going to make a run for the second spot. Meet us there as soon as possible." Reggie nodded, sparing only a second to give Roman a puzzled look. An alarm blared at the top of the hill, and Lottie disappeared as the door closed.

"Where's the second spot? Are they going to be okay?" Cosmina demanded.

"No time," Reggie said. He grabbed Cosmina's arm in one hand and Roman's in the other and teleported them back to the cottage.

Cosmina felt dizzier than she ever had. When they landed, she fell to the ground on her hands and knees, shouting as shocks of pain traveled up her arms. She rolled onto her back, clutching her aching ribs.

Nix bent over her, reaching to pull the drying fabric off her face. "That's an interesting way to wear a shirt."

She opened her mouth to retort but didn't have the energy to think of a good one.

Cosmina woke from a nightmare, the sound of shattering glass ringing in her ears long after she'd gasped awake. She disentangled herself from the blanket and threw her legs over the side of the bed, flinching as her bare feet made contact with the cold floor. She was in one of the private rooms in Tiz Agathe's cottage, barely big enough for a twin-sized bed and a small, ratty armchair in the corner.

She took a few tentative steps toward the door. The world swayed, but not so much that she lost her balance. Encouraged, she made her way to the bathroom.

Someone had removed her pants, but she was still wearing the same underwear she'd worn for their last raid. Judging by the odor, entire days had passed since then. She scowled and peeled them off, turning on the water to fill the small tub.

She removed her bandages and inspected her wounds. Nothing too severe, but she was covered in bruises. When the last bandage had been dropped unceremoniously into the sink, she grabbed a few washcloths and a bar of soap and scrubbed at her skin. She threw her filthy underwear out the window, vowing to burn them later, then grabbed a towel and headed for the loft, where the rogues kept their clothes.

Meg and Lottie were there, lounging on their individual cots. They scrambled to Cosmina's aid when they saw her.

"I'm fine. I just need clothes."

"You should have called for help," Meg said.

Cosmina shook her head. "Where's Roman?"

"In the other room. Nix locked him in." Lottie whispered something to Meg, who hurried downstairs. Cosmina fished in the drawer for something comfortable and loose-fitting and didn't ask.

"Let me help you," Lottie said as Cosmina closed the drawer and made her way to her cot. "I know you don't want help, but you aren't doing anyone any favors by over-exerting yourself."

Cosmina relented. Most everyone else considered Lottie and Meg to be practically the same person, but Cosmina had always felt more comfortable with Lottie. There was something about Meg that demanded to be impressed. Lottie, however, was accepting and sweet.

"How long have I been out?" she asked as Lottie dried her back and helped her wriggle into a sports bra.

"A little over thirty hours."

"And how long was I in that prison?"

"Three days. After we returned all the children, we got to work on a rescue plan."

"How did that go?"

"Returning the children? Perfectly. No issues at all, though we all felt watched."

Cosmina exhaled with relief. "I'm glad to hear that. And how is Roman doing?"

"Better. The Council really roughed him up. His arm was infected, but it's healing now. He'll have some ugly scars, though." Lottie cringed as she finished putting on Cosmina's last sock. "The Council never ceases to amaze me. He was one of their own."

"Not after he protected me from an attack."

Lottie's eyes widened. "Is that what happened? But why—"

Someone cleared their throat at the top of the stairs. Both women turned to find Nix standing with Meg, who held a plate of food and a piping hot mug of ishti.

"You look better." Nix eyed Cosmina expressionlessly.

Cosmina nodded, her breath caught in her throat. Nix had a gnarly black eye, fading now into lighter blues and purples, as well as ugly browns and yellows. Next to his black eye, his temple had a healing gash in it, with a matching one traveling from his cheekbone to his jawline. His right hand was wrapped in white bandages, and the bulge under his loose-fitting shirt made her suspect his ribs were as well. For him to still look this rough four days later, even with immediate care, his injuries must have been brutal.

"So do you."

Meg perched next to Cosmina on her cot and passed her the mug. "It has a painkiller." Cosmina ignored the burn and downed the entire thing in a few gulps. Her stomach growled, and she grabbed the plate off Meg's lap.

"I'm also curious about why the prisoner turned on his brothers to defend you." Nix's voice was cold as ice. Cosmina lifted her eyes to find his gaze was as hard as his tone. She hesitated, confused.

"He's a weird guy. During the attack, he swore in an ancient language called Helkesian. I studied it as a child, so I answered him in the language. And it turns out the guy's obsessed with his heritage. Said the minute I showed I might be Helkesian too, his blood ties meant more than any job. So he protected me, and they punished him for it."

"So you think he's one of us now?"

"He's our prisoner. He said he had information that would be valuable to us."

"I've no doubt he does, but he refuses to speak to anyone but you. So now that you're awake, you'll need to visit him and determine if his knowledge is worth keeping him around. We don't have limitless resources."

Cosmina tried not to flinch away from the steel in his words. "I'll go after I eat."

"Good." Nix turned and left.

Cosmina turned to Lottie, her hand frozen halfway to her mouth. "I take it he is not happy about your mission to rescue me."

"It's not that." She glanced uncertainly at Meg. Cosmina followed her gaze.

Meg dropped her voice. "Scorpia told him that she saved his life after you wanted to leave him for dead. I guess she thought you were never coming back, so it didn't matter if she lied."

Cosmina laid her toast down on the tray and stared at it. "And no one told him the truth?"

"We didn't know she told him that until we returned. Scorpia was horrified that we'd brought you back."

Rage flashed in Cosmina's icy blue eyes. "That lying, scheming, praying-mantis-looking pad-hopper. I'll kill her."

Lottie snorted, then covered her mouth with her hand. Meg grinned. It was the first time someone had insinuated aloud that Scorpia was trying to romance Nix *and* Destiny, though they'd all noticed it. "We'll back you up. Nino, too. So many of us saw what happened, but Nix has been avoiding everyone since the mission. Something is up with him."

"I'll get it out of him. I'll talk to Roman first, though." Cosmina stood and dusted off her pants.

Roman was sitting on the bed with an untouched tray of food beside him. He eyed the door warily as it opened, then brightened as he recognized her.

"Cosmina! You're awake! How are you feeling?"

Her heart sank as she took in the sight of him. He looked much cleaner, with no trace of dried blood on his face. His head had been shaved, and his wound covered with thick white gauze as hers had been. He wore gray sweatpants and a white T-shirt, borrowed from the group's stash. His right arm, wrapped in bandages, rested in a cheap sling. The rough strap had been fed through a sock with the toes cut out, providing a barrier against his neck. He looked pale and thin, with dark circles under his eyes and a fragility she had not noticed in the prison.

She waved away his concern. "Much better. How are you?"

With his unbound hand, Roman scratched the back of his head and smiled sheepishly. "Better than we last met."

"I heard your arm was infected."

"Yeah. There was an old woman, she came in with some Magic salve and potions. She's checked in on me a couple times, but I'm afraid to eat or drink anything brought to me by anyone else."

"They won't poison you. That's not how we operate." Then again, how would this brainwashed man know that? "When was the last time they let you bathe?"

Roman grinned. "Do I smell?"

"We all smell here. Too many people, not enough water. Come on, I'll walk you to the bathroom."

She helped remove his bandages, then stood outside the bathroom as he washed and brushed his teeth. Then she took him to the kitchen and let him get some food and a healing potion. They returned to his room, where she rebandaged his arm and head and helped him back into the sling before he ate. She watched, waiting until he looked a little better to speak.

"Roman, we have to talk about that information you promised me."

He placed his apple core back on the plate. "I'm familiar with the inside of many facilities. I'm acquainted with some of the higher-up officials within the Program. I would be more than happy to tell you what I know. I can also help you plan your future raids. I can tell you about the guard rotations, which areas will be the most secure, how to locate and disable the alarm systems."

"Why would you do that? The last time we spoke, you were convinced we're all criminals. You called me a murderer."

"I've changed my mind since then."

"Why?"

"I've seen more now. I understand more."

"Elaborate."

Roman shrugged. "Your group is too big for this place, but you make do. You've given up your lives to fight for this cause, so you must believe in it. You have meager resources, yet I've not been treated unkindly as your prisoner. And you'll think I'm crazy, but I had a fever dream the first night I was locked in this room. Aranthos appeared and told me I was finally making him proud. That I'm right where I'm meant to be now. And who am I to disobey the great Aranthos?"

Cosmina very carefully did not roll her eyes. Helkesian bloodline obsession was one thing but having faith in Helkesian religion was worse. Still, if he believed a god was telling him to switch sides, he might be more loyal.

"I don't want to ditch you somewhere," Cosmina said. "But they aren't going to be patient with you. They want you to prove your worth before we use more of our resources on you."

"How should I begin?"

"Wait here." Cosmina left, locking the door behind her. From the locked bookcase in the gathering room, she took the binder of blueprints she'd stolen from Frank Egert's office, a pen, and a highlighter. When she returned, she tossed the binder onto the bed beside Roman and reclaimed her spot at the foot of it. He opened it and studied the first few pages.

When he looked up at her again, his eyes were wide. "Where did you get this?"

"Not important. Are they accurate?"

"No. Some of these must be a decade old, maybe more. But I can help you update them."

She handed him the pen and highlighter.

"If you've got a blank page, I can also give you a list of names to look into."

Cosmina returned to the bookcase, but there was no blank paper, so she ripped the insignificant pages from a couple of books and took those back to his room. "I'll be back with your dinner later. Do you think you can make some progress for me to share with the others by then?"

"Yes. Thank you, Cosmina, for saving my life."

"Don't thank me prematurely. Just work on convincing us you're on our side."

She found Nix outside, building a fire in the pit. The sack of raw meat from the day's hunt rested on the ground beside him. He ignored her as she waited, watching the muscles in his shoulders as he worked. Finally, she did what they both did best and got right to the point.

"Scorpia lied to you."

He paused, only briefly, but she saw it. "About what?"

"About who saved your life."

"Why would she lie about that?"

"Because she also lied about who wanted to leave you for dead."

For a moment, she thought he was going to ignore her. But, once the fire crackled pleasantly and he'd placed the meat on the grill above it, he rose to his full height and turned to face her.

"Why should I believe you?"

"You already believe me. You just don't want to face it yet."

Nix studied her. She stared back, arms folded across her chest.

"I know you love her. We all know and have for a long time. But if Scorpia had been the one to fight off your attackers, wouldn't she have been taken prisoner? The truth is, she escaped with Destiny while shouting at me to leave you because you were too far gone. And I ignored her, and I saved your life."

"And got yourself captured. Looks like Scorpia was right."

Cosmina shrugged. "I took a chance. The group needs you more than it needs me."

"I disagree."

"Do you believe me?"

"You said yourself, I already knew the truth."

Cosmina huffed. "Then why are you angry with me?"

Nix turned away from her. "You got yourself captured. We had to send a rescue team, and you brought a Councilguard back with you."

"I wasn't expecting to be rescued. And I really think he can help us."

"He sounds delusional."

"There are those who say that of us. Rinna, for instance."

"Touché." He flipped the meat on the grill.

"I'm sorry. I know you don't want to talk about your feelings, but I also know it must hurt." He stiffened but otherwise did not respond. Cosmina waited a long time before giving up. "Well, I'm always here if you need to get anything off your chest. Or off your mind." She went back inside. Nix stared after her, the insinuation she'd left making his heart rate quicken.

Roman came through. By the time she arrived with his dinner, he'd updated three blueprints and added notes explaining where to find the alarm systems and how they might be disabled. He highlighted the areas where they would find the heaviest guard presence. He wrote on one of the torn book pages a list of three names, with job titles and locations, as well as whatever details he could recall about them.

"I also need to tell you," He said as Cosmina was leaving with this evidence, "the Council has power lines set up all over the planet. They detect Magic usage. Whenever there's an unexpected or unexplained surge of Magic energy in one place, they send someone to investigate. This has led the Council to your group a few times already."

Cosmina ogled him for a moment, then promised to return later with late meal. She found Nix by the fire pit again, sitting silently as Lottie, Meg, Xia, Sam, and Nino entertained themselves with a card game. She passed him the pages, then repeated what Roman had told her. "We should warn Rinna right away."

"I'll handle it," he said, wandering into the forest with the pages she'd given him.

"You really think we can trust the prisoner?" Lottie asked.

Cosmina tore her eyes from the dark space where Nix's back had vanished. "It's too soon to tell. But I think he knows his best chance of survival is to help us. Just be careful not to say too much."

When Nix returned, he passed the torn book page to Sam. "Can you fact-check this?"

Sam went inside with Xia. Meg sighed and dropped her cards on the ground. "I was winning."

"Go replace Destiny on kid duty. Tell her I need to know what she knows about this facility." Nix handed her one of the blueprints. Meg scowled again as she left, followed by a somber Lottie.

"Kid duty?" Cosmina asked. Nix ignored her, studying one of the other two blueprints as he went inside the cottage. She glared after him.

"The rescued fledglings are in the back building until we can vet their families," Nino explained. "We haven't been able to start yet, considering your rescue mission and your prisoner. Destiny and Scorpia have been out there all day, interviewing and entertaining them."

"If we haven't even finished vetting these families yet, why is Nix already planning our next raid?"

Nino shrugged.

It's Time We Waged War

Gladio 318

Tiz Agathe promptly ended Nix's plans to conduct another raid.

"We cannot continue to rescue prisoners when we have nowhere to put them." She would hear none of anyone's objections. "And with this news of the power lines throughout the planet, I have been concerned. But I believe I may have a solution."

They waited for her to continue.

"There are places on Earth that remain secluded. Places we can use to our advantage. If we find somewhere to use as a home base of sorts, we will have a safe place to house and train new rescues. We will also have a safer place to hide if something happens."

"On Earth? Transport between planets is no simple matter," Cosmina pointed out.

"Between Reggie, Eric, and myself, I think it may be feasible. I plan to make a trip to explore our options. I leave tomorrow morning, and I am unsure how long I will be gone, but I will send word when I have some."

With nothing else to do, they busied themselves returning the missing children to their families and researching the Eradication Program, as Roman called it. The fact it had a formal name made the whole scheme more sinister.

The girl Cosmina had taken, Ava, was afraid of going home.

"I don't want to go. My old parents didn't want me, and they sold me to Mama and Papa Lincoln."

Cosmina paused, taken aback. "Is that what they told you?"

"They had proof. They showed me the receipt. Signed by my old parents."

"Oh, honey, receipts are easy to fake. Signatures are easy to forge. Your real parents have been missing you terribly," Cosmina said as reassuringly as she could. "I met them. They told me themselves."

On the night she returned Ava to her family, she teared up a little, watching them wrap her in their arms and shower her with kisses. She chastised herself for getting soft.

After the children were gone, life for the rogue group was tedious. They hunted, fished, and gathered. They tended to Tiz Agathe's garden and her few livestock, arguing every day over whose turn it was to exercise the horse. They alternated guard duty, bathed in the river, took turns training their Magic, exercised, hosted sparring matches, and did research until they were cross-eyed. Reggie and Eric sent groups of two into towns to visit libraries or scout locations, then went later to get them. Roman continued to update blueprints and answer questions. He began to trust other group members, eating food and taking potions brought to him by Lottie, Meg, Hiroto, and Nino.

Cosmina and Nix continued to meet, but there was now less discussion and more silent review of information. Cosmina found herself grateful when Xia interrupted one such meeting with the craziest idea any of them had had to date.

"...Assassination missions?" Cosmina echoed, sure she'd misheard.

"Hear me out." Xia held up both hands and looked between the skeptical faces of the group leaders. "In my research and scouting, I've realized we could make a big impact by eliminating some of the top-level people in this scheme. Some people are important to the process—directors approve or deny all experiments. Medical professionals must be present for them. Scientists come up with experiments and determine their validity. Eliminating these people would hinder the Program's function."

Cosmina was still in shock. She turned to Nix, who was studying Xia thoughtfully. "Have you identified any of these individuals?"

"Aside from the three Roman gave us, we've identified five more."

"We?" Cosmina asked.

"Sam and I."

"Well, you certainly have my interest." Nix leaned forward in his seat, elbows on his knees. "Convince me further."

Xia launched into a well-rehearsed speech about a good candidate's requirements for these positions. She detailed how it was challenging to find someone morally gray enough to accept the role or someone oblivious enough to believe lies. She explained how eliminating the top scientist on an experiment would effectively put it on pause, maybe even rendering it useless since so many depended on time and consistency. She suspected losing a Director of Facilities would halt everything from hiring and promotions to prisoner transfers. By the end of the speech, even Cosmina saw the appeal.

"I have questions," she said the moment Xia finished. "How do we know the targets you've identified are willing participants in the scheme? I don't want to kill innocents."

"Sam thought of that, too." Xia pulled a wad of paper from her pocket, unfolding and smoothing the pages before passing them to Cosmina. "So we verified it. We had a list of seventeen names until we did that. These eight, we can say with confidence, believe in what they're doing."

Cosmina took the pages and flipped through them. Nix rose to stand beside her and look over her shoulder. She could feel the nearness of him, making her skin prickle. The first page was a list of eight names, next to basic information. The following pages were evidence. Dr. Olivette Wells had written an article in a medical journal about the dangers of dark Magic and the factors to consider when treating a patient with a dark affinity. Director Orson Caswell had been arrested for inciting a riot the year following his graduation. The attached news article and arrest record detailed his efforts to get a member of the Council of 7 removed for "being inherently evil." Dr. Paula Kingsbury had claimed to invent a medication that would inhibit the development of dark affinities in fledglings. Suspiciously, she'd been employed soon afterward by a sizable facility in Timberglen.

Cosmina handed the papers back to Xia, but the other woman shook her head. "You'll need them to convince the others."

"I don't want to force anyone to kill." Cosmina addressed this statement to Nix, whose face had settled into a resolution she knew well.

"Then we'll only take volunteers."

Xia gasped and clapped her hands.

"We'll do it once," Nix said, glancing sharply at Xia. "We'll see how it goes and re-assess afterward. That is, of course, only if we can get enough volunteers for it to matter."

"I volunteer, of course. Sam will too. And others will. You'll see."

"Go summon everyone else," Nix said. "We'll meet by the fire pit right now to discuss it."

Once Xia had left the room, Cosmina turned to Nix with a sick feeling in her stomach. "You realize, of course, that asking others to do this means you and I have to be willing to assassinate targets as well. Otherwise, we're hypocrites."

"I know. I'm fine with it, and I assume you are as well. I heard you killed two people."

"That was different. That was to save your life."

"And this is to save lives, too. Some people are genuinely too evil to live, Cosmina."

He brushed past her out of the cottage. She stared after him, unsure if she could kill a person outside the heat of battle.

"Absolutely not," Scorpia said, already on her feet to walk away. Destiny grabbed her arm and pulled her back to her seat.

"We've already decided to do this," Nix said without looking at her. "But we aren't going to force anyone. Cosmina and I are volunteering, as well as Xia and Sam.

We've identified eight targets, but we don't have to hit all of them."

"This is disgusting. Are you listening to yourself?" Scorpia's eyes were as full of rage as her voice. Nix ignored her.

"We'll start planning our attack tomorrow evening. The idea right now is to hit all our targets—however many we can—in the same night, for the same reason we returned all of the missing children to their homes on the same day. Xia came prepared with an explanation for why this is a good idea, as awful as it may seem." Xia's eyes rounded, but she regained her composure as Nix turned the meeting over to her. She had not expected to do this in front of everyone.

The moment she finished speaking, Scorpia began shouting. "It's still murder, no matter how many provocative words you put in front of it! Are we really so bored we have to stoop to *murder*?"

"Some people are too evil to live, Scorpia," Nix said, addressing her for the first time.

"But who are we to determine that?"

"We're their victims."

"Not anymore. We all got out. We need to focus on rescue missions—"

"Your overall plan is just to rescue every prisoner they take? Follow the Council around with a broom, hoping they never catch on?"

Even Cosmina wanted to squirm under the weight of the cold glare he'd fixed on Scorpia.

"The more children we return to their families, the more people will start to talk—"

"Rumors are not enough."

"But—"

"And we can't keep only rescuing children. Most of the Council's victims are adults, like us."

"Nix is right," Nino interrupted. He rose to his bare feet and turned to Scorpia. "We said we wanted to wage war. I say it's time we did that."

"How many of us have they killed like we're nothing?" Hiroto added. Murmurs of assent went around their group.

Scorpia's gaze traveled over all of them with a look of stark horror, skipping over Cosmina. "I cannot believe you people."

Nino turned to Nix. "I volunteer."

"Are you sure?" Cosmina asked. "Everyone who volunteers must be absolutely sure they can follow through when the time comes, and relatively sure they can live with themselves after."

"And somehow convinced you're still better than they are, after you stoop to their level," Scorpia said.

Nino nodded. "I can do it."

"Me, too." Hiroto stepped forward to stand by Nino.

"Then we have two more spots," Nix said. "We'll meet again at sundown tomorrow, right here, to discuss the plan. Please see Cosmina or me before then if you wish to volunteer, but I second what she said. Be absolutely sure. Meeting dismissed."

The group dispersed with much whispering and a bit of angry ranting.

Enchanting

Draco 318

No one else volunteered, but six was plenty. Xia was thrilled to have contributed an idea, even if it was controversial. The plan they created involved a lot of scouting and spying, and everyone was willing to help with that. Even Scorpia agreed to provide a few potions, but nothing more.

In their second week of scouting, Nix and Cosmina assigned themselves to tail Dr. Quinn Fellowes to her Sven vacation home. They were thoroughly bored. As suspected, the "solo vacation" she'd told her family she needed was an excuse to visit the Northern Fairrest Correctional Facility. The doctor had gone inside at sunup and hadn't left in seven hours. Cosmina hugged her light coat tighter around her thin body and hid her gloved hands inside her armpits. Their lifestyle made time difficult to track, but it was clearly Ytterfic. All the buildings were decorated, and everyone they saw wore festive makeup and plaid. They'd been silly not to anticipate this. They stood out in their all-black clothing, so they were forced to freeze on rooftops and in alleyways, staying out of the public eye whenever possible.

Cosmina stiffened as she recognized Dr. Fellowes exiting the facility. She shot an excited red spark into the air to signal Nix, then rushed to the edge of the rooftop to follow the doctor's movements.

Like most of their targets, Dr. Fellowes had been doing her job for so long she'd stopped feeling shady about it. She didn't look around in fear she was being followed or wonder if the faces in the street harbored knowledge of her actions. She was confident in her work and comfortable in her life. Comfortable enough to stay alone, without security, even with the rumors of the group freeing prisoners. She thought herself untouchable.

In her defense, the group had never harmed anyone other than guards who got in their way.

So far.

Nix appeared at Cosmina's side. "Finally," he muttered. To punctuate his statement, his stomach growled.

Cosmina grinned up at him. "Me, too. If she goes straight home, we should take a break to get warm and eat something."

She knew Nix would refuse under normal circumstances, but the cold and boredom affected both of them. Dr. Fellowes would be an easy target. She had a predictable schedule, a husband who relied on sleeping ishtis, and one child, far too young to hinder their mission in any way. She didn't have security guards at home, bodyguards for her person, or even escorts in and out of work. She was overconfident, and it would be her downfall.

They split up to tail the woman, Cosmina on rooftops and Nix on the street. Dr. Fellowes took a bus to Sven as she had done that morning. Nix got on the bus with her, hiding behind his hat and a book. Cosmina waited for the next one.

"Not very festive, eh?" The driver asked as she boarded, grinning from ear to ear.

Cosmina laughed and said, "Just running errands, didn't feel like dressing up." She took a seat near the front.

When she got back to their hiding spot in a small cove on the beach near Dr. Fellowes's neighborhood, Nix was already waiting with a fire built, scaling the second of three fish. Cosmina recoiled. "How the hell did you catch three fish already?"

"I put out a net this morning. We also caught a crab and a turtle, but I freed them."

"Kind of you. So she went home, huh?"

Nix nodded. "She is the most boring person I've ever encountered."

Cosmina couldn't argue with that. She shrugged out of her coat and sat as close to the fire as she could, trying to control her shivering. The rocky cliffs on three sides protected them from some of the icy wind buffeting the beach, but the air coming off the ocean was brutal. She politely ignored the fumble of Nix's numb hands as he scaled the last fish.

"I still have some bread," she remembered aloud, unzipping her pack and digging inside for the lumpy loaf she'd swiped from the cottage before they'd left. "No butter or jam, unfortunately."

"Beggars can hardly be choosers." Nix shoved sticks through the three scaled fish and passed one to Cosmina. She joined him in roasting their dinner. "Besides, I prefer honey."

"All sweet, no tart? That seems out of character for you," Cosmina teased. He ignored her, but she was used to that. "You know, I bet we could get away with spending the night inside the doctor's house. I have yet to see her go into the basement, and it's gotta be warmer than out here. Less wind, at the very least."

Nix studied her, turning his fish over slowly. "That's risky. But tempting, I won't lie. Do you know a way in?"

"Yeah. When she takes her hour-long hot bath with wine and a book, we go in any window or door we like. She doesn't bother with the alarm system unless she's sleeping or leaving."

"We have to make sure the neighbors aren't watching."

"Yes, all the neighbors visiting their beach houses in the dead of winter." Cosmina rolled her eyes and took a big bite of her fish.

Nix grinned, but only for as long as her eyes were closed.

They walked into town to buy water and snacks. The store was empty, and a cashier with a black bob and radiant smile flirted with Nix as she rang up his items. Cosmina took the opportunity to swipe two plaid sweaters, two plaid scarves, a pack of underwear, a pack of socks, and an armful of high-quality gloves in black and shades of gray. She slipped out the door without the cashier even noticing and waited for Nix, who exited a moment later with a free salted pretzel. "Want half?"

Once they had traveled a couple of blocks, he side-eyed her and asked, "So what did you steal?"

"How very dare you." Cosmina lifted her chin to the sky. "What an awful accusation to make."

"It would be, if I weren't completely correct."

Cosmina gasped and yanked him into an alley between two buildings. They pressed their backs against the walls and stared at one another with wide eyes.

"What is it?" he hissed.

Cosmina leaned out of the alley and pointed. "Look."

Nix followed her gesture and was startled when his eyes fell upon Cosmina, or a girl just like her. The only difference was this girl was several years younger and still had the long, wild blonde curls Cosmina had when he first met her.

"Okay." He forced a sheepish grin at an older couple that walked by and scowled suspiciously at them. "You must be related to her."

"That's Daisy." Cosmina's eyes were huge and round. "That's my little sister. But what is she..." She clapped one hand over her own mouth.

"Cosmina," Nix said warningly.

"She must go to Karin Svensdotter's now."

"We need to get out of here. We're drawing attention to ourselves." Nix did not want to be insensitive, but he also would not risk sabotaging their mission.

Cosmina continued to ogle her lookalike until Nix reached over and took her hand in his. Brought back to reality, she swallowed. "Right. Sorry. Let's go." She led the way out of the alley and down the street but did not release the death grip she had on his hand. He allowed it, his heart swelling with pity. He had not encountered anyone from his past since his imprisonment, but he had to imagine it would be hard to walk away.

As usual, Cosmina was right. Dr. Fellowes did not set her home security system before getting in the bath. The light jazz she blared through the house masked the sounds they made when unlocking the cellar door and entering the basement.

Once inside, they used battery-operated flashlights to avoid Magic and looked around. It was everything one would expect a basement to be: dark, damp, dusty, and scarcely used. Boxes filled with random home items were stacked against the wall. A sizable dining room table was propped on its side against the adjacent wall. A well-worn sofa pinned the table to the wall, a matching loveseat pushed up against it like an oddly shaped bed. A couple of recliners rested on either side of the sofa.

"Ooh, look," Cosmina whispered. Nix walked over to find her pulling aside a beaded curtain and shining her flashlight inside a bathroom even smaller than the one in Tiz Agathe's cottage. It contained a toilet, sink, and standing shower that was small even by standing-shower standards. Before Nix could say anything, Cosmina turned on the water and began stripping off her clothes.

"What are you doing?" he hissed, glowering at her.

"Relax. She's still in the bath and will be for a while."

"This house is probably old enough that she can hear the water running through the pipes in the wall," Nix said, but Cosmina was already down to her underwear and digging in her bag for soap. "You are crazy." He left the bathroom as Cosmina's hands reached to unclasp her bra.

As she cleaned herself, he snooped through the boxes and located a couple of sheets. He shook them out and spread them over the sofa and one of the recliners. Cosmina exited the bathroom in a plaid sweater and clean leggings and tossed an identical sweater to him. "I got this for you. She'll probably be in the bath for another twenty minutes if you want to wash too. I left the soap."

"I knew you stole something."

"Why do you sound so disappointed? We paid them plenty. Besides, we need to blend in better during Ytterfic." She crawled over the arm of the sofa and reclined regally, her cheek resting in her hand. "Thank you for the sheet. You're always thinking of me."

Nix rolled his eyes. "We paid them for food. Clothes are more expensive. And we need to steal the sheets when we leave. Can't risk leaving behind DNA or Magic residue." He'd been opposed to the shower before, but now he found himself wandering toward the beaded curtain.

"If you're so bothered by the sweaters, don't check what else is in my bag." Cosmina giggled. Nix groaned inwardly and climbed into the shower.

By the time he got out, though, his curiosity had won. He left the bathroom in pants slightly too big and his stolen sweater and checked Cosmina's bag. She watched from the sofa, where she sat reviewing her notes by flashlight. As he pushed aside the scarves to see the socks, gloves, and underwear, she waited for the lecture.

Nix stood up, a pair of socks in one hand and gloves in the other. "You couldn't have stolen some men's underwear, too?"

"Those can be men's underwear, if you really want."

"Not enough room." He approached the recliner and sat, then nodded at the small notebook in her hands. "Finding anything good?"

The amusement faded from her face. "I was thinking about how to assign the targets. Who do you think is the least resolved of our volunteers?"

"Nino," he replied, without hesitation. Nino was the youngest and thought he had something to prove. Nix had been worried about the kid since he volunteered, but could hardly tell him no.

"I agree. I think we should assign Dr. Fellowes to him. She'll be so, so easy. And she's one of the less-important targets, so if he loses his nerve…" She trailed off with a shrug.

"That makes sense to me."

"And Xia will never forgive us if we don't give her someone important, so I think Director Caswell should be hers."

"He's a tough one."

"Yes, but she's familiar with his home and routine. She scouted him before we even agreed to do this. And I think she feels strongly that he deserves to die, so she's unlikely to back out."

"I think she's unlikely to back out anyway. She's too excited about this, if you ask me."

"Yeah, there's that." She paused, taking a deep breath as she stared at the floor. "Listen, Nix, I... have a favor to ask."

His eyebrows lifted. "Is it about your sister?"

"Yes."

"What?" he asked warily.

"I want to cast a protection spell over her."

Nix closed his eyes. "Cosmina, absolutely not."

"Hear me out."

He waited while she arranged her thoughts.

"I heard her mention Dusk Hall to her friend. I used to live there too. It's on the very edge of campus, almost right up against the wall. If we can find a way over the wall and into the building, I think I can find which room is hers."

"Are you listening to yourself? You could put her in real danger by talking to her. And I don't mean to be insensitive, but you don't know what she believes. She could turn you in."

"I know," she said softly. Sadly. "That's why I'll do it while she's sleeping, and then leave."

"You're talking about breaking onto a Primary School campus. It's impossible. We'll be caught and arrested."

Cosmina shook her head. "I think I know how to do it."

Nix knew he should not entertain this conversation, but his curiosity was piqued. "How?"

"You know how Tiz Agathe makes a living going around wherever she's summoned and performing illegal Magic for asinine prices?"

"...Yes."

"She's often summoned to school campuses. And I know the spell she uses to get through the protections. I've never tried it before, but I think I can do it."

"Cos, KS is different."

"She's been to the KS campus more than once since we've lived with her," Cosmina argued, lowering her voice. A creaking above their heads indicated Dr. Fellowes was coming downstairs after her bath. They fell silent, waiting tensely as light filtered through the crack in the door at the top of the stairs. A cabinet banged shut. Dr. Fellowes said something they couldn't make out in her cheery, high-pitched voice. They felt the Magic security barriers shoot up all around the house, and then the light at the top of the stairs went out. A moment later, more creaking told them the doctor was retiring to bed for the night.

They both unwound their nerves. After a minute or two, Nix said, "Would you allow anyone else in the group to break onto a school campus to cast a protection spell on their sister?"

"No," she admitted. "But no one else in the group would know how to do it. Aren't you even a little curious to see if I can pull it off?"

He was, but he would not give her even an inch. "It's too risky."

"I can do this. I want to put a protective enchantment on her, so what happened to me doesn't happen to her."

"Affinities are not genetic. You have no reason to think—"

"I know it's illogical, but...please."

Nix hesitated. The more she pleaded, the weaker his resolve became. "I'm only trying to keep us safe. Both of us."

She said nothing. She put her flashlight and notebook back inside her bag and laid flat on her stomach across the sofa. Nix waited a moment, then reclined his seat and relaxed into it the best he could.

They woke well before dawn to gather their things, fold the sheets as small as possible and stash them in their bags, and ready themselves for escape.

They listened as Dr. Fellowes came downstairs, then deactivated the security system to take her breakfast on the covered porch as she liked to do. It was freezing out, and the doctor would soon go inside, so they wasted no time exiting through the cellar door. They locked it behind them and slinked away through the yard.

Nix waited unhappily as Cosmina tucked herbs and seeds into a small terracotta pot of soil. They stood in the middle of the woods behind the campus of Karin Svensdotter's Primary School for Young Witches. It was the middle of the night. In about three hours, they were supposed to meet Reggie in their beach cove to teleport back to the cottage. For the time being, however, it seemed Cosmina had convinced him to attempt to break onto the campus.

The larger, but unfortunately quieter, part of him said this was a stupid idea, and he should put an end to it. But his curiosity had gotten the better of him.

She'd avoided his gaze for the last twenty minutes as she prepared her spell. Now, she turned to him and said, "That's it, then. Are you coming with me?"

The knot in his stomach tightened. This was his last chance to save himself, even if he couldn't stop her. Just because she would not listen to reason did not mean he had to go down with her.

The stark hope on her face would not be ignored, though, and neither would the way her face lit up when he heard himself say, "Tell me what to do."

"Stand on the other side and hold both my hands." She placed her feet firmly on the ground on one side of the terracotta pot. Nix did as he was told. Her hands were cold and dry in his calloused ones. "Now chant with me. *Arachi aflen lugen lugen ben. Arachi aflen lugen lugen ben.*"

Nix paused, surprised to recognize most of the words. He hadn't known what to expect, but it had definitely been something more mystical and ancient and complicated than this. Maybe requiring a blood sacrifice or something else awful.

When he joined her in the chant, plumes of smoke began to waft from the pot. They started out thin, wispy, and pale gray, but soon turned navy blue and thick enough to choke them. Nix followed Cosmina's lead and continued to chant even as his eyes and lungs began to burn.

He was relieved when Cosmina stopped and released his hands. He doubled over and coughed several times to clear his lungs of the smoke. His eyes watered.

Cosmina passed him a wet cloth. He wiped his eyes and opened them against the lingering sting. "What now?"

"Now we hurry. This is a very temporary spell, and Tiz Agathe would say it is unwise to dawdle." She grabbed his hand and pulled him through the woods in the opposite direction from which they'd come, closer to the campus.

Primary School campuses were the safest places on Cantamen. They were heavily enchanted to prevent and detect intruders. The punishment for even attempting this was one of the highest a person could receive. This was riskier than anything else they'd ever done, and for a sillier reason.

The rational part of him was growing louder.

Cosmina stopped just shy of the woods' edge. A clean, straight border of trees and a six-foot strip of crunchy, frozen grass separated them from the formidably tall stone wall that bordered Karin Svensdotter's. They stood and stared for a moment.

"It's taller than I remember," Cosmina admitted.

Nix released her hand and approached the wall, running his palms over it to feel for potential handholds. "It's also too smooth to climb."

"There must be a spot where it's shorter." Cosmina took off, sprinting to their left. Nix waited, watching as she turned and ran past him in the other direction, before returning to stand by his side and catch her breath.

He opened his mouth to tell her there was no way over, as he'd said, and then the moonlight reflected a teardrop rolling down her cheek. She turned away, but not fast enough. His chest tightened. "I can give you a boost over the wall, but that means I won't be able to follow you. You'll be on your own once you're over."

She turned to him with wide eyes. "That's fine. Maybe even safer."

"And I want to be clear...if you get caught, I'm running."

"Of course. The group needs you back." She shrugged out of her backpack and dropped it at his feet. "Everything in there is valuable to the group and dangerous in the wrong hands, so take it with you if you have to run."

He sank into a squat, lacing his fingers together and holding his hands palm-up in front of him. "Ready?"

Cosmina retreated to the woods for a running start. When she planted her foot in his hands, he pushed upward with all the strength in his legs and arms, propelling her as high into the air as he could.

She didn't quite clear the wall. She hit the top of it on her pelvis and released a wheezing grunt.

"Are you okay?" Nix hissed up at her.

"Fine," she said through gritted teeth. She wriggled, and he watched as the lower half of her body slithered over the wall until her feet disappeared. An instant later, he heard a loud thud on the other side.

"Still good?" he called softly.

"Never better. Landed on my feet," she said in a tone that made him doubt the validity of the statement. "Okay, I'm off."

Nix found himself straining to hear footsteps he knew she was too skilled to make.

After a couple minutes had passed, he scooped up her pack and made his way back into the woods. He found a fallen tree trunk that seemed sturdy when kicked and sat, their bags at his feet. His lungs still burned from the smoke.

It occurred to him that Cosmina had no way back over the wall, and he groaned. Why had he allowed any of this tomfoolery to occur?

On the other side of the wall, this had yet to occur to Cosmina.

She crept to the back of Dusk Hall and crouched behind the building. Her x-ray vision deprived several students of their privacy, but she had no time to waste. She found Daisy sleeping in the first room on the building's backside, on the second floor. The roof of the wraparound porch would nearly get her there.

Cosmina hoisted herself onto the porch railing and, from there, the roof. She managed to tiptoe along the frieze while clinging to the top for dear life and nudged the window open with her foot. It creaked, but she relaxed when she heard a little snore from inside.

She managed to wiggle inside with little bruising, crashing in an ungraceful heap on the floor, then disentangled her long limbs and rose to her feet. As she inched to the bed, her breath caught in her throat. Even in the moonlit room, there was no mistaking her sister.

She placed a tentative hand on Daisy's glorious blonde curls, recalling a photo her parents had kept framed in the living room of the day they'd brought Daisy home from the hospital. In the photo Cosmina, who had gone by a different name then, was five years old and wearing a yellow dress. Their mother knelt by her, her head cut out of the photo, holding baby Daisy in her arms for Cosmina to see. She'd had that crown of pale golden curls even then, fresh from the womb, just like Cosmina before her.

Daisy had always been so much like Cosmina. They said most sisters were opposites, but that hadn't been true of them. Daisy was every bit as smart, willful, imaginative, bossy, determined, and take-charge as her big sister.

Cosmina was terrified for Daisy's future. They'd already falsely convicted one Frazier daughter, so if they decided to take the other, they would probably fake her death.

Cosmina closed her eyes and began to whisper the enchantment.

It was a dark-aligned spell, one Tiz Agathe had taught her and a few others when they first began training at her cottage. Back when the group was still intact and led by Rinna. She knew other protective enchantments, of course, but this one resonated with her. It felt like the powerful, all-encompassing, ruthless protection her sister would need in the world.

She had no idea how long she stood there, touching her sleeping sister's hair and letting her tears fall as the Magic drained from her body. It hardly mattered. If she gave every ounce of it to Daisy and promptly died, it would be worth it. Cosmina's fate was sealed; her life had been marked as waste. But Daisy had all the potential in the world, and Cosmina wanted nothing more than for her sister to enjoy the life she couldn't.

The door creaked open. Cosmina's blood ran cold. Before she could react, she was thrown backward into the wall and a shimmering, soundproof barrier appeared around Daisy and her bed. A petite witch with porcelain skin and enviable jet-black tresses stepped into the room. The door slammed hard enough to rattle the wall but made no noise as it did.

For a moment, Cosmina thought she'd gone deaf; and then the witch stepped forward, hand forming a thick cloud of red Magic smoke, and demanded, "Who are you?"

Cosmina tried to answer, but her strong emotions combined with the shock of the witch's entrance had her stunned. The witch stepped closer and froze, her expression melting from hardened fury to unveiled surprise. "You're Daisy's sister."

Cosmina nodded weakly. Why bother lying when she was caught? She was in no condition to escape, having used most of her energy on the spell.

The witch looked over at Daisy and lowered the barrier for a moment to sniff the air. Cosmina furrowed her brow. The witch erected the wall again before speaking. "This is protection Magic."

"I saw her in Sven yesterday, and I just wanted to protect her."

The witch dissipated her Magic and helped Cosmina to her feet. "Follow me. If you try to run, someone other than me will catch you, and believe me, you don't want that."

Cosmina did believe her, so she followed the intimidating little witch from the room and down the stairs. They made their way down a candlelit hallway to a large wooden door that opened as the witch approached. Cosmina looked around in awe as she recognized a magister's living quarters.

"This was extraordinarily reckless of you." The woman turned to face Cosmina. "And also extraordinarily clever. I daresay it would've worked on any other dorm head." She smirked, and Cosmina ogled her in confusion.

"I'm Ezra Barnes. Your Magic is well-veiled, but the veil is fading. We need to get you out of here." Cosmina blinked dazedly, and Ezra smiled as though she were making perfect sense. "First, tell me why Tiz Agathe has not responded to my summons in two weeks."

Cosmina took a startled step back. "Say again?"

"I know Agathe well. She always responds to my summons. I've been worried about her."

"I'm guessing the Education Council doesn't know about your relationship, or you wouldn't have this job," Cosmina said dryly.

"Many of us have secrets. Will you at least tell me if she's safe?"

"She's fine, as far as I know. She's been traveling."

"Ah, I see. To find a place to hide the rescued witches, am I right? She spoke of that last time. I'm going to help you get off this campus, but promise me when you next see Agathe, you'll tell her I must speak with her urgently."

Cosmina nodded, unable to believe her luck. "Why would you help me?"

"I'm an ally to your cause. Think of me as a spy. Now, quickly. We need to go." The door opened on its own again, and Ezra ushered Cosmina through the kitchen and out the back door. Ezra approached the wall and waved her hand over it, creating solid iron footholds for Cosmina to climb.

"Why has Tiz Agathe never mentioned you to us?"

"Because it would endanger me. You have to go now, or you'll be detected when you cross."

"Right. Thank you."

"Do not be so reckless in future, Miss Frazier."

Cosmina said nothing and hurried over the wall.

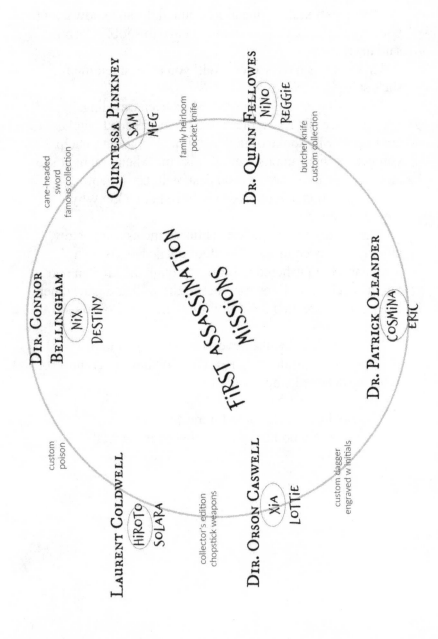

FIRST ASSASSINATION MISSIONS

QUINTESSA PINKNEY
SAM
MEG
family heirloom
pocket knife

DR. QUINN FELLOWES
NINO
REGGIE
butcher knife
custom collection

DIR. CONNOR BELLINGHAM
NIX
DESTINY
cane-headed
sword
famous collection

DR. PATRICK OLEANDER
COSMINA
ERIC

LAURENT COLDWELL
HIROTO
SOLARA
custom
poison
collector's edition
chopstick weapons

DIR. ORSON CASWELL
XIA
LOTTIE
custom dagger
engraved w/initials

Burning Leather

Papilio 318

The rogue group was as prepared as they were going to get. More than three weeks of scouting, spying, research, planning, and rehearsing had them feeling confident. They had back-up plans for their back-up plans. Everyone knew where they were supposed to be and when, and what they were supposed to be doing there.

Xia and Lottie left after breakfast. Eric and Reggie teleported them to the northern part of Goldcastle, where Director Caswell lived with his boyfriend and their familiars. Due to the boyfriend's lion living in the home, Xia's mission was being conducted more publicly than most.

Nix and Destiny left after lunch. Their mission was the most dangerous. Cosmina suspected that was why Nix had insisted on taking it himself. His target was Connor Bellingham, the very director he'd drugged with truth serum in their first raid. Connor lived in Lochspring Correctional Facility, which had increased its security since their attack. Roman had been instrumental in the planning of this mission. He was familiar with the facility and told them where the central communications room was and how Destiny could disable it. Destiny could do this from a safe distance of several blocks while wearing a disguise inside a public building. Once she disabled the comms and the security system, Nix's job was to get over the wall into the director's bedroom window, complete the assassination, and get out again. He was equipped with suction handles to help him scale the building rather than navigate the interior, which had far more guards than before.

The other teams departed at intervals throughout the day: Hiroto and Solara to Sagewynne, Sam and Meg to Graymore, Reggie and Nino to Swyncrest.

Cosmina and Eric waited another half hour. Like Xia's, their mission was public. Doctor Patrick Oleander also lived inside his facility, but it was high-security, and they couldn't break in with just the two of them. Fortunately, the doctor had a clear pattern of behavior that made things easier for them.

They appeared atop a building half a block from The Three Borders, a ratty old bar at the borders of Fogmount, Valmeadow, and Svensdotter. Cosmina wore a pink dress, a size too big to hide the weapons belt secured around her upper waist. She'd stolen a leather jacket from a thrift store to keep her warm. Her shoes added a challenge, but she needed to play her part, and she had some practice running and fighting in heels. She was also wearing makeup, applied by Lottie to make her look forty years older. They'd dyed her hair a bright and vibrant red using beets. There was nothing to do for the length of it, but it didn't matter. She looked enough like the doctor's ex-fiancée, Elise, to throw a drunk man off his game.

Eric's job was to wait on the rooftop, ready to make a quick getaway after the deed was done. Aside from that, she was on her own.

"You got this," he told her, but they were both uneasy. Everything had felt surreal all day, all of them waiting to see if anyone would actually do this.

"Thanks." She cleared her throat and shook out her arms and legs, trying to get rid of some of her nerves. "Be back in an hour or so."

"If you're not back in two, you know where I'll be." He sat with his back propped against the safety rail, feigning nonchalance. Cosmina threw one leg over the wall onto the fire escape.

The minute her heels hit the ground, she was in character. She strode the half-block to The Three Borders and let herself in, expecting the obnoxious music that played when the door opened and behaving as an experienced patron would. She made her way to an empty barstool, scanning the room and noting Dr. Oleander in the corner. After confirming his presence, she didn't look at him again. She took her seat and smiled at the bartender, who looked at her without interest. She ordered the first mixed drink that came to mind and used a bit of Magic to stopper the alcohol bottle as the bartender poured inattentively. He sat the glass in front of her and she sipped it, chatting with patrons around her over the thunderous music in the bar.

It took longer than she'd hoped, but three drinks later, she felt a hand caress the small of her back. The doctor had arrived to occupy the empty stool by hers. "Can I buy you a drink?"

She smiled. "You can buy me as many as you'd like."

The doctor smacked the bar to get the bartender's attention, a rude gesture Cosmina forced herself to ignore. The man behind the counter turned to him, and the doctor eyed Cosmina's drink. "We'll take two more of these."

Cosmina plugged the bottle again, then turned her attention back to the doctor. She removed a tiny capsule of sedative from a pocket sewn into her left sleeve. To anyone else, it would look like she was scratching her forearm. She'd practiced this movement a thousand times over the past weeks, knowing she'd only have one chance to get it right. She tucked the capsule into her closed hand.

"What's your name?" Dr. Oleander shouted over the noise.

"Elsie." Cosmina used the accent from the doctor's ex-fiancée's hometown in Northern Valmeadow. It had the effect she'd hoped. The doctor recoiled and blinked dumbly at her, his mouth open. It was well-known that he and Elise had been happily engaged for some time before she left him abruptly. No one seemed to know why, and the doctor's own explanation changed with the telling. But he was still haunted by the loss of her. He frequently visited Valmeadow hoping to find her and couldn't resist redheads in bars. "What's yours?"

"James," the doctor lied, mumbling gratitude the bartender couldn't hear as their drinks arrived.

"What?" She leaned closer.

"What?"

"Your name? I missed it."

"Oh." Cosmina noticed a twitch in his cheek and a drooping eyelid. He was already drunk. "Paul."

"It's nice to meet you, Paul." Cosmina reached for his drink and ran her index finger around the rim. He watched as she lifted her finger to her lips and sucked off the salt, maintaining eye contact. She saw his breath hitch in his chest, and her smile widened.

He snatched his drink and downed the whole thing, oblivious to the powder she'd dropped inside. She checked the clock. She was behind schedule, but still had time.

She downed her own drink before turning back to him. "Do you want to get out of here?" She slid off her stool, smearing a handful of Mag-away cleaner across the seat as she did. She also waved her hand and stacked their glasses before levitating them into the sink with a coy smile to the startled bartender. Another couple flicks of her wrist covered them in soap and hot water.

"Let me just pay." The doctor eyed her cleanup with confusion. He removed his wallet from his coat and produced an obnoxiously large stack of obnoxiously large bills. He separated one of them—enough to pay for all their drinks two times over—and laid it on the counter. Cosmina took note of which pocket he kept his wallet, then accepted his offered arm and escorted him outside.

Another couple leaned against the building, kissing. They paused long enough to take a long look at Cosmina and the doctor as they passed. Cosmina studied them in return, deciding they were both drunk enough to be unreliable witnesses. She winked at them as she led the doctor around the back of the building.

He was already leaning on her as she steered him down a nearby alley. He stumbled and squinted ahead of them, and she knew his vision was going dark. "Where are we?" he tried to ask, his words more slurred than before.

Cosmina swore under her breath as he sagged against her, nearly knocking her down. She used more Magic to levitate him into a fenced area around a dumpster. It wasn't the space they'd designated for the mission, but she deemed it acceptable enough now that she needed an alternative. She lowered him between the overflowing dumpster and a pile of stinking trash bags started by some obstinate people. His entire body was limp, and he began to snore.

Cosmina suspected Scorpia had done this on purpose, but she didn't have time to linger on it. She donned a pair of black leather gloves, dousing them in Mag-away to cover her DNA and Magic. She removed the doctor's pants and underwear to his ankles. He mumbled something unintelligible and attempted to sit up, but she ignored him. She wrestled him out of his coat, then loosened his tie and unbuttoned his shirt.

Then she removed the butcher knife from the weapons belt around her waist.

Her hands and legs trembled as she knelt before the sleeping doctor. She forced herself to think of Amara, Henry, Conley, and everyone in their group whose lives had been ruined by people like this man. All the people he'd made the conscious decision to hurt in his career. The witches who had died under his "care," possibly dozens of them.

She pressed the blade against his throat.

Some people are genuinely too evil to live, Cosmina.

She dragged the blade across.

The blood made a squelching sound as it escaped the laceration and sprayed her head, torso, and legs. She allowed herself a moment to gag before dropping the knife onto the doctor's lap.

This had been her morbid idea, and she was proud of it. The knife was stolen from a customized set of kitchen knives in Dr. Fellowes's home. The pocketknife being used to assassinate Dr. Fellowes was a family heirloom swiped from Quintessa Pinkney, a prominent researcher and Sam's target for the night. Quintessa herself would be taken out by a cane-headed sword from Connor Bellingham's famous collection. Connor would be killed by a special type of poison invented by Laurent Coldwell, a seedy politician who did an excellent job of covering the Council's more suspicious operations with his influence.

Each target would be murdered with a weapon stolen from another of tonight's victims. Provided no one failed, they made a full circle. Cosmina had suggested this to send an even louder message to the Council and was pleased when the idea was well-met. Even Nix was impressed.

She grabbed a wad of alcohol wipes from her pocket and scrubbed at her face, neck, and chest. She donned a beanie and cleaned as much blood as she could from her clothing and legs before re-pocketing the wipes. Then she grabbed the doctor's coat and put it on. It was far too large for her thin frame, but it would cover the remnants of blood on her clothes. She buttoned it halfway, patted the wallet to ensure it was still there, and took one last glance around the crime scene before she fled.

She was halfway to Eric when her legs began shaking enough to impede her progress. She was forced to slow down to keep her balance. By the time she reached the building, she'd removed her heels. She chucked them one by one onto the rooftop before climbing the fire escape, not caring how much it rattled. Eric was waiting in a defensive stance, his eyes wide.

"Are you being chased?"

"No, no, let's go," she gasped, her lungs burning. Eric responded instantly, grabbing her shoes in one hand and her forearm with the other before teleporting them away.

They reappeared in the clearing outside the cottage. Eric asked Cosmina if she was alright. She waved away his concern and stumbled to the fire pit, stripping off her clothes. She moved the doctor's wallet to her bra and wadded everything else, shoes and all, into a pile, before igniting the whole thing with a bit of Magic. As she watched the items turn to blackened ash, she realized her face was soaked with tears. She wiped them away furiously and cleared her throat of the lump that had formed in it.

Eric stood behind her and placed a gentle hand on her bare shoulder.

Eric was not one of the closest people to Cosmina. Aside from planning missions, she rarely interacted with him. Still, she didn't want to be alone, so she grabbed his hand and squeezed it. "Please don't tell anyone."

"Of course not."

They sat like that until shivers wracked Cosmina's body so much they couldn't ignore it anymore.

"You're going to freeze to death out here."

"Right. Wouldn't want that." Cosmina took a breath and pulled herself together.

Eric insisted on giving the house a precursory safety check before letting her inside. Scorpia was supposed to be guarding the place in everyone's absence, but neither of them had seen her. Cosmina bitterly hoped she'd returned to Rinna.

She fetched some clothes from the loft, then went to the bathroom to scrub as much blood as possible from her hair and body. She felt a little better after counting the money she'd stolen from the doctor, which she returned to her bra for safekeeping.

Outside again, Cosmina was relieved to find Xia, Reggie, Nino, and Lottie inside the clearing. Her second observation was more alarming since there were no back-up plans that called for it: Reggie had as much blood on him as Nino did.

Her third observation was that Scorpia was now standing with the others, griping that anyone would have the nerve to accuse her of abandoning her station. Cosmina didn't know who had accused her of this and did not care.

"Strip," she ordered. "All clothing with blood gets burned."

Xia and Lottie turned to her in alarm. "We don't have enough clothes to just burn them," Xia objected.

"I robbed my target. We can get more clothes." Cosmina waved away their protests. "Strip, burn your clothes, then go inside and clean yourselves up. Lottie, can you grab clean clothes for them? Eric, you have to leave in two minutes to get Solara and Hiroto."

Everyone scattered. As they did, an owl descended from the night sky and dropped a crumpled piece of paper into her outstretched hand before retaking flight. Everyone stopped to watch her, but she didn't even notice as she smoothed the page and stepped closer to the fire to read it. Her body sagged with relief as her brain absorbed the words.

"Nix's mission went as planned, and he and Destiny are safe for the night. They should be back tomorrow afternoon, right on schedule."

As everyone expressed their relief, Cosmina looked up to see Scorpia glaring at her. Cosmina didn't need to wonder why. Nix's decision to enchant the bird for Cosmina spoke volumes to the two women staring at one another across a firelit clearing in the woods, the stink of blood and burned leather in the air.

By the time Nix and Destiny reached the cottage the following afternoon, even Scorpia was itching to know how the missions went. Cosmina insisted on letting them bathe and eat before everyone settled around the fire pit to tell their stories.

Cosmina's most burning question was how Reggie got covered in blood during Nino's mission, but she waited as Hiroto detailed the dinner guest that had caused Laurent's children to go to bed late, forcing them into Plan B. Despite the delay, the collector's edition chopstick weapons stolen from Director Caswell were placed through his eyeballs as planned.

Xia went next, sheepishly explaining that her mission had gone awry from the start. If not for Lottie and her quick thinking, she would've failed. Her target had been warier than expected and difficult to approach. After an hour of trying to seduce him with increasing desperation, Lottie stepped in to lure the man away from the crowd and into an ice sculpture garden. Then Lottie stood guard as Xia slit his throat from behind. This resulted in blood-soaked snow and ice but little blood on Xia or Lottie themselves. They'd been forced to escape as casually as possible through a crowded town square before anyone discovered the body.

Sam and Meg detailed the flawless execution of their Plan A, followed by Nix and Destiny. They had also been successful with no apparent setbacks. Reggie and Nino went next, explaining that a fussy toddler had kept Dr. Fellowes and her husband awake later than anticipated. They ran out of time, and Reggie locked the father in the room with the crying child while Nino attacked the half-awake, struggling doctor. Reggie had come to his aid, and the two of them escaped disappointed but ultimately successful.

Following the debrief, there was silence as everyone waited to see who would speak first. In the end, it was Xia. "I don't think this could've gone better."

"Well," Eric said, "aside from a few setbacks."

"No, come on." Xia began to pace. "No one really expected *all* these plans to go perfectly, did they? That's why we made the back-up plans. All the targets are dead, and no one got caught, so could we have asked for things to go better?"

Various levels of agreement sounded around the group. The next person to speak was Scorpia, who stood with her arms folded. "This entire mission was abhorrent."

Only Cosmina maintained eye contact, a passive look on her face.

"Don't any of you feel guilty? You killed someone last night! Orid, it wasn't even Cosmina's first time murdering someone in cold blood, and at least she *cried* when she got back."

Cosmina picked some fuzz off her shirt as several people turned to her. "Is it really considered 'in cold blood' if you were saving a friend's life when you did it?" she asked, achieving the air of aloofness she wanted.

Scorpia scowled. "You know, I had a little bit of respect for you when I thought murder actually made you feel bad."

"Scorpia, for me to care whether you respect me, I would first have to respect you, and we really aren't at risk of that here." Cosmina lifted her eyes threateningly. Scorpia worked her jaw; whether out of anger, surprise, or nerves, Cosmina couldn't tell.

"Okay, that's enough," Nix said. "What's done is done, and there's no need to hash it over like this. No one will ever be forced to participate in something like this, even if they've done it before. If it comes up again, it will be voluntary as always. But I think, for now, the best idea is to lay low until we see how the aftermath of last night plays out. Any objections?"

There weren't, but one look at Xia and the impatience in her eyes was enough to tell Cosmina there would be soon.

SPRING

Boredom

Muraena 318

Winter went out with a bang, with a parting gift of snow and ice storms. As it turned out, they were all impatient. Xia was the worst, her temper out of control. Sam did his best to provide a much-needed cushion between her and the rest of them, but she was still like a livewire that someone frequently made the mistake of stepping on. Nix and Cosmina rearranged schedules to keep Xia away from others.

Scorpia also became a nuisance, deciding it was in everyone's best interest for her to manually drum up some guilt. There wasn't enough work to keep Scorpia and Xia both busy, and tensions ran high as the two women made their teammates uncomfortable.

Cosmina and Nix did their best to keep everything under control as they waited for news from Tiz Agathe. Two seasons had passed since they'd heard from the old woman. Eric and Scorpia teleported into town with the money stolen from their targets to purchase clothing and supplies. Lottie sat for hours each day and worked with Roman to update their blueprints and pick his brain for information. Meg, Solara, and Reggie busied themselves with whatever hunting, gathering, gardening, soap-making, and bread-baking they could manage. Hiroto and Nino chased the rest of the team down for regular training. Cosmina and Lottie asked everyone ten times a day if they'd eaten. Someone teleported Destiny into town nearly every morning for research.

As expected, the news reports were vague in the beginning. Cosmina and Nix reviewed them together in the gathering room while Destiny installed new braids for Xia.

`"Body of Local Man Found Uptown;`
`Officials Investigating."`

`"Terrifying Home Invasion Apparent Cause`
`of Death for Celebrated Doctor and Mother."`

`"Night of Drunken Debauchery Unfortunate`
`Final Decision for Doctor Found Deceased by`
`Dumpster."`

Cosmina wrinkled her nose at the article. "That headline is gross."

Destiny nodded. "Not a great source. Less than reputable. Most of the so-called details are just baseless speculation. But more reliable and well-written articles are soon to come, with comments from law enforcement. They just need some information to give the public first."

"How long do you think it'll take to make connections between the cases?" Xia asked.

"Not long. A season, maybe sooner. But they won't release those details to the public unless they get leaked."

"Why not?" Cosmina was unable to hide her disappointment that the whole world may never know her morbid brilliance.

"Damage control," Nix answered. "It doesn't serve the Council for the public to know there's someone making waves. It doesn't exactly instill confidence in the government if a small, untraceable band of anonymous faces can do all this without getting caught." He folded the newspapers and tossed them into the kindling pile.

The excessive hunting and gathering became wasteful. They ran out of storage for all the extra soap, spices, and bread, leading them to build another shed behind the cottage. Even that only kept them busy for a couple of days. Their research and planning began to make them bleary-eyed. The games they played to pass the time grew redundant. Tempers flared.

On one of the many afternoons when the camp felt too small to breathe, Scorpia and Destiny separated themselves. Stubborn patches of snow and ice clung to the forest's shadowy parts, but it was sunny by the river where they sat with their overseasoned meal that had gone cold because they'd waited so long to eat.

"Do you think they'll do more missions like this?"

Destiny hesitated, lowering a strip of meat back to her plate. "Like the...assassinations?"

Scorpia scoffed and sat her entire plate aside. "You can't even say it either, huh?"

That wasn't the problem, but Destiny let her think that. "I don't know if we will. I guess it's too early to say."

"You think they might?"

"It's possible, depending on how the next few weeks play out. It was a bold move, and it will have drawn attention. The question is whether the benefit outweighs the risk, I suppose."

"The benefit and the risk?" Scorpia's dark eyes were wide. "Des, they killed people, and you're talking about benefits? They deprived children of their parents. People of their siblings. Parents of their children. They tore apart families, and for what benefit could that be?"

Destiny set her own plate aside, holding in a sigh. "Weren't you in the same facility as Nix, under Director Bellingham? Making one of the targets partially responsible for the undoing of your own family? For the separation of you from your parents, and their daughter from them?"

"It was a terrible thing that happened to us, but it doesn't give us the right to play god."

"Then, your issue is with the action rather than the outcome?" Destiny hugged her knees to her chest and studied her friend's face. "If you think we should just take what happens to us lying down, without fighting back, why did you leave Rinna's group to do something more proactive?"

"Are you saying you think I should go back?"

"Of course not! I would miss you if you left. I just don't understand, I suppose. Nix made it perfectly clear that we'd be taking drastic action under his guidance. I guess I always assumed nothing was off-limits."

"Of course Nix made everything perfectly clear. Nix is always perfect," Scorpia drawled, her voice dripping with sarcasm. Destiny arched an eyebrow and waited for the comment's awkwardness to come full circle and reach Scorpia herself. When it did, she just laughed bitterly and shook her stringy black hair out of her eyes. "I think maybe the group idolizes Nix too much."

"Uh-huh." Destiny picked up a stick and began to draw pictures in the dirt to have somewhere to look besides Scorpia. The dark circles under her eyes and the sallowness of her cheeks were starting to make her look haunted.

"Don't you feel bad about the part you played in this?"
Destiny stiffened.

"I mean, I feel bad just for knowing about it. But you
played a much more active part and continue to do so. I
can't imagine how I would feel in your place."

"Don't you think that's a little insensitive?"

Scorpia blinked, replaying the comment in her head.
"Orid, you're right. I'm sorry. I guess I've become a little
jaded because no one is bothered by what they've done."

It did not escape Destiny's notice that Scorpia had yet to
use the word "we," separating herself from the group with
her words. "Everyone feels bad about what we did. Every
single person here. But you're making it impossible for
anyone to process what happened because you're constantly
putting everyone on the defensive."

Scorpia ogled Destiny, dropped jaw and all. "So you
don't think anyone should feel bad? You think it's okay
they got together and planned the slaughter of six people?
And we still call ourselves the good guys. We should just
pretend that's normal and fine?"

"No, I think a certain amount of guilt is normal and
necessary. But I don't think what we did is as bad as what
the Council is doing. And I also don't think we need to
drown in our guilt, or we'll all go mad. Which is why you
need to back off a little. Give people some space to process
what happened. No one wants to be vulnerable or admit
any sort of weakness with you hawking around, just
waiting on an opportunity to make them feel worse."

"You really think I'm in the wrong here!" Scorpia
scrambled to her meager five-foot height to put some space
between them.

"I don't." Destiny stood as well, only slightly taller. "I
know your heart, and I understand where you're coming

from. I just think there's a healthier way for everyone to deal with this, including you."

"You're talking about this like it's something that happened to them and not something they did, and that bothers me." Scorpia folded her arms across her narrow chest and glared at the ebony-skinned woman she'd come to respect so much. "I expected more from you."

Destiny rolled her eyes. "Why did you join this proactive group, Scorpia?"

"I wanted to do more for the cause."

"Did you? Is that true?"

"Of course it's true. It's why everyone betrayed Rinna. None of us would do that lightly."

"That's the other thing. You still think of it as 'betraying Rinna.' None of us did anything to Rinna. We just made different decisions for ourselves than she wanted us to. Even in her anger, she understood it wasn't her place to control us. She's even helped us as much as she can. We have continued camaraderie. None of us betrayed her."

"Then why do you think I joined the group, Des?" Scorpia rubbed her temples.

"For Nix."

Scorpia flinched, a gesture as good as confirmation.

"But he still wouldn't prioritize you. His focus has never been you, and when that didn't change, you took it personally."

"How could I not take it personally? If things had even just stayed the same, I could've handled it. But he replaced me."

"Is that true? I think the timeline might be a little blurry in some people's minds."

"Whose minds?"

"Yours. His. Mine."

Scorpia braced herself to argue, then deflated. "I don't know what to think or feel."

Destiny paced for a minute before responding. Scorpia watched impassively. Her body shivered with cold and something more threatening. They were on the cusp of something she wasn't sure she wanted to touch, a truth she was not ready to face. But Destiny was here and ready to face it, and she'd run out of time to straddle the line.

"I think," Destiny began, her mouth pinched in a way that said she wasn't happy to be saying this, "you agreed to join the proactive group for Nix, at first. But his goals were bigger than yours. Meanwhile, you and I partnered for a lot of work, and we grew closer. He noticed, but because he's unrelenting in his separation of pleasure and work, he stayed detached in a way you couldn't. You've never been convinced that love cannot be a normal part of our lives, and after a while, you started taking his convictions personally. But you can't do that. Nix is who he is, and you are who you are, and even in this crazy whirlwind life we're all forced to live, love remains fluid. But I don't think Nix is ever going to choose you, not over the work we're doing. No matter how loud you are about it. No matter how agreeable you try to be. No matter what."

"What about you?" Scorpia whispered.

Destiny stared back at her.

"Would you choose me?"

Destiny remained still, terrified of making the wrong move on this tightrope she hadn't expected to walk today. "Surely you know how I feel about you."

"That isn't what I asked."

"I choose you every day. I choose you every time I see you staring after Nix, and I look the other way. I choose you every time you upset someone, and I defend you. I choose you every time they ask for volunteers to work with you, and I leap on the opportunity. I choose you every time I grab you a snack, or prepare an extra bit of food, or grab your favorite scent of soap before we go down to the river. When I heat your towel on cold days and light the fire a little brighter when you're returning from guard duty. I'm always choosing you, day in and day out, over and over again."

"But?" Scorpia asked, feeling it coming.

"But I joined this group to fight the Council. I joined this group to save lives. I didn't do this for you, or to find love, and I can't give you what I know you really want. I won't abandon them for you. Their lives, and all the lives we'll save in the future, matter more than my feelings."

"It sounds like we're back to the original topic, then. You think what we did is okay."

Destiny, who thought they'd made some progress, threw her hands in the air. "Are you serious right now?"

"Of course I'm serious! This is bothering me, and everyone is so dismissive of me like I'm insignificant! I am not insignificant!"

Destiny gathered the remnants of their meal, now inedible. "I think the best advice I can give you is to leave people the hell alone about it for a while. Let everyone process their own feelings in their own way, and do your own soul-searching while you're at it. Because it seems like maybe you and this group have reached an impasse." She left in the direction of the cottage with their plates. Scorpia watched, feeling her entire body deflate as the woman she had begun to love walked away.

Within the hour, Scorpia enchanted a bird to find Rinna with a message.

When it returned with a response containing coordinates and a meeting time, Nix agreed to have Reggie teleport her there. An undeniable sense of relief came over them upon her departure, a feeling that chipped at Destiny's heart no matter how she tried to ignore it.

Scorpia had only been gone a few hours when Xia and Sam wrangled Nix and Cosmina together for another impromptu meeting in the gathering room.

"I know we agreed to lay low for a while," Xia began, passing around a paper with hastily-scrawled notes, "but we're wasting precious time now. We're losing momentum, and that's one thing we don't want."

"How are we losing momentum?" Cosmina asked.

Sam steepled his fingers and met her gaze. "We succeeded in our initial goal, which was a big, shocking slaughter of six important officials in one night. And we are still in agreement that it was wise to wait before taking further action."

"But we're confident now that things went well," Xia finished for him. He nodded for her to continue. "Now, the longer we wait, the more time we give them to get scared. Pay for extra security. Increase guards at facilities. It makes things more difficult."

"I would expect the reverse to be true." Cosmina leaned forward in her seat. "We have to give them enough time to relax again after our initial ambush. Make them think our sights are elsewhere for the time being."

"We've discussed the timeline, and it is tricky," Xia agreed. "The key is finding that sweet spot where we're maintaining momentum without crashing and burning."

"And I take it you have an idea for that sweet spot?" Nix asked in that way of his that commanded the room's attention in an instant.

Xia's face was resolute. "Yes. We won't do any big group assassinations for a while, but we'll pick off targets one or two at a time. Sam and I are happy to volunteer so no one else has to. If we can get help with scouting, teleporting, and all the other details, we can keep striking blows to their ranks without putting anyone in too much danger."

Cosmina crossed one long leg over the other and looked at Nix as she passed him the page with the notes. The lights in the room brightened as he read, taking his time. Xia and Sam turned impatiently to Cosmina, who only shrugged.

"There are nine names here," Nix said finally.

"Yes," Xia said.

"The two of you believe strongly in these assassinations."

"Yes, we do," Sam said.

"The right kind of people for the Program's purposes are not easy to come by," Xia said. "In a way, many of these people are irreplaceable to them. If we further limit their pool—"

Nix held up a hand, silencing her. "I understand the logic, and I agree with the benefits." He passed the page back to Cosmina and gave them each a stern look. "My concern is more with your willingness—or, perhaps enthusiasm is a better word—to take on more of these types of missions. Everyone else has reservations about doing this again."

Xia and Sam exchanged a look. Nix waited on them to fumble through an explanation, but they surprised him again.

"I have no reservations about it," Xia said.

"Nor I," Sam agreed. "Is this not what we're here for? No one changes the world by following its rules."

"And you'll never convince me to feel bad for ruining the lives of evil people," Xia added, her jaw set.

Nix studied them for another moment, then turned to Cosmina. "What do you think? Pick a couple potential targets, and send scout groups tomorrow?"

Xia was unable to stifle her gasp, betraying her glee. Cosmina eyed her sharply as she handed over the page of notes and said, "Pick two names tonight. The entire group will convene after breakfast in the morning to discuss. First scout groups will be two or three people and will leave after lunch. If a potential target doesn't feel right, we'll bring the scouts back and pick someone else."

"Understood," Xia said with an eager nod. She grabbed Sam's wrist and dragged him from the room.

Nix and Cosmina sat inside the dimming room for a moment, staring at the back of the door Sam had closed behind him.

"Should we be worried about them?" Nix asked. The lights, which had dimmed to nearly off, brightened again.

Cosmina shrugged. "If you mean their mental well-being, no. None of us are stable, are we?"

"No. But I also don't want to find out anyone in this group is a monster."

Cosmina turned to him, half-smiling, and touched the back of his hand. The lights flickered. "We can't be monsters, Nix. We're the good guys."

Destiny was not happy about the new missions. She was the only one bothered, though, so she let it slide like always. Scorpia had left because she couldn't deal with this, and she wasn't even gone an entire day before they'd decided to do more of it. It felt disrespectful.

As much as it hurt to witness, she could only be grateful Scorpia wasn't around to feel it.

Everyone else was excited to have something to do, even if there still wasn't enough work to go around. Destiny, for her part, had plenty to keep her busy. Most mornings, Reggie or Eric teleported her into one small town or another, and she'd find a coffee shop or library and set up her laptop. Maintaining her own security while hacking government firewalls was tricky, but also her specialty. Once she was in, she scoured police reports and browsed the news. She never stayed in one place long or went back too often, especially after once being recognized by a cute and chatty barista who insisted they hang out later. It was hard to explain her lack of a cell phone and not within Destiny's nature to be rude, so she'd avoided that entire town since then.

The investigators had connected the dots on the murder weapons within a week. The Copperville authorities had made the connection first, which did not surprise her. They seemed competent up there.

Public reports on the murders had run dry. Destiny thought this meant they suspected the rogue group's involvement and stopped talking to the press. At any rate, they were scrambling to save face. Dr. Fellowes's murder was reported as a home invasion gone wrong, her husband touted for his bravery and quick thinking in protecting his baby. Director Bellingham's death was never mentioned in the news, but when she hacked the employee email system,

Destiny learned it was reported within Lochspring Correctional Facility as "an unfortunate accident." An investigation had been launched into rumors he'd been living in the facility, but Destiny knew that was a formality intended to cast blame on the victim.

The authorities had even embraced the "night of drunken debauchery" theory about Dr. Oleander that Cosmina found distasteful, despite that being the plan all along.

There was only so much new information each day, so Destiny had adopted the secondary mission of exploring the separation between authority lines. Not every branch of the Council could be involved in the Program. Having too many moving parts would make it impossible to keep secret, and the Program could not function if it was not a secret. The public would never accept it.

It also couldn't function without *some* influence over the rest of the Council. She thought it necessary that they better understand the nuance between the branches. The more knowledge they had, the more they could accomplish. Unfortunately, it was a tedious and thankless task, and one with which she rarely had help or revelations.

As Destiny kept warm in a cafe, sipping a cappuccino and ignoring the call of the pastries, the rest of the group split a giant skillet of eggs and potatoes outside the cottage and discussed the assassinations. Solara and Lottie were concerned it was too soon; Hiroto and Reggie thought they'd already waited too long. Meg thought perhaps two targets was not a big enough statement, while Nino thought it made more sense to focus on one target and have plenty of back-up if things went wrong.

Cosmina tapped her foot and prodded at the fire pit and worked to unclench her jaw as Nix handled the discord perfectly. It was decided that Eric and Xia would travel to the home of Dr. Nelida Burns for a few hours. First, they would send Destiny back to the cottage. Reggie would accompany Sam to Dr. Anthony Jenkins's home on Goldgrass Island and be back before late meal.

"Please remember this is purely observational. If these don't feel like reasonable targets, we can always pick others," Cosmina reminded them as the meeting concluded. "Today's mission should not be risky." They departed the moment Lottie and Meg arrived with their supplies.

Ten minutes later, Destiny appeared in the clearing, undisguised irritation on her face.

"Oh, no," Cosmina said, "please tell me we didn't ruin any major breakthroughs?"

"No." Destiny placed her backpack of precious cargo on the ground with a gentleness that contradicted her tone and sank onto a stump. "It isn't that, although I was in the zone this morning."

"Then what's wrong?"

Destiny wrinkled her nose. "They caught me splurging on a chocolate croissant and made me split it with them before they would send me back."

Cosmina gasped. "Those absolute bullies."

"I know." Destiny sighed and shook her head. "Did I miss anything good at the meeting?"

"Just a lot of arguing. Good thing Nix is here. He always knows just how to handle them. My first instinct is always to yell back."

"He's a good leader."

"He is, which is why I'm sure he'll agree that Xia and Eric are getting too comfortable and mean together and must be separated from now on."

Destiny laughed and watched as the long-legged blonde walked away, marveling at how different a person could be from Scorpia.

Nelida Burns was a well-respected doctor and researcher with twenty published articles and eight studies to her name. Before accepting a formal position with the Council in her seventies, she had already made a career of working with Magically volatile fledglings. Her work centered around the idea that medication could be used to dilute fledglings' abilities until they could master them. The theory was interesting, but volunteers for the studies were hard to find. Magic could be dangerous under the most stable conditions, and society was resistant to change. After attempting to self-fund two studies with little success, Dr. Burns agreed to a partnership with the Council to test her medications on dangerous Variant Idealists.

The problem was, there simply weren't that many dangerous criminals, and they were forced to supplement minor ones. Many were quite young. The doctor had always claimed her drugs were intended for children, so she turned a blind eye.

On the surface, she maintained the squeaky-clean image of the good doctor working hard to make schools safer. It was only within the well-guarded walls of the Program that the ugly truth of her character festered.

Midway through her eighties now, Dr. Burns had a slew of adult children who no longer lived at home and would not get in the way. She was twice-divorced but civil with both ex-husbands. Currently, she had a girlfriend who resided in the doctor's home, maintaining an organic garden in backyard greenhouses. The girlfriend made a small income by teaching local children about gardening and selling a few rarer plants for exorbitant prices.

Dr. Anthony Jenkins lived alone with his wife. He was one hundred and twenty-four years old and boasted that he had no intentions of retiring anytime soon because his work was too fulfilling. His wife spent more time with their children and grandchildren than with her workaholic husband. Their youngest daughter was expecting a baby any day now, and Mrs. Jenkins was planning a long trip to Sagewynne to help the family adjust. The doctor had told many of his neighbors and co-workers that he'd join them for a few days once the baby arrived, but he saw no real point to all the fuss. They already had a dozen grandchildren, and families had been doing this without his help for centuries. His work, however, could not flourish without him.

Sam returned with an odd respect for the old man. "His candidness is refreshing. You don't see that often."

Reggie rolled his eyes. "I hate him. I'm convinced he deserves to die."

"We aren't in the business of killing people because they're unlikeable," Cosmina reminded him.

"Yeah, yeah. He sucks, and he's an easy target. Better?"

"Much."

When Dr. Jenkins' youngest daughter went into labor and Mrs. Jenkins departed for Valmeadow, the doctor asked a neighbor if they would mind dropping by to check on the house and water the plants Saturday through Monday. Upon hearing this, Reggie and Sam returned to the camp to explain they needed to act by Friday.

They arbitrarily selected Wednesday night for the mission. Plans were made, but the whole thing was very straightforward. Xia and Eric teleported into Swyncrest

Wednesday afternoon and walked right into the unguarded Burns home while the doctor was at work and her partner was teaching a gardening class. From there, it was a matter of camping out in the basement until time to attack.

Reggie and Sam left soon after to wait for Dr. Jenkins's return from work. He stayed late as usual, then grilled steaks alone on the patio while Reggie and Sam snuck in the back door and hid comfortably in a spare bedroom. After dinner, the doctor reclined with a book for half an hour before heading into the bathroom. As he washed his thinning hair in a steamy shower, Reggie stood guard outside the door, and Sam slipped in unnoticed. He slit the man's throat, blood spraying the tile wall and running down the drain. His lifeless body slumped to the floor, sloshing waves of pinkened water over the lip of the shower. Sam scowled at his drenched shoes, then hurried to seal his bloodied gloves in a plastic bag and swap them for clean ones from his pack. He used no Magic, so there was no residue. He stole two towels and wrapped them around his shoes to avoid leaving wet footprints through the house.

Sam's feet felt frozen as they ran through the small, quiet neighborhood of upscale homes, careful to cover their tracks. When they thought they were far enough away to avoid being traced, they teleported back to the cottage.

Dr. Nelida Burns also liked to take long, relaxing showers every night. Xia let the memory of every bitterly cold river bath she'd taken fuel her as she entered the lavish, humid bathroom and took the morally impaired doctor's life. The woman's partner cluelessly enjoyed a stroll through the greenhouses, bestowing care on plants as her lover took her last wet breaths atop a metal drain. These women took the luxury of their privileged lives for granted, and it disgusted Xia.

Even given the circumstances, the camp was abuzz with excitement as they returned. Lottie had prepared meals, Meg was ready with clean clothes, and Solara brought soap and hot water and insisted they wash before eating.

"What is that?" Reggie asked, squinting into the treeline at a new shape rising out of the dark.

"Just a small structure we're adding," Nix said. "Tell us how tonight went."

"What sort of structure?" Xia asked.

"Let's focus on this for now."

When every detail had been wrung from the stories, they fell silent for a time. An owl hooted in the distance. Bugs chirped all around. Spring was upon them, but the nights were still cold, and they huddled near the fire for warmth as the weight of the assassinations increased. No one felt miserable, but they also knew murder was no small matter.

"What's the structure?" Xia asked again.

"A combined prison and shed," Nix answered, his quiet voice resonating as always. "Two underground cells with a workspace above them. It'll free some room inside the cottage for us."

"We're moving Roman underground?" Eric's eyes widened.

"Until we figure out what else to do with him, yes." Nix's tone was a reminder that Roman was an outsider and a prisoner, and not one of them, no matter how helpful he'd been.

They had cause for celebration the following afternoon when Tiz Agathe appeared amid their work on the new shed.

"What is this in my yard?" she asked as though she hadn't been gone for seasons.

"Your yard?" Nix arched an eyebrow. "I was beginning to think you'd abandoned your property to us."

"Do not be ridiculous. It would take years to perfect another location where I cannot be easily detected. Are you doing me the kindness of building a new and improved shed?" Her eyes twinkled in amusement.

"If you'd like it."

Within ten minutes, everyone had gathered to hear the latest.

"I have delightful news about a crumbling old fortress on Earth," she began proudly. Not since Nix had announced they were separating from Rinna had more stirring words been uttered in these woods.

"It took some time to be sure, but I feel confident this fortress will aid you in your success. I cannot offer you the manual labor the task will require, but I can offer guidance and Magical assistance. Unfortunately, this one will require physical work more than anything else."

"At least it'll give us something to do." Solara tugged excitedly at the cuffs of her khakis.

"You have not had enough to keep yourselves busy?" Tiz Agathe feigned surprise. "Why, then I should not need to make soap or hunt for a year at least."

"You won't," Meg muttered. A few snickers rose.

"Tell us about the fortress," Nix said, failing to hide his impatience.

Cosmina, too, listened on the edge of her seat as Tiz Agathe detailed her struggle to find a suitable location for their needs. It had to be secluded enough from society to allow for secrecy, but near enough to allow them access to people, electricity, and the internet. She had imagined they would need to build the structure from the ground up, but fate smiled upon them and provided them with a partially destroyed fortress constructed centuries ago. It would give them the bones for the project and a bit of added security.

"I would like all of you to see it, but unauthorized teleportation to Earth is quite a feat to accomplish. There will be challenges. And we are, of course, limited to the abilities of only three of us."

"Just teach us how, and we'll get it done," Reggie said.

Tiz Agathe smiled. "Unfortunately, it is not that simple. I will teach you, of course, but it will be harder than you expect. We will begin this afternoon. We will create a transport schedule once I believe you can do it. It will take weeks to get everyone to Earth, so we must discuss and prioritize."

"Obviously, Nix and Cosmina should go first," Xia said. Everyone turned to her. She blinked. "Well? Shouldn't they check it out and confirm this is something they think we should do?"

"I do hope I did not waste my precious time and money securing a fortress, only for you to decide you do not want it."

Xia blanched. "Of course not! I only meant—"

"Xia's right," Nix interrupted. "Cosmina and I will go first to start putting a plan in place, and the rest of you will join us later."

Tiz Agathe nodded. "As soon as the boys are ready, I can take the two of you to the fortress. From there, it is not unreasonable to expect that two more people may join us every four or so days."

"Two people every four days?" Hiroto asked, his brow furrowed.

"Well, we are teleporting to another galaxy, not across the ocean." Tiz Agathe eyed him. "What did you expect?"

Most of the group had not expected such a long timeline, but her words put an end to their objections. No one wanted to get a tongue lashing from Citizen Agathe Thoreau.

Cosmina said nothing, too busy being horrified by the intrigue she felt at four days alone with Nix. She tried to tell herself she was just excited at the prospect of making some real progress. And it was exhausting to be surrounded by people all the time. The quiet would be a respite.

The timeline was more disappointing than they realized. Tiz Agathe began training Reggie and Eric right away as promised, but neither had ever attempted intergalactic teleportation. There had never been a need for it, and it was both forbidden and dangerous.

The first step was to give them a realistic idea of how much Magical energy this would consume. Even that was a challenge when her students were overconfident and eager to prove themselves. On the first day, Tiz Agathe attempted to convince them Earth was farther away than they thought, and she could tell on intuition alone they had not accumulated enough energy to try it. They argued Earth could not be farther than multiple trips around Cantamen in a single day with multiple people in tow. To teach them a lesson, she gave them permission to attempt it, then begrudgingly began the hunt for them. She tracked Reggie to Umbra, where he was lucky she found him before the phantoms discovered his illegal intrusion. Eric ended up on some uncivilized planet where he would've died from lack of oxygen in another few hours. Cosmina was furious with Tiz Agathe for risking their lives, but Nix found the harsh lesson amusing. Eric was recovered and ready to get back to work within a day, and it was easier to convince them of the seriousness of their task after they'd been rattled by their harrowing experiences.

Humbled, they worked harder and more obediently. In a week, Tiz Agathe told them they were ready to attempt teleportation to Earth. Eric made it to the fortress. Reggie landed somewhere in the nearby jungle, but close enough. They restored their strength for three days, then returned. This time Reggie landed in the clearing outside the cottage, and Eric crashed through a weak tree branch onto the ceiling of the now-complete new shed.

Roman, huddling by a torch for warmth in his new underground quarters, flinched at the sound. Lottie, who was sanding the wooden counters to smooth, splinter-free perfection, ran to investigate.

After Eric's sprained ankle was treated and the group had spared a moment to celebrate, Tiz Agathe announced she would take Cosmina and Nix to the fortress the next day.

"I will return in a couple of days to assist the boys with their first transports to Earth, so we will need two brave volunteers for that." She grinned mischievously. "Then it will be a matter of returning to fetch two people every few days. We must decide who joins us sooner, and who later."

"You're the only one who's seen the fortress, so what's your recommendation?" Nix asked.

Reggie cleared his throat. Everyone ignored him.

"Security and manual labor will be priorities in the beginning," Tiz Agathe said. "The Magic-detecting barriers are weaker on Earth, and less prevalent, so I believe we can work around them if we are careful. But the Council will still be able to detect us if we use too much Magic. We also will not have access to much electricity, so it will not be terribly different from living here, but perhaps a bit more...antiquated."

"My immediate thought is Destiny needs to stay on Cantamen because of her work here," Cosmina said. She'd been concerned this would offend the other woman, but the width of the brown eyes that turned to her indicated gratitude.

"That makes sense to me," Nix said.

"What skills can everyone offer?" Cosmina asked when no one said anything else.

"Hiroto is really good with setting traps and security measures," Solara said.

Meg nodded. "And Nino is great with strategy and scouting. They'd make a great team for setting up security around the fortress."

"Solara is great with construction," Lottie added. "She grew up helping her dad's company, right?"

"I did," Solara said, surprised someone remembered.

"No one will get the place comfortable and livable faster than Lottie," Hiroto said.

Lottie smiled. "Thank you, but I'm too afraid to be one of the first to go."

"I, too, prefer not to be a...test subject," Meg agreed. "I'll go once Reggie and Eric have made at least one more successful trip."

A few chuckles went around the group as Reggie and Eric scowled.

"Nino and Hiroto, do you feel comfortable joining us first? You can share control of security around the fortress while Cosmina and I get started on the manual labor," Nix suggested. They agreed with shining eyes.

Cosmina and Nix spent the rest of the evening packing, preparing, and doling out instructions. A rough draft of their teleportation schedule was posted on the wall. Nix met with Destiny and explained that he planned to assess the fortress for realism, but he trusted Tiz Agathe's judgment. He would send word with Reggie and Eric when he was ready for Destiny to contact Rinna.

"Don't put too much in the letter," he reminded her needlessly. "Make her meet with you for the real details, or she can wait to meet with me, but I'm not sure how long I'll be on Earth."

Destiny promised to hold down the camp in their absence. She was nervous about the responsibility, but part of her hoped news of the fortress would bring Scorpia back.

As they stood in the clearing waiting on Tiz Agathe to take them to Earth, Cosmina watched Nix fiddle with the lock on the new shed door. "Are you nervous about leaving them alone?"

"Yes," he admitted.

"They're all adults. Well, practically. And you can't protect them from everything. They didn't join this group blindly."

"I just hope they can behave like adults when unsupervised. It would be a shame to lose all our progress because they get reckless."

"Are you worried about Roman?"

"Partly. Lottie spends a disproportionate amount of time tending to him, don't you think?"

"Yes. But I think you can trust her to follow the rules. And he's been well-behaved thus far."

"I think we should bring him to Earth as soon as we can create a cell for him there. Decrease his chances of escape."

"Okay," Cosmina agreed because there was no point in arguing. "Anything else?"

"Yeah. It bothers me that Xia and Sam are waiting so long to join us on Earth. They've been so vocal about wanting to stay busy that I expected them to leap on the opportunity."

"A lot of people are nervous about the teleporting part of this."

"You don't really believe that's the reason, do you?"

"Do you have suspicions?"

"Yes."

Tiz Agathe stepped into the clearing with a messenger bag slung over her shoulder, looking around for them.

"Then we'll ask Tiz Agathe to check on them when she comes back in a few days, and we'll ask Des to keep an extra eye on them," Cosmina murmured as they hurried to the old woman. "You don't think it's that serious, do you?"

"Time will tell," Nix said as the old witch spotted them and began to hassle them for making her wait.

It took a moment for Cosmina to recover from the teleportation. She'd never traveled to another planet, and without the safety of authorized travel, the trip was rough. Once her vomiting stopped, she found her first impression of the fortress underwhelming. Dilapidated stone walls surrounded a partially rotted wood structure that had once stood atop a brick foundation. The air was heavy, wet, and bug-infested. She scowled at Tiz Agathe's misleading use of the word "fortress." Even with "crumbling" and "old" before it, the term brought to mind something more substantial than this.

At least it smelled like the ocean. Everything else was awful.

"You've slept here?" Cosmina asked skeptically, nudging a chunk of concrete free with her toe and gazing nervously into the jungle around them.

Tiz Agathe laughed out loud. "I told you living here would feel more antiquated."

"It doesn't seem safe."

"People lived like this for centuries, and with less technology and weaponry than we possess," the old witch pointed out. "Though I do believe a roof is a priority."

"Why bother? People lived in huts with banana leaf coverings for centuries," Cosmina muttered, raking her hands through her already-damp hair. Nix pulled his back into a short ponytail, turning aside to hide his grin.

"I have always liked you, in spite of yourself." Tiz Agathe smoothed her own coarse gray hair back into its tight bun as it began to frizz. "If you will follow me, I will give you the full tour."

Cosmina pressed her lips together and focused on not tripping over any of the loose bricks and dead branches littering the ground. Nix's dark eyes were bright, his face open to possibility as he surveyed the area. Cosmina took a breath and willed herself to adopt his attitude. "Who owns this island?"

"Technically, an impoverished and under-established country with few immigration laws," Tiz Agathe replied vaguely. "They should be friendly enough, provided we are good neighbors."

"They won't know we're here, will they?"

"It will be impossible to reside here as a group without having some interaction with the locals."

"How big is it?" Cosmina took note of the distant ocean view in all directions.

"Small," Tiz Agathe said. "But it is close enough to other islands nearby. A short boat ride from most of them."

"That's good," Nix said. "Seclusion is possible, but we'll also have some access to civilization and supplies. Although it sounds like civilization may not be what we expect."

"It is a poor human civilization," Tiz Agathe said. "Fortunate we have no need for human doctors because you will not find that here. But they will be happy to trade with and sell to us."

"And their government?" Nix asked.

"A small monarchy, located in the center of the largest island. They are enamored with their luxury and will not be meddlesome, I am sure of it."

"Sounds perfect for us, but unfortunate for the people who live here," Cosmina said.

"We can't save the whole world," Nix reminded her.

"I know, but doesn't it feel weird to bring part of our mission to save Cantamen all the way to Earth?" Cosmina shook her head. "I feel like a colonizer."

Nix turned to hide his laugh, but he snorted, and she punched him roughly on the shoulder.

"Children," Tiz Agathe said sharply. "We are not here to overthrow this government or deplete the resources. If we are respectful, we can be good neighbors. Still, it will be up to you to ensure we do not lose our heads and take this gift for granted."

"You're right." Nix straightened. "The Earth has provided us with a resource in our fight to save the innocent. Even if this is the home of humans, Earth doesn't work against the witches she also created. This is the homeland of our people, and there's no reason we shouldn't accept her aid."

"Now you are thinking like a real witch," Tiz Agathe said, her blue eyes appraising him proudly. Cosmina balked at her motherly expression. "Where should we begin?"

"I'll take clean-up if you want to start thinking about a roof," Cosmina said.

"My thoughts exactly," Nix agreed, with one of the warmest smiles she'd ever seen grace his angular face. It stopped her in her tracks in the middle of donning a glove.

By the end of the day, Cosmina had cleared most of the dead branches and plants from the inner area. She managed to make some progress on the bits of loose concrete and brick after Tiz Agathe made a trip to the nearest island for a wheelbarrow. A local man who felt concerned for the ancient woman buying supplies had accompanied her back over in his boat. He introduced himself as Thilo and spent a few hours acquainting Nix with the area. Nix committed to memory the information about venomous reptiles, fish, and plants to avoid. Thilo demonstrated the proper set-up for fishing nets to passively catch food, and Nix promised to find Thilo and his brothers when they were ready to begin building.

"So much for discretion," Cosmina muttered as they watched Thilo and his brother set off in their boat.

"I like him," Nix said.

"Yeah, but now he's going to tell the entire island that a strange family is building here, and we don't want that to spread."

Nix shrugged. "We'll work around it."

She eyed him warily. Never had she known him to be so relaxed. Where was the guy who resisted rescuing her because she hadn't suffered like the rest of them? Where was the man who vetted everyone Rinna saved for worthiness? Now he was letting strange humans traipse through their sacred refuge and spread rumors that could get them all killed.

The change was unsettling.

Thilo's visit delayed their plans for a roof, but Nix propped a wooden cover against an intact fortress wall and used some twine and rope to fashion a makeshift lean-to. They insulated their shelter with a canvas tent they'd brought from the cottage, for added protection from the relentless rain. Even though the hard, wet ground was uncomfortable, Cosmina was tired and sore enough to eat her dry crab and doze off quickly.

Nix lay awake for a long time, listening to sheets of rain pelt their meager shelter and the rhythm of Cosmina's restful breaths. Occasionally, unpleasant choking and hacking sounds came from Tiz Agathe's old throat and lungs. He couldn't help wondering if every sound he heard was a wild animal on the prowl or a local human intending to kill them.

They were sore when they rose the next morning. Nix got to work on the fishing nets as Cosmina struggled to ignite a fire in the rain. In the end she used Magic, heating the skillet with her hands to scramble a few eggs and a couple bell peppers they'd brought from Cantamen.

Desperate to feel dry, Cosmina insisted they work on the roof together. The rain was worse today but provided little relief from the heat and humidity. With determination, they erected a small room with four walls and even a wooden platform elevated off the ground. Cosmina was so ecstatic she stripped to her underwear and lounged on her dry sleeping bag as though she were living in the absolute lap of luxury.

They built a fire in the center of their room and pretended it wasn't full of irresponsible kindling. As they heated their dinner, Tiz Agathe reminded them more people would join them in a few days, and this shelter would not be big enough for everyone.

Cosmina picked a fishbone from her mouth and scowled. "Maybe we can sleep in shifts." Though she couldn't imagine how they would accomplish anything in the dark on this island.

"I'll go into town tomorrow and see if Thilo and his family can help us," Nix said. "I just don't know how we can pay them. I don't know where we are, or the currency." He looked pointedly at Tiz Agathe, but the old woman only smiled and fished a coin purse from her jacket, tied at the top with a bright red string. She tossed it to him, and he caught it neatly.

"I believe you will find Thilo quite receptive to this payment," she said. "I will depart from you in the morning, so I do urge you to be careful. I will return in two days, if all goes well, with your reinforcements in tow."

Cosmina suppressed a shiver. Being alone with all this freedom and wildlife was scarier than slitting any man's throat.

Tiz Agathe was gone when they woke. Cosmina stretched her legs and showered in the rain as the sun peeked over the horizon. She started a fire in their shelter, which already smelled smoky all the time, and made breakfast for Nix before he took a boat to the mainland. She swallowed the bitterness of bile down her throat as she watched his black jacket and topknot disappear between sheets of rain in the gray morning. It wasn't his fault this was probably the closest she'd ever get to taking care of a husband before he left for work in the morning. She tried to recall if she'd ever wanted that but couldn't remember now what she'd planned for her future. She'd been so privileged it was possible she'd never bothered to ask herself. She would've believed she could have anything.

Since being forced into this life, a normal future with a husband and children felt like the most wonderful and unattainable thing in the world. But maybe anything at all sounds better than a life of survival.

She cast the fishing nets herself, then resumed the unending and thankless task of clearing storm debris from their camp. She wondered if it rained year-round on this island. They might even experience monsoons, she realized with a sudden weight in her stomach. Just surviving here would be more work than on Cantamen, and they planned to fill this place with rescued and traumatized people, some of them fledglings. How long before one of them fell to a venomous insect bite or panther attack?

Her mind traveled to the memory of Nino's mangled leg when he'd been attacked by the wolf. Wolves were manageable compared to what little she knew of wild cats. Wolves tended to avoid people, but cats hunted individually and stalked their prey. There could be one watching her now, waiting on the right moment to strike.

A gust of wind tore a branch from a nearby tree. A shrill scream escaped Cosmina's throat, along with a small part of her soul.

She swore and stamped her foot, willing herself to get it together. She was not a helpless child. She was a grown woman, a witch who could use Magic. Not to mention well-trained in physical combat, loaded with weapons, and in excellent physical condition. Her chances of survival were good, even in this relentlessly wet jungle. Her biggest fear should still be the Witching Council, not some theoretical animals lurking in the trees.

Cosmina dug a hole a ways from their camp and wrapped their Magical paraphernalia and many of their weapons in an extra tarp before burying them. She walked around their base and attempted to think big picture. Where could they put prison cells? How many of those would they realistically need? How many bedrooms, and how big should they be? What about bathrooms? Was indoor plumbing a radical idea? How would they preserve food when it probably never got cold enough here to freeze? Would they have any electricity at all? How many people were likely to live here at once, and how would they keep them safe and contained? What were the chances Rinna would choose to keep her group here, and how could she and Nix maintain the trajectory of their mission if they allowed that to happen?

Nix returned with Thilo, six strange men, three strange women, and, inexplicably, four small children. Cosmina hurried to greet them, embarrassed that all she'd done was overwhelm herself with variables.

She kept her questions to herself while Nix conversed with Thilo, his omnilingualism proving to be invaluable. A young girl who could not have been older than seventeen but carried a toddler on her back approached Cosmina with a kind smile and a word she did not know. She stammered an apology and attempted to back away, but the girl continued to smile and repeat herself as she gestured between Cosmina and Nix.

Cosmina repeated the word blankly. The girl beamed and gestured between herself and one of the men speaking with Thilo. Cosmina thought the word must indicate a relationship, perhaps marriage or sibling. She doubted this woman was looking between Nix's features and her own and guessing they were siblings. The idea of this child being married turned her stomach a little, but human cultures were different, and seventeen was not as young when your lifespan was half the length of a witch's.

Cosmina forced a smile and nodded. Did it matter if the locals assumed she and Nix were married? Could she help it if they did? Maybe it would make things easier.

She had thought that might be the end of it, but she was wrong. Thilo's family were strong, strapping men who were pleased to help Nix with manual labor. The women they'd brought along were just as adamant about keeping busy. They were unflustered by the language barrier, working through it whether Cosmina liked it or not. By the end of the day, she'd learned a dozen basic words, a new trap for catching jungle rodents and another for small birds, and a more efficient way to set and empty the fishing nets. The teen with the toddler taught her to braid large leaves into makeshift rugs and tarps, and pointed out a few edible and inedible plants.

When the family returned to their boat at dusk, Thilo promised to come back in the morning for their second day of work. The toddler gave Cosmina a straw doll and a shy smile before going back into her bundle on the teenager's back.

Every fiber of Cosmina's being felt raw and exposed as she watched the small boat depart for the mainland, rowed by the tireless, tanned arms of men long accustomed to harsh island living.

"Really kind people," Nix said from behind her, and it surprised her to hear a faint huskiness in his voice. She turned and tilted her head up to his.

"Yeah." She cleared her throat of the lump in it. Nix smiled in a way that indicated understanding. "They did an amazing job."

They walked back to camp side by side, surveying the progress with appreciation. Thilo and his men had made short work of the crumbling bricks and stones, tearing them down and clearing them away in no time. They had then erected a protective barrier from the rain and started laying new bricks. The walls to three sizable rooms stood drying in the evening's misty waning light.

The shelter they'd finished the day prior had also been reinforced. Two of its walls were salvageable, and their touch-ups were already almost dry. Thick layers of banana-leaf carpeting cushioned the wooden floor around a deep clay pot that served as a far less hazardous fire pit.

"This is going to be much more comfortable." Cosmina thought of the pains she'd already developed after just two nights on the hard ground.

"I'll go check the traps," Nix said.

Cosmina was already weary of dry crab, but at least they seemed plentiful. When they'd finished eating, a drowsy, lazy quiet settled over them. She reclined on her arms and asked the question that had been burning in her mind all day.

"How are you explaining to Thilo what we're building here?"

Nix didn't take his eyes from the fire. Cosmina watched the embers reflect in the deep blackness of them and wondered at the warmth in her belly. It was incredible how fleeting moments of contentment could be found even in situations as wild and improbable as theirs.

"Many of the locals believe this island is sacred land," he said after a long moment. "Some think it cursed, some think it blessed, but all leave it untouched because the treasures hidden here are not for humans to behold."

Cosmina gave the news a moment to settle. Any witch knew better than to discount the rumor of a curse. It could be human superstition passed down among fearful locals, or it could just as possibly be an actual curse placed by a Magical species. "Then why would they help us?"

"Because apparently, Thilo's father is a seer. He took one look at me and told Thilo I'll be the one to bring divine glory back to these islands."

Cosmina laughed. "You're exploiting the superstitions of poor, uneducated people."

"Not necessarily." He feigned offense. "You think it's so far-fetched that there might be some godly missive in my destiny?"

"I didn't say that. I just highly doubt there's two of them."

Nix arched one thick black eyebrow at her. "Maybe they're more connected than we know."

"And how do we explain all the other people joining us?"

"We don't. Most of us will never meet the locals, and very few of them will ever step foot on this island. Once Thilo and his family help us get things set up, I'm hoping Tiz Agathe will manipulate their memories. They should only remember that we sometimes visit to explore the island, and we pay generously in our dealings with them."

"And if they do come here?"

"One of our initial security measures will be to mask the appearance of this place. It should be simple for Hiroto and Nino to do." He sat up and unbuttoned his shirt. Cosmina averted her eyes, though she'd been lounging in her sports bra and a pair of loose shorts for over an hour. Nix noticed the shift of her gaze and smiled to himself.

"I still don't feel great about this," Cosmina said as he settled back into a reclining position. Her eyelids felt heavy.

He studied the long, lean, flickering shadow cast upon the wall behind her by the dying firelight. "Do you remember the Ethical Magic classes they made us take in Primary School?"

Cosmina blinked. She had started to doze, and his question felt like it was pulling her back from the start of a delightful dream. "Of course."

"There was one exercise in particular that stuck with me. An advanced simulation. I failed it four times before I figured out what they wanted the answer to be. Even then, I only passed because I realized what they wanted from me, not because I agreed. And what it really taught me is there's no way to be ethical all the time. There are hard and fast rules, of course. Don't kill, don't cheat, don't steal, don't lie. And then there are gray areas around every rule. And those gray areas are where depth of character lives."

Cosmina's brain felt fuzzy. She knew she should debate ethical nuance with him, but the warmth in her belly and the husky sound of his voice in the dark lulled her into a sense of peace.

"Do you know why I asked you to lead this proactive group with me?"

Her heart missed a beat. "Does it matter?"

"It does to me." He paused. "It did to Scorpia."

Cosmina had long suspected this, though she wasn't sure what it meant, and she didn't pry. "I'm guessing she didn't find it very ethical."

"To say the least."

"You're in love with her," Cosmina said, the lull making her bold.

"I was," Nix agreed readily, because he was always bold.

"Then why did you do it?"

"Because it was a lose-lose situation, and I was willing to be the bad guy."

Cosmina furrowed her brow. "What does that mean?"

"Scorpia has always been special to me, and I would've died for her in an instant. But I can't live in hiding, pretending things are normal because I managed to escape, no matter how hard I try. I thought she understood. I thought she felt the same way. We worked well together for so long because we had a common goal.

"And then, she wanted something else. And I don't begrudge her that. She has the right to change her mind. But when we no longer want the same things, what's more ethical? To go on pretending, to preserve her feelings for a short time, until it becomes unsustainable? Or to sever the relationship and work toward a new understanding?"

Cosmina closed her eyes and settled against her pillow. The last of the fire had died, and it felt more like bedtime than ever. "So you picked me because I was the furthest person from asking you to date me?"

Nix laughed out loud. "No. The first part of the story is that Scorpia and I had reached an impasse, and it would have been wrong to deceive her. The other part..."

His long fingers brushed her jaw, and her eyelids flew open. His face hovered inches from hers, his inky black eyes taking note of the hitch of her chest and the tremble of her lip just before he steadied it with his own.

A blinding clarity erupted inside her brain. Her pale cheeks flushed as she grasped for Nix's skin in the dark. For a few hours, they added to the heat of the night.

It took just over a day for the group to run amok in the absence of leadership. Destiny refused to teleport into town because she wanted to preserve Eric and Reggie's energy. She justified this by saying there wouldn't be many updates now, anyway. By spending more time with the others, she realized the structure Nix and Cosmina provided was invaluable.

Without Nix's prying eyes, Lottie snuck extra food and small comforts to Roman. Destiny noticed she disappeared during her hunting shift, only to emerge from the new shed three hours later with a couple of updated blueprints. Reggie and Eric were bored. They weren't allowed to do much, making them cranky. On the first day without Nix and Cosmina, Eric lost his temper and threw acid at a nearby tree, which Meg uprooted and threw at him. Xia and

Sam disappeared while on guard duty, forcing Nino and Hiroto to cover for them.

On the third day, Solara limped into the clearing with a broken arm, sending everyone into a panic. Destiny ordered Lottie and Nino to search for Meg and Hiroto and make sure they were safe. Solara laughed and said they'd have trouble finding Meg. It was true; Lottie found her two hours later, suspended in a tree by Solara's webbing. When they returned to the cottage and Meg lunged for Solara again, Destiny threatened to lock everyone in the cells with Roman if they couldn't behave. Never had she felt so much like a mother.

Destiny retired to bed early, grateful beyond measure that Tiz Agathe would return the following day.

Unfortunately, she returned with a note from Nix to keep an eye on Xia and Sam. Destiny's mouth went dry. The two of them were still missing, but she couldn't bring herself to tell Nix she'd already failed at the most basic task of keeping everyone in line. She claimed they went into town for supplies, walking to preserve Reggie and Eric's energy. It was a good lie, and one everyone believed.

Tiz Agathe stayed one day and night. Once the next group departed, it would be days before anyone knew whether their transport was successful. Due to the inexperience of the young men, Nino and Hiroto traveled lighter than Nix and Cosmina. However, Tiz Agathe refreshed the supplies in her messenger bag and packed two chickens and a rooster in a cage. The sight of her was comical, especially once she slung a small bag of seed over her old shoulder. She turned to the sweating young men. "Ready?"

They nodded nervously. Tiz Agathe watched as they secured their meager packs to their bodies and linked arms. The four of them closed their eyes and disappeared.

Everyone in the clearing held their breath as she leaned forward and sniffed the air. "Maybe," she grunted before vanishing herself.

"Maybe," Meg repeated. "Can you believe that woman?"

Destiny shrugged. "It's probably hard to tell where they ended up on smell alone, don't you think?"

Meg scowled and went inside the cottage without another word. Destiny chewed her lip. She considered reminding her to make lunch, then decided to just do it herself.

The young men crashed ungracefully into the ocean. They were close enough to shore to swim, but Reggie had a panic attack when Eric told him about sharks, and Hiroto got stung by a jellyfish. Tiz Agathe made quick work of their ailments, and within the hour, a tour of the fortress was underway. Nino was dismayed that Nix had been careless enough to invite humans to the island. As he ranted, Nix flashed Cosmina a smile behind his back.

After the initial tour, Tiz Agathe forced Reggie and Eric to eat and rest. Nino and Hiroto got to work circling the compound and brainstorming security measures. Nix and Cosmina continued to help Thilo and his family build the fortress.

The rain brought a steady stream of debris into their compound, but it was manageable with routine maintenance. They now had multiple rooms, some with windows. Most even had ceilings. Cosmina and the local women had arranged an indoor bathroom for them. Though it was no modern facility, it certainly beat walking a hundred yards, digging a hole, and squatting in the rain.

On their first day, Nino and Hiroto determined the official perimeter and cast protective enchantments around it. Their first priority was hiding from the Council, so they needed to find out how much Magic was safe to use on the island. Earth's sensors were weaker than Cantamen's since the Council had less interest in Earth. Still, a sudden influx of Magic in one place—even this place—would alert them to the rogues' presence. Basic protective enchantments used small amounts of Magic and were unsuspicious, but they would eventually need to train witches here.

This would be more work than they'd anticipated. It would take time to obtain supplies and complete the structures, especially without Thilo's help. Nino and Hiroto wanted tall stone walls to border the grounds, locking gates, meandering halls, deceptive doors, guard towers, barred windows, vantage points for long-range weapons and observance. They also needed a prison, preferably underground and hidden deep within the compound. Cosmina was quick to mention they would need more livable quarters and meeting rooms for research and planning.

"We've crashed on cots in one room for years, so we don't need private bedrooms right away. But we also don't have enough sleeping space for everyone, so we need a few more rooms. And another bathroom or two." Eric scowled at the tiny wooden shack. "We all can't share that thing."

"If we want it done quickly, we need more help from Thilo's family before we alter their memories," Cosmina said. "I don't see why they can't help us build a few more rooms and start the border walls. They've been nothing but lovely."

"I agree with that," Nix said.

Nino furrowed his brow. "I'm surprised at you two. It was stupid to bring the locals here and show them our inner compound. They've likely told the entire population of this country about us, and it's bound to draw unwanted attention."

"Well, it's a little late to take it back now," Nix said with a shrug. Cosmina stifled a grin.

Tiz Agathe swept into the room, the wind banging the wooden door shut as her jacket dripped water all over their banana-leaf floors. "The locals can be trusted," she said firmly, taking her long gray braid in both hands and wringing it free of water. "They have a generational connection to Magic here, and they recognize it in Nix. They will not betray him."

"Oh, orid." Nino rolled his eyes, but Hiroto, Reggie, and Eric looked intrigued.

Rather than explaining, Nix changed the subject. "Are we in agreement, then? Walls and rooms are the immediate priority, and Thilo and his family return for a few more days to help us out?"

Nino was eventually convinced.

Please Tell Me That's Animal Blood

Arma 318

It had been three days. Destiny was about to go into town to check for news of Xia and Sam and nearly cried with relief when Lottie ran into the gathering room to announce their return.

She dragged them into the new shed before anyone else noticed them. "Where the hell have you been?" She padlocked the door and whirled on them in one motion, taking in the sight of their black clothing and boots, crusted with faint, flaking, rust-colored stains that stank of metal and decay. A strangled wheeze escaped her chest as she understood.

"Please tell me that's animal blood," she said, her mouth agape as she looked between them.

"It's animal blood," Sam said, too lightly. Destiny lunged and seized him by the collar with both hands, causing both Xia and Sam to yelp in surprise.

"Have you lost your minds? Did you actually do what I think you did?" Her voice rose shrilly with each word.

"Des, we don't have to do this." Xia reached to pry Destiny's hands from Sam's shirt. "You can just pretend—"

"Oh, yes, we do have to do this, because Nix specifically asked me to keep an eye on the two of you in his absence!" Destiny released Sam's shirt so roughly he stumbled back against the wall. The jars on the shelves rattled.

In his cell beneath their feet, Roman stared at the ceiling and strained to make out the words being said.

"Are you kidding me?" Xia's brown eyes were wide. "Now Nix thinks we need a babysitter?"

"And not for no reason! How could you do this without clearing it? Who was it?"

"Thalia Holland and Samuel Fitzgerald," Xia said.

Destiny furrowed her brow and tried to recall the names. "Thalia Holland, Head of the Middlebrook Tribune?"

"Yes."

"And who is Samuel Fitzgerald?"

"One of their biggest influencers, financially and socially." Xia tucked a loose box braid back into her ponytail.

"Why bother killing two people with the same issue?"

"Because we can only travel so far without teleporters, they were both local, and they were easy," Xia said.

"*And*," Sam said, sparing a moment for a quick eye-roll at Xia, "because they were equally important to the issue, in different ways. Fitzgerald provided most of the funding, while Holland was extremely good in her role as the project's brains. Taking out either would have been a good blow, but taking out both almost guarantees the Middlebrook Tribune will go under."

"Why do we need a newspaper to go under?" Destiny massaged her temples.

"They've been targeting Amara and her blog, putting resources into finding her identity and exposing her," Xia said.

"I've been monitoring that, and they haven't even gotten close," Destiny said. "Amara is doing an excellent job." Before returning to her family, Amara had told Destiny she was good with computers and asked if there was anything she could do to help their cause. Nix had suggested she run a blog exposing their stories and researching new disappearances, getting these accusations against the Council in front of the public in a way the government couldn't trace. Destiny had taught her about cybersecurity and firewalls, as well as watching from afar to make sure her identity was never compromised, but Amara had done far better than any of them had expected.

"Yeah, but now we don't have to worry about it anymore." Sam shrugged.

"This is insane. You had no planning. No backup. Very little, if any, scouting. Did both murders occur on the same night? How did you do it? You're still covered in blood. How do you know you weren't seen?"

"Everything went perfectly!" Xia insisted. "When we were scouting, they took a convenient little working lunch to a restaurant together. We incited a bit of car trouble, lured them into an empty parking lot, and staged the crime scene to look like they were having an affair. They never saw it coming, and we never needed access to their homes or families."

"How did you cause car trouble?" Destiny asked. "With Magic? Can it be traced?"

"Des, we're good at this," Sam said. "We thought of everything, and we covered our tracks."

"You cannot do this again. I cannot allow it."

Xia inclined her head. "Can you actually forbid it?"

"Yes." Destiny felt her cheeks grow hot. "Nix placed me in charge—"

"Yeah, but he can't actually think—"

"Xia," Sam cut her off. She looked at him, opened her mouth, then closed it again. For a long minute, no one said anything.

"You won't do it again, right?" Destiny asked, hating how it came out like a request.

"We won't do it again," they said together. Destiny ordered them to find clothes and change before anyone saw the blood, then readied herself for an early morning trip to check the news.

When Tiz Agathe, Reggie, and Eric returned to the cottage, they found it poorly attended. Destiny had gone into town and planned to stay the night. As to the whereabouts of Xia and Sam, no one was sure. Scorpia was also still missing, though no one mentioned her.

"Orid. This place needs Nix back," Reggie said.

Lottie rolled her eyes. "We are just fine doing absolutely nothing without him, thank you very much."

"How's the prisoner?" Eric asked, relaxing for the first time since they'd left the cottage four days earlier.

Lottie handed him a bowl of steak, eggs, and vegetables without meeting his gaze. "He's the same, I suppose. Why do you ask?"

Eric shrugged. "You seem to like him the best. Nix wants us to bring him to Earth next time we go."

Lottie froze in place. "What? Why?"

"Dunno. That's just what he said to do."

"Is he planning to hurt him?" Meg asked. Lottie paled.

"I don't think so?" Eric screwed up his face in confusion. "We built a prison cell for him there, so I think he just wants to move him somewhere he's less likely to reach the Council if he escapes."

"But he's never once tried to escape," Lottie objected. "He's grateful to be here. He knows the Council are not his friends. When is Nix going to figure out Roman can be trusted?"

"Probably never, knowing Nix," Meg reminded her gently.

"I don't know about that," Reggie said. "On Earth, he's letting humans build the fortress."

Shocked faces peered back at him in silence.

"It's true," Eric said. "It was shocking for us, too."

"Humans?" Solara's blue eyes were round in her face. "He's letting humans into our fortress?"

Eric nodded. "You'll see for yourself in a couple days. Is it true no one knows where Sam and Xia are?"

The rest of them shared uneasy looks.

"Man, Nix is not going to like that." Reggie chuckled.

Destiny returned the following evening and was more horrified than anyone to find Sam and Xia gone. Before allowing the teleporters to leave again, she scrawled a quick plea for Nix's help and gave it to Tiz Agathe for safekeeping.

Roman was unwilling to transport to Earth via unsafe means, forcing Tiz Agathe to sedate him. Lottie stood nearby and wrung her hands for a long time after they left.

With Xia and Sam missing, only Lottie, Meg, and Destiny remained at the cottage. They alternated ten-hour guard shifts and strayed from the clearing minimally. They dared not discuss where Xia and Sam might be. Destiny was furious with them for lying to her.

It wasn't in the plan to split up, but it became necessary when Ella Walden and her cousin, Oslo, got into an argument at the dinner party and left separately. Xia tailed Ella through the park on foot while Sam made his way through town in a stolen car behind Oslo's limousine.

Xia felt as calm as she ever did before a kill. She had come to think of herself as a natural predator, controlling the population of a destructive species. It was ugly work, but nothing she would shy from or feel guilty about.

Sam felt a bit differently. Though he agreed to help Xia, he lost sleep over the matter.

He abandoned the stolen car several blocks from Oslo's mansion and made the rest of the journey on foot. The home was well-guarded, and law enforcement presence in the area had increased after their last kills. He didn't know how he would get inside. They'd hoped for an opportunity as the pair left the party and hadn't planned beyond that. Playing things by ear had worked well for them over the years, and they preferred it to endless scouting and backup plans.

Neither of them worried as they tailed their targets. They had absolute faith in each other.

When Ella Walden and her bodyguard stopped beneath a grove of trees to wait for the car she'd called, Xia released the sleeping dust she'd brought, blowing it through the trees and into their faces. Within moments, they were snoring on the ground.

The grove was well-lit, and a car was on the way, but she only needed a moment. Xia stepped over the bodyguard, sliced the lady's throat, and fled with the weapon.

She reached the rendezvous point in the woods in no time, the sound of sirens at her back propelling her feet with urgency. Her heart raced as she crouched in the dark, willing Sam to appear so they could escape town. It struck her suddenly as stupid, how publicly she'd just murdered a prominent socialite.

The sirens faded, only to return in uncomfortably close proximity. Flashing lights filled the wealthy neighborhood behind which she hid. She realized with a sinking feeling that she was very near the Oslo Walden mansion.

She rose to her feet.

These sirens weren't for her.

As more law enforcement vehicles sped through the neighborhood, lights came on in houses. Nosy residents peered through windows and walked onto porches. Xia stood frozen, unsure whether to flee or run to Sam's aid.

She heard shouting and saw red sparks shoot into the air somewhere far away, illuminating the area. Dogs barked, birds screeched, people shouted, and something exploded with enough force to rattle the ground on which she stood. Her quaking knees held her upright by muscle memory alone.

The scene subsided as the vehicles left. People went back inside their extravagant homes.

And Xia knew the worst possible thing in the world had happened.

Xia crashed through the door without warning, sending Destiny into an attack. The noise brought Lottie and Meg from their cots in seconds. It took a minute of scuffling, but they realized who she was and dropped their fists with considerable irritation.

Then they saw the wild-eyed look on her face and the blood on her clothes, and noted Sam's absence. The mood shifted to panic.

"What happened?" Destiny demanded.

"Sam was captured."

Lottie clapped a hand over her mouth.

"You said you weren't going to do it again," Destiny said hoarsely. "You promised me."

"We lied!" Xia threw both arms into the air. "We lied. We were always going to do it again, and you should've known that. But who cares now? We have to go get him!"

"Xia," Destiny said, shaking her head slowly, "it's not that simple—"

"Why not? Everyone rallied around Cosmina when she was taken!" Xia's eyes flashed with unbridled fury. "Is Sam less important than she is?"

"Of course not, but the situation was wildly different!" Meg shouted. "For starters, every single one of us was still on the same planet then! How are the four of us supposed to organize a rescue mission with no teleporters?"

"It'll take days just to find out where they're holding him," Lottie said softly.

Xia clenched and unclenched her fists. "No, it won't. Just look it up. Give me your laptop." She whirled on Destiny.

"No." Destiny felt like she was forcing the word up through shards of glass in her throat. "It isn't safe here. It can be traced. There are precautions we have to take—"

"This is Sam's life! I don't give a damn if they locate the cottage!"

"This is all of our lives!" Meg stepped between Xia and Destiny. "This is Tiz Agathe's *home*! We can't just throw caution to the wind because you and Sam decided to be reckless!"

"Oh, forgive us for actually *working* while the rest of you lounged around for seasons!"

"Working! Ha! You clearly get off on killing people, for some sick reason, and now Sam's been captured because you thought you were immune to consequences!"

Xia threw a punch, but Meg blocked it and countered with an upward elbow jab. Lottie grabbed Xia and Destiny grabbed Meg, both screaming to stop.

The women separated. Xia sniffed and wiped her bloodied nose on her jacket sleeve. She glowered at Meg, who matched her gaze.

"That's enough," Destiny said. "We're not going to turn on each other. I'm going into town to see what I can learn about Sam's arrest and where he's being held. But if they've identified him as a member of our group or an escaped VI, they may keep it quiet."

"Why? They reported on Cosmina's," Xia said.

"Yeah, but that was an attack on an orphanage, and one that drew the attention of the neighbors. They had to make a public statement."

"This drew attention too. He was arrested in a wealthy neighborhood. There were sirens and even fireworks—"

"Good. That'll help us find where he's being held. But orid, Xia, don't make this worse. Stay here until I get back. Don't leave the camp at all. Swear it."

"Maybe we should put her in Roman's old cell," Meg muttered. "It seems like the only thing that might work."

"Fuck you." Xia spat on Meg's bare foot.

Lottie moved to restrain her friend, but Meg just laughed darkly and left the cottage. Lottie and Destiny shared a stricken look.

"Do I need to lock you up, or will you swear to stay put?" Destiny asked.

"I'd like to see you try." Xia arched an eyebrow. "But I'm not going anywhere until we find out where Sam is."

Destiny hesitated, then ran to pack her bag. "Send a bird if something happens," she told Lottie. Lottie nodded, and Destiny disappeared into the dark woods.

Destiny arrived shortly after dawn and stopped in the first cafe she found. She bought a black coffee, added a splash of cream, and settled in with her laptop. She kept an eye on the morning news playing above her head as she hacked her way into the local law enforcement's system. She had done this a thousand times before, but it was always risky, especially if they'd identified Sam as part of their group. They might have had the bright idea to put extra precautions around their systems or flag certain keywords in anticipation of another rescue mission. And Sam had attempted to murder a Program Manager for the Council's Law Enforcement Community Outreach Program, after several other murders of prominent Councilwitches. They underestimated the rogues, but they weren't stupid. They had probably guessed his connection to the group by now.

On the morning news, an in-studio anchor named Barbara Lincolnshire detailed a midnight arrest in the Yesteryork neighborhood. As she half-watched the TV, the jingle of the cafe door drew Destiny's attention. She stiffened as two police officers entered the cafe and scanned the place. She backed out of her incomplete hack. She was in the restaurant corner, where they couldn't yet see her, but she needed to keep it that way. She averted her eyes as they circled her booth.

"How may I help you this morning, officers?" a sweet voice asked loudly, drawing their attention to the barista behind the counter. Destiny locked eyes with her and realized with a start that it was the too-chatty one she'd been avoiding. She looked away from Destiny and said, "You have perfect timing, because we're offering a free pastry with the purchase of a coffee for all law enforcement today. To show our appreciation."

This intrigued the officers, and Destiny could hardly believe her luck as she slipped unnoticed from the cafe, the bell on the door oddly silent as she went.

Maybe she should come back and see the pretty barista again, after all.

Destiny didn't bother to stop anywhere else. They had no avenue into the department's database until she had time to investigate the new security measures and work around them. She wouldn't be able to do that safely for weeks. Barbara Lincolnshire had stated the suspicious man was being held locally for questioning as a person of interest in a string of recent murders.

He may be right there in town, but there was no way the four of them could rescue him themselves. The police in the cafe made her suspect this was a trap. The Council hoped they would stage a rescue mission, and they would be ready when it happened.

They had to abandon Sam.

Xia would never accept it.

Destiny stopped running and hauled herself up a tree. Sitting in the branches, she placed a hand over her heart and breathed.

She needed Nix back, but there was no way to get word to him soon enough. Her best hope was that he would take her message seriously and return in two days. But she couldn't contain Xia for that long on her own.

She tore a sheet from her book and scrawled a note, then captured and enchanted a bird to find Rinna.

"I don't give a damn if it's a trap! I will not abandon Sam!" Xia's box braids flew as she whirled to face Destiny.

"Xia, I'm sorry!" Destiny truly was sorry. She was even crying. "There's no way we can help him with just the four of us, knowing it's a trap!"

"Sam knew the risks of what he was doing," Lottie said gently. "We all know the risks."

"We even swore to it," Meg said. "If someone can't be saved, we leave them behind. And we know we get left if we're too far gone."

"Bullshit." Xia spat on the floor again like a curse. "Those rules didn't apply to Nix and Cosmina."

"We had the entire group available to help Cosmina!" Lottie protested. "The timing was just better. She was luckier."

"And Cosmina got captured because she was saving someone's life, not because she was trying to kill someone," Meg added.

"Sam was only doing necessary work to help our cause. Work everyone else was too weak and scared to do. He is the bravest and most loyal person in this group, and I refuse to let you treat him like he's less important than anyone else!"

"No one thinks he's less important, Xia," Destiny said. "I love Sam. He's as close to me as any brother I might have had. I want more than anything to help him."

"Then just do it!"

"It's not that easy! We have to think about everyone else, of all the work we've put into this, and how we can still salvage it—"

"I don't give a shit about any of that! I care more about Sam than anything in this world, and if the rest of you plan to abandon him, then I'll just have to save him myself." Xia turned on her heel and started upstairs to the loft.

Destiny hurried to stand in front of her. "Xia, you know I can't allow—"

"Destiny, you know you can't stop me." Xia's voice was as cold as ice. "And, for the record, after I rescue Sam, we'll be returning to Rinna. You can tell Nix his particular brand of loyalty just doesn't sit right with me, and his idea of leadership in his absence is a joke."

Destiny froze with her mouth open, looking as though she'd just been slapped. Meg lunged for Xia, but Lottie grabbed her hand and pulled her back. The three of them left the cottage and sat around the fire pit in silence.

When Xia came out wearing some of their most high-quality black clothing, a weapons belt, and a backpack of supplies, they knew they should stop her. They should consider it stealing. Instead, they watched her leave, resigning themselves to the fact they would never see her again.

Moments after Xia departed, Scorpia and Rinna appeared in the clearing with a couple of other witches. The three proactive members scrambled to their feet. Scorpia raced to Destiny and threw her pale arms around her, and she dissolved into tears again.

"Tell me what happened," Rinna said, taking a seat at a spare stump around the fire pit.

Xia was surprised no one tried to stop her, especially after she made it clear she would not return. She decided to walk rather than run to preserve her energy. She also needed time to think.

It stung that no one was willing to help her rescue Sam, but maybe going solo was an advantage. She only needed to get herself inside the prison, find Sam, and get out. She wouldn't have to worry about sneaking a bunch of physical bodies past cameras. There would be less risk of their Magic being detected.

Sometimes it just made more sense to work alone.

The sun had set by the time she reached the outskirts of town, giving her the cover of night. Her feet dragged despite the energizing potion she'd consumed. She had another, but would save it for just before she entered the prison. It had been forty hours since she'd last slept, and that was a mere nap.

She found a spot in a field outside the prison and sat in the shadows. She forced herself to eat a protein bar and study what view she had of the facility, which was more of a police station than a prison. Sam was being held for questioning, so maybe he was in an interrogation room.

She watched the parking lot for signs of transport vehicles but saw nothing. Rubbing her eyes, she willed the fuzziness in her brain away. If she was honest with herself, she was in no condition to attempt this, and more likely to get herself killed than anything. Still, she had to try.

She got to her feet as a back gate near her opened. Dropping to a crouch, she scurried across the field, keeping low to the shadows. If she could get inside now, then she would just need to find him.

And he could be anywhere.

She reminded herself not to panic. To take it one step at a time. A medical truck from a local hospital was idling, waiting for the gate to finish opening. She opened the back and found herself face-to-face with a wide-eyed nurse in a crisp brown uniform.

"Orid." She rendered him unconscious with a quick pressure-point technique, then unclothed him and pulled his uniform over herself. She stowed his unconscious body behind a stretcher propped against the side of the truck, swearing again as she banged her shin against a table. This was already not going well.

"The hell's going on back there?" the driver demanded, yanking open a window that separated the front cab from the back. "You're supposed to be sat the hell down."

"Sorry!" Xia called in a deep voice she hoped sounded manly and not at all fake. For the first time ever, after seasons of privately mocking her for its uselessness, Xia envied Cosmina's voice manipulation. "Lost my balance."

"Just sit down!" The window slammed shut again. Xia rolled her eyes, but sat.

The truck came to a halt. Xia braced herself to fight off any attackers if her feeble disguise failed her, but it soon became clear the driver did not know the nurse he was transporting. Maybe he'd never seen the white guy before, because he didn't blink when he opened the door to a black woman with box braids in an oversized uniform. "They want us in and out quick."

Xia helped him unlatch and remove the stretcher before wheeling it out together.

"Sick prisoner?" she asked, no longer faking the man's voice.

"Dead one."

Xia flinched. "Dead?"

"Yeah. Guess they need us to keep up appearances, but the prisoner died a couple hours ago."

"How?"

"Don't ask too many questions, kid. Curious ain't a look they like."

Xia struggled against rising bile as they walked the dim concrete hallway with a guard and their stretcher between them.

They reached a morgue, a cold room with sliding shelves built into the walls. Xia could see a cloud of her own breath form with each exhale. A man in a lab coat led them to a shelf door, which he opened to reveal a body covered in a white sheet. He helped them shift the body onto their stretcher, then warned them to keep it covered. "It's not a pretty sight."

Xia managed to contain her vomit as they left back through the hallway. She needed to find a way to ditch this scene and look for Sam. She tried to look for a door she could duck through, but there were none, only the occasional dark hallway that branched off this one. She'd have to try her luck with one of those.

The nurse's scrub pants were too long and had started to fall over her shoes, creating a tripping hazard. She cursed her overexhaustion. If she'd had any sleep at all, she would have noticed in the truck and cut the extra fabric before entering the jail. She pinched her thigh and tried to tug it higher without missing a step, succeeding only in kicking the stretcher. It lurched sideways. She and the driver reacted quickly, catching it before it toppled over. Xia opened her mouth to apologize, then spotted the arm that had slid from beneath the sheet.

When Sam had first learned of his dark Magic affinity, his older brother had said it was unique and cool. He'd taken him to get a tattoo to commemorate it. It was a simple design, a symbol from an olde coven that represented the perfect harmonic balance between dark and light powers. A lash-rimmed eye, representing wisdom to know when each type of Magic was best, containing a partially shaded, nine-pointed star inside the pupil.

The tattoo was faded, and it was dark in the hallway, but it didn't matter. Xia knew it was his. She grabbed the white sheet in both hands and tore it from his body. The entire hallway blazed with light, temporarily blinding them all and leaving her in a brilliant white haze with Sam. His skin had distinctive bruises consistent with boiled blood.

Blood boiling was quite a rare ability, but Sam had it.

A large pattern of bruises across his abdomen created the appearance of a pair of lips with a slash through them.

I'll never talk.

He'd killed himself rather than being tortured for information. Xia felt something snap in the back of her mind, and her lungs sucked in a painful amount of air all at once.

"What the hell, kid?" The driver stooped to pick the sheet off the floor.

Xia heard herself release a shrill scream that froze the driver and the jail guard just before she threw knives into their brains. They dropped to the concrete floor, and she flung herself over Sam and sobbed. Deep, agonizing wails racked her body. The stretcher collapsed under their weight, and she fell atop him. She cradled his head against her chest, screaming his name with every ounce of grief she possessed.

Distantly, she was aware that people were coming. Her survival instinct was louder than she would have expected after losing Sam. She touched his face, tracing the outline of his jaw and lips with her fingers. She kissed his entire face, drenching him in her tears.

And then she released him, leaving him on the floor as she rose and ran down the hall on shaking knees, away from the approaching guards.

She retraced her steps through the jail, kicking herself for not stealing the keys to the medic truck. But she knew how to hotwire an engine with a bit of Magic, and they already knew she was here, so she didn't need to bother with stealth.

She ran past a couple of guards enjoying a smoke break and climbed inside the unlocked truck. The sirens started to ring, and they leaped to their feet, but they were too late. She already had the engine running. She whipped the truck around and aimed it at the gate.

The back was still open, and she felt things sliding out as she sped away. She spared a moment to hope the poor nurse would be alright, and then she floored the gas and crashed headlong into the weak spot where the gate connected.

She bounced off the roof and the door, wrenching her shoulder as she clung desperately to the wheel. The gate broke free and, after a minor stall, the engine revved again. She was able to peel out with other vehicles hot on her tail.

A high-speed chase ensued through town. After nearly hitting two pedestrians and destroying a storefront when two stretchers slid out the back of the medic truck and through their windows, she managed to lose her pursuers. She drove straight into the nearest forested area and abandoned the truck, wishing she could check on the nurse but not daring to risk it. She could still hear the alarms of law enforcement vehicles, too close for comfort. She sprinted for several hundred feet, then climbed the first tree that looked promising. Moving through the canopy was slower and more difficult but provided better cover.

When she had traveled a couple of miles, a pair of witches she vaguely recognized appeared on the ground beneath her, looking right up at her.

"Are you Xia?" one of them called.

Xia said nothing. She squinted down at the witches, trying to decide where she knew them from. Her vision blurred in her exhaustion and grief.

"We're with Rinna. Destiny called on her for help. Come on. Let's take you back to the cottage."

Xia hesitated.

"You'll never make it back on foot." The witch's voice was kind, and Xia relented. They were right. She was also too weak to fight off both of them, so if they intended to hurt her, she could do nothing about it.

She dropped to the ground, her knees buckling under her. She cried out softly as she fell.

The witches knelt beside her and each took one of her hands in theirs, whisking her to safety in an instant.

Xia did not return to the cottage right away. Once she and Rinna's teleporters arrived in the clearing, she made a sharp left and beelined for the river. She could feel their eyes on her, but she ignored them. The wind chilled the hot tears on her cheeks as she ran. The forest seemed unusually still, as though nature itself made space for her grief.

When she reached the riverbank, she stripped to her underwear and threw herself in the chilly water. Gritting her teeth, she submerged her entire body as the first penance for her sins. She held her breath until she saw stars, rose for a gulp of air, then pulled herself back under.

In the darkness behind her eyelids, she saw Sam. The ferocious pattern of blood blisters defacing his skin would haunt her memory for as long as she lived.

She opened her eyes and allowed the cold water to sting them. She deserved this. She deserved worse. She should have been the one to die. Sam had never been as committed to the assassinations as her. She had exploited his loyalty for her own selfish ambitions, and he'd been the one to pay a brutal, infinite price.

Quite of its own accord, her body dragged itself from the river when her vision went black. She flopped onto the bank, still halfway in the water, and her chest heaved as her lungs fought to fill. She stared distantly into the sky. A flock of birds passed overhead, and her gaze focused on them until they were gone.

She crawled from the river and wrapped herself in her hoodie. Her body trembled. She wasn't sure if it was from the cold, the shock, the exhaustion, or all of the above.

It was another hour before she could stand and put on the rest of her clothes. Her feet and hands were so numb she could hardly dress, but she deserved it. She needed to pay in every possible way for the end of Sam's life.

She wandered back toward the camp but still did not return to the cottage. Instead, she went to the small shelter they'd thrown together when they'd first settled here and kicked open the door. They'd taken most of the supplies back to the cottage, but it contained a few raggedy blankets, a couple cheap kid-sized sleeping bags, and a thin, lumpy pillow.

She opened the sleeping bags and zippered them together, making one larger bag, then crawled inside and hugged the pathetic pillow to her chest, curling around it as her body shook with sobs. She didn't know how long she cried or what she planned to do when she finished, but eventually, she fell asleep.

When she woke, it was light outside, so Xia assumed she'd slept through at least one night. She hoped it had been a week. She wished someone had shown up to cut her throat in her sleep.

Her stomach growled, but she ignored it. She would pay for Sam's death with hunger too. Maybe she'd try again to drown herself in the river today. Perhaps she'd stand barefoot in the fire pit. The possibilities were endless, and she had nothing but time.

First, though, she needed to do something good in Sam's memory. Her head was a bit clearer after sleeping, and she knew she owed him an altar, right here in these woods where they'd been safe and played soldier for so long. Before she'd ruined everything.

She spent hours trudging through the forest for the ingredients she needed. She could find many of them in Tiz Agathe's cottage, but she still didn't want to go back. She didn't want any of this to be easy for her.

Once she had everything she needed, she went to the thick copse of trees where the two of them would steal private moments whenever possible. Being here without him brought tears back to her swollen, raw eyes. She allowed herself to cry as she worked and whispered her thoughts aloud to him. She poured her love for him into her Magic, then let it drain from her body into the fire that flickered in the center of his altar. She reminded him of jokes he'd made, the private mockery they shared of certain other people, the first time they admitted their love. She talked about the dozens of adventures they'd had together, in both groups.

"I'll never again know someone like you," she whispered, her voice scratchy and painful against her dry throat. "We were perfect." She paused. "You. You were perfect. And I deprived the world of you. I'm sorry. I am so, so sorry, Sam."

She took another log from her unburned pile and a knife from her belt and carved "Demarcus Rockford" into it. Because that was his real name, and Demarcus had also deserved to live. She hadn't taken Demarcus from the world, but she had guaranteed he could never return.

She thought of her own real name, her own real past. She'd hoped that someday she would be Nikita Rockford. She and Demarcus would own a home in an oceanside town in Crystalcliff and have babies named Ariel, Brandy, and Oliver. She would probably work in military reform during the government rebuild. For years, they'd accidentally call one another Xia and Sam, and they'd laugh about it and tell their babies they were pet names.

She told Sam all of this now. She'd never told him these dreams when he was alive. Any sort of hope for the future felt silly and far-fetched, given their situation. But in her own head, she knew exactly what she wanted.

She wished she knew what Sam had wanted. She wished she had asked him, just once.

Maybe it was better that she didn't know, she thought, trying to blink away the fuzzy second altar that appeared in her vision. She felt her body slump against a tree. The Magic still flowing from her sputtered. She would always wonder, but never be sure, what she'd taken from him.

She closed her eyes.

When she woke again, Xia was in a private bedroom in Tiz Agathe's cottage. She sat up and threw the covers from her body. She tried to stand and the world swayed beneath her. Shouting in fear, she shut her eyes against it.

The door opened, and Rinna stepped inside. She took Xia by the shoulders and steered her back to the bed, urging her to sit.

Xia cried from her closed eyes. "No, let me suffer. Please."

Rinna wrapped an arm around Xia and pulled her close. "Your suffering benefits no one."

"It does. I deserve it. I deserve it."

Rinna said nothing, only sat and held Xia for a while. The door was open, and they could hear someone moving around in the kitchen. When her sobbing ebbed, someone brought a plate of food and an ishti and left them in the armchair. Rinna whispered her thanks and instructed them to run some hot water in the bathroom. They closed the door behind them.

"I'm not eating," Xia said. "And I'm not taking a bath."

"You haven't eaten in four days. You drained all your Magic. You're going to kill yourself."

"Good."

"Xia, no one wants to lose you."

"I killed Sam."

"You did not kill Sam."

"He would still be alive if not for me, and everyone knows it. Meg even said so."

"You haven't spoken to Meg. She did not say that."

"You know what I mean."

Rinna pulled away. "I know Meg said Sam got himself captured on a reckless mission, but I do not believe she or anyone else blames you for his death."

"I do."

"And you will for a while. I've lost people over the years, and I know how you feel. I also know what you need. Please trust me."

Xia looked up. Rinna smiled, her brown eyes crinkling at the corners. Xia considered that. If Rinna had given up when she lost someone she loved, she never would have rescued Xia, or Sam, or a dozen other people. Had she also felt back then that there was no purpose in living? Could there be more purpose left for Xia, too?

"Will you eat? And drink the ishti?"

Xia hesitated, then nodded.

"Thank you." Rinna grabbed the meal, then sat with her, both as she ate and as she bathed.

"I have to return to my group tomorrow," Rinna said when they were back in the room. "You're welcome to come with me if you'd like."

"I think I need to stay here for a bit...close to Sam's memory."

Rinna smiled gently. "Send a bird if you change your mind."

Lottie and Meg left for Earth, leaving Xia alone with Destiny and Tiz Agathe. Destiny went into town regularly to work, but Tiz Agathe stayed close to the cottage and Xia. By now, everyone knew what happened, and Xia was humiliated. She also felt guilty that her grief kept her from being any help. Destiny reminded her to eat, bathe, and sleep, but Xia only resented her for it.

After a few days, restlessness joined her grief. Xia asked Tiz Agathe when she could join the others on Earth.

The old woman blinked in surprise. "Do you want to?"

"Of course." Xia furrowed her brow. "I'm no use here, am I?"

"I will send word to Nix. We will see what he says."

Later that night, alone in bed, Xia changed her mind. The idea of being surrounded by people, knowing they were judging and pitying her, was unbearable. She could not suffer Nix and Cosmina keeping an eye on her because they no longer trusted her. Nor could she go back into hiding with Rinna, even if no one knew why she'd returned. She would know she was a coward.

No, what she felt now was anger. What she wanted more than anything was revenge.

She packed a bag and snuck out of the cottage.

(Amelia Schmidt) Director, Lochspring – replaced Bellingham

(Florence Dunne) blogger & writer, Lochspring

Sadie Poole doctor, lives coastal Beachwall

(Rukhsar Cousins) Director, Goldgrass — involved in child kidnappings?

Gianni Goodwin doctor, lives central Ebonpoint

Ritik Wheeler Head – Prison xport system, organizes victim xports

BOTH LIVE NEAR COUNCIL HQ

Sonny Beckett Head – Prison xport security, escorts victim xports

(Oslo Walden) southcentral Timberglen – yesteryork

Save Her from Herself

Militus 318

Xia had a list of eight names. She would complete the mission that ended Sam's life. And if she died in the aftermath, so be it.

Amelia Schmidt had just replaced Director Connor Bellingham. Xia had anticipated this. The woman had served directly underneath him and was corrupt to the core. It was an obvious and seamless replacement, but Xia would not let it stand.

Florence Dunne was a well-known blogger who supported the suppression of dark affinities. She was also one of the most prominent voices stoking public fear of them. Florence had built a comfortable little career for herself on the backs of Xia's people. Having read much of the woman's work and studied her extensively, Xia had a personal goal of silencing this woman.

Sadie Poole and Gianni Goodwin were doctors employed by the Program, known within its walls for being aggressive in their experiments. Ritik Wheeler was the Head of the Prison Transport System across Cantamen. He was responsible for the top-secret exchange of falsely convicted prisoners. Sonny Beckett was the head of a subdivision known as Prison Transport Security. Officially, he was in charge of safety measures for prison transport. Unofficially, he escorted the false prisoner transports organized by Wheeler.

Rukhsar Cousins was another facility director who harbored no qualms about experimentation on children. While the group had not yet been able to discover which organization arranged the kidnappings, Xia felt Cousins had a heavy hand in it. He, too, was a personal target of hers.

And then, of course, she would end the life of Sam's failed target, Oslo Walden.

There was something liberating about the idea of death. She no longer cared if the targets were easy or practical. She didn't need a clean escape because it didn't matter if she got caught. And since she no longer affiliated herself with the rogue group, she felt no pressure to protect anyone else.

She was just an assassin with a personal vendetta.

The lack of secrecy opened methods of travel as well. It had been years since she'd escaped from the lab. She'd been abducted as a child, labeled a missing person rather than a Variant Idealist. If she used her Magic DNA as an identifier to teleport, it might flag the Council, but not before she was gone. If she did this sparingly and kept her destinations erratic, they couldn't track her.

Amelia Schmidt and Florence Dunne lived in Lochspring. It was the farthest of her target destinations, and they were both high priorities, so she decided to start there. It was early in the morning when she reached the transport center, with few people traveling. Security scanned her palm and waved her through and joined the line that would take her far away.

The moment she touched down in her new location, she pushed through the crowd to get the hell out of the transport center. Not caring where it led, she found the nearest exit and hit the street, careful to blend with a crowd whenever possible and check street signs discreetly. When she'd gained her bearings, she made her way to the facility now run by Amelia Schmidt. It was time to see the new security measures they'd put in place.

Destiny tried not to panic when she couldn't find Xia in her room, but she hadn't exactly given her much reason for trust lately. She went to the river first, but Xia wasn't there. She checked the spot where they'd found her collapsed after draining all her Magic in an altar for Sam, despite knowing the Council monitored for such extreme emissions. Destiny and Tiz Agathe were still waiting with bated breath and twelve escape plans for the Council to show up one day.

The altar was unattended, so Destiny checked the makeshift shelter, also empty. She returned to the cottage, checked the sheds, then studied the treeline for any sign of her pacing the woods or hiding in a tree.

"Do you seek Xia?" Tiz Agathe asked, exiting her private shed to stand beside the younger witch. "She is not here. I do not know where she has gone, but she has taken money and supplies and departed my home."

"Do you think she went to Rinna?" Destiny asked, already knowing the answer.

"No, but I have sent a letter asking as much." Tiz Agathe's voice was heavy-laden with sadness, and Destiny reached between them and took the old woman's hand, despite never doing such a thing before.

"We have to hope for the best," Destiny said unconvincingly.

"Yes, but that girl has much darkness inside her right now. I fear she will be lost to it forever, and her memory used as an example of the exact type of problem the Council is attempting to solve."

Destiny scowled. "What a burden we all bear. Be perfect, or be an example of why people like you deserve to suffer. As though only witches with dark affinities have ever committed crimes or lost themselves to evil."

"Indeed."

"Are you going to send for Nix?"

"Not yet. I would like to believe Xia may yet return without causing further trouble."

"Well. I suppose hope is all we have."

Amelia Schmidt made the mistake of leaving work late. She had a security guard escort her to her car, but Xia had only to linger nearby until the guard walked away, and the new director was alone.

Xia opened the car door and blew sleeping powder in the woman's face. She was too startled to do more than gasp, and fell asleep in an instant. Xia held her breath as she finished her kill and darted into the night.

It wouldn't be long before the director's body was discovered, making Florence Dunne's kill a pressing matter. Xia swapped her bloody jacket for the clean one in her pack, ignoring the stains on her pants and shirt.

Florence's home was surrounded by neighbors in a gated community with security guards. An alarm system protected the house. Given what she knew about the woman, it was not unreasonable to expect additional guards hired privately.

Outside the Dunnes' fenced yard in bloody clothes, Xia faced the house and scanned the windows for vantage points. This was reckless, but it was for Sam.

"We have a serious problem." Tiz Agathe appeared in her gathering room with a newspaper crumpled between her hands. Destiny lifted her eyes from her notes warily. Tiz Agathe passed her the paper and Destiny scanned the article, feeling sick but unsurprised.

"Did she get caught?"

"No."

"We have to get Nix. She's going to lead them right back to us."

Tiz Agathe nodded. "I will be rested enough to leave tomorrow. I need you to send a letter to your friend Rinna, telling them to stay away until further notice. Xia knows little about the fortress on Earth, so we should be safe there. We will take what we can with us."

Destiny went outside to find a messenger bird.

Ritik Wheeler and Sonny Beckett were surprisingly foolish, for heads of security in an industry where prominent people were being picked off. It was too easy to get them in a hotel room alone, then execute them in front of one another in humiliating positions. They carried obscene amounts of cash, which she thanked them aloud for doing as she pocketed the funds. Xia left the hotel freshly showered, wearing clean clothes they'd purchased for her.

She felt more confident and less stable with each kill. This inspired her to use the teleporter again. Again, she swiped her DNA. Again, they waved her through, and she felt an exhilarating rush as she joined the line to her next destination. How long was she actually going to get away with this?

One by one, her targets fell in plans that got sloppier as she went. Staying on the move and seizing opportunities worked perfectly until she only had one mark left.

Oslo Walden.

She had to go back where she'd started and complete the mission that took Sam from the world.

In a way, it felt blasphemous. What right did she have to survive something he hadn't?

On the other hand, what right did Oslo Walden have to keep living when Sam could not?

"I should have brought them with us first," Nix said, raking his hands through his hair. "This is a disaster."

"What's done is done," Cosmina said gently. "We have to decide what to do now."

"I knew she was unstable. Both of them. I could've prevented this."

"Listen to Cosmina. Do not lose your head," Tiz Agathe said.

"I'm sorry, Nix." Destiny's voice shook.

Nix turned to face her and noted the trembling of her hands. Destiny was one of the strongest people he'd ever met, but she did not like disappointing people. He sighed and willed himself to calm down. "It's not your fault."

"What do we do?" Cosmina repeated. "Do we risk going to get her, or do we abandon her?"

"We're all on Earth now. How would we even go get her? There's no way she expects to be saved," Destiny said, hearing the same words they'd used for Sam and hating herself for them.

"Cosmina, we'll go get her," Nix decided. "Reggie and Eric should be able to teleport us anytime, and we'll find a hotel or campground where they can rest while we track her."

"How can we possibly find her? She could be anywhere, killing anyone."

"I think she'll target Oslo Walden, the man Sam was captured trying to kill," Destiny said. "She may kill a dozen others too, but that's my only lead."

Nix nodded. "It's the best we have. We'll do what we can, but I can't promise to save her from herself. I'm not even convinced we should try, after she's done so much to put us all at risk. But I feel partially responsible for allowing this at all, so I think we have to."

Cosmina stood, resisting the urge to put her arms around him. "Let's leave soon."

They teleported into southcentral Timberglen, where Oslo Walden lived. They booked a sketchy motel for Reggie and Eric then went to the library, using public records to find the man's exact address. The photos of the gated community filled with sprawling mansions and well-tended properties were dismaying. They were also old, meaning there were probably more neighbors now. The Yesteryork area had become popular with wealthy old socialites in recent years. With dread in their stomachs, they made the long trek on foot to see if there were any vantage points at all.

One look at the neighborhood told them this was a suicide mission for Xia. The Waldens and their neighbors had felt unsafe enough to take action after Sam's arrest. Guards kept watch at every house, with more patrolling the street and sidewalks. Law enforcement vehicles circled the nearby neighborhoods. There was zero chance that a single home in this area didn't have their alarm systems set at all times. The one surrounding the Waldens' house, in particular, felt shiny and new and extra-sensitive.

"Is it too much to hope she's seen this herself and given up the dream?" Cosmina whispered, leaning her head on Nix's shoulder and giving his gloved hand a squeeze as they pretended to be out for a lover's stroll around the lake and its fountains.

"Yes," Nix said darkly. "She'll feel compelled to finish this or die trying."

Cosmina closed her eyes. "I cannot imagine how she's feeling right now." She was trying not to think about it, but she couldn't say with any certainty that she wouldn't behave exactly as Xia was.

"This has happened before, and it's exactly why it's so important for all of us to not get attached." Nix glanced down at Cosmina's blonde head. "Though I understand it's difficult."

Cosmina looked up at him. They hadn't discussed their relationship or what had transpired between them, and she suspected doing so would only hurt her feelings. "This has happened before?"

"Yeah, about a year before your trial. A couple of people got caught on a scouting mission and re-arrested. One of them had a boyfriend who left the group to rescue them. Long story short, we don't know what happened to any of them, but our hideout was raided the next day and we lost three more people in that fight. A few seasons later, right as we were getting back on our feet, one of our newest rescues betrayed us to the Council when we wouldn't go help their roommate escape, and our hideout got raided *again* and we lost two fighters. We had a string of bad luck for a while."

"There," Nix interrupted himself. She lifted her head in the direction he indicated with his chin.

Xia was thinner, dirty, and wild-eyed, but it was her. Her box braids were wound into a knot at the back of her neck, and she dressed as suspiciously as possible in black cargo pants, hoodie, and boots. At least her hood was down.

She lurked behind a fancy black car, crouching to avoid detection as she circled the opposite side as the driver. As he climbed inside to wait on the family he'd just dropped off in the park, Xia entered the trunk.

"Orid," Nix and Cosmina said together, their eyeballs huge in their sockets.

"She's going to get herself killed," Nix said.

"Is that Walden's family? It looks like it could be his wife and grandkids, maybe." Cosmina glanced around for ears that may be too close.

"I have no idea. I barely know what he looks like."

"I hate being this unprepared." Cosmina released his hand, her irritation making her walk faster. "So maybe she found a way onto the property, but how does she plan to get past his guards and security system? Where does she plan to hide while she waits for him to get home?"

"Don't be silly. She doesn't have a plan. She's being stupid, and I have no idea how we're supposed to save her."

"We'll just have to do what we can without getting ourselves killed," Cosmina said. "Come on. We need to find our own way onto the Walden property."

They managed to break onto the property caddy-corner from the Waldens' and hide on the roof, where they had a partial view of the Walden home and driveway. Their arrival triggered alarms, but the guards never thought to check over their heads. Cosmina exhaled in relief when they shrugged and ruled it a false alarm.

They had no way of sneaking onto the Walden property, but Nix thought there would be no need for stealth once Xia attacked. When she made her presence known, the goal was to get her out without anyone being captured, to hell with Oslo Walden.

Their perch on the rooftop was uncomfortable. Cosmina wondered about Xia in that trunk. The sunny evening folded into dusk, and the Waldens' car finally returned from the park. They watched tensely as the driver walked around and assisted Mrs. Walden out of the car. The children tumbled from the vehicle, shouting and chasing one another inside. Mrs. Walden took the hand of the smallest one and steered him after the others. He followed obediently, flying a toy airplane through the air and making whooshing noises.

Cosmina's chest tightened.

Soon after, another car pulled into the driveway. The passenger in this one waited until the driver and another guard did a precursory scan of the yard before getting out. The man's gray hair was unkempt, sweat curling it around his hairy ears and the thin silver frames of his enormous bifocals. His suit was well-fitted and stylish, with navy pinstripes and well-shined shoes. It was as though his wife had dressed him while lamenting that she could never convince him to cut his hair or shave.

Oslo laughed out loud at something one of the guards said, then waved and said something about just wanting to see his wife and grandkids for dinner. Cosmina kept one eye on the trunk, wondering if Xia was still in there or if she'd been caught. They were behaving too casually, so probably the former.

The trunk popped. Cosmina gasped, drawing Nix's attention. They watched in horror as Xia leaped from the vehicle and launched into a pressure-point attack on the nearest guard. He grunted and collapsed with a thud, drawing the attention of Oslo and his other guard.

Both men shouted. The guard sent a wave of fire at Xia, who ducked behind the car and ignored him completely as she set her sights on Oslo. He made a mad dash for the house.

Nix slid down the edge of the roof and sprinted for the stone wall separating the gardens, hurling himself over in one neat leap. Cosmina wanted to find it less sexy than she did, given their current situation. She scrambled clumsily after him, cursing herself for getting distracted. Their departure triggered as many alarms as their arrival.

The guard was not expecting more intruders, and Nix wrangled him into submission quickly. Cosmina went for

Xia, who ignored her unrequested assistance. She caught up to Oslo and tackled him to the ground.

The old man was surprisingly nimble. Thanks to the distraction of children screaming inside the house, he was able to throw Xia off him and hurl a stone statue from the nearby garden at her chest. She grunted, knocked to the ground, the wind expelled from her lungs.

"More guards," Nix called, already leaping to meet them. Cosmina's stomach tightened. She attempted to levitate Xia into the air.

"Time to go."

Oslo, who had been poised to fling more statues at his attackers, turned to Cosmina with a baffled expression. "Who the hell are you? Do you work for me?"

"Orid, no," Cosmina said. Xia took the opportunity to blow a blast of smoke in Cosmina's face and send her into a coughing fit. She lost her focus and dropped Xia. The confusion gave Xia the upper hand, and she used her smoke to blind and choke Oslo Walden as she bore down on him again.

Sirens sounded too close for Cosmina's liking. She heard Nix grunt and turned in time to see him hit the ground and slide several feet, his jacket sleeve on fire. She smoothed her razor-sharp Magic to a blunt edge and sent a large wall of energy at the men advancing on him. It knocked all four of them a dozen feet through the air and onto the ground.

"What is it you think I've done to you?" Oslo cried, pinned to the ground with Xia's knees on his shoulders. Children still screamed inside the house. The front door opened, and Mrs. Walden ran out with her hands raised and fury on her face. Cosmina did not want to hurt this woman, nor any of these guards who were just doing their jobs. She grimaced as she shoved the woman back in the house, pinning the door in place with her body. "Please stay inside."

"You know what you've done, you absolute bastard." Xia spat in his face. "Does your family know? Are they proud of your evil? Is the money worth your very soul? Is it worth theirs?"

"Don't touch my family," Oslo said, lifting his arms to block a punch to his face.

"XIA!" Nix bellowed as the sirens got closer. "IT'S TIME TO GO."

Oslo chuckled darkly. "It doesn't matter if you kill me now. It's too late for you to escape."

"Then I'll be joining Sam, which is exactly where I belong."

Oslo screamed. A brilliant white light exploded in the center of Xia's black smoke, blinding everyone and bringing an eerie, silent calm over the area.

The moment shattered like glass, and they realized just how close the sirens were as cars sped to the locked front gate of the Walden property. A guard hurried to open it as the others advanced on the trio again.

Xia knelt weakly over the butchered Oslo Walden, thick sheets of blood covering her body as it heaved with silent sobs.

Nix dodged the guards and ran to Xia, levitating her into the air. She didn't fight this time. Cosmina sent another burst of energy to throw the guards and police backward. This one didn't work as well as the first, but it helped. She added her levitating power to Nix's, and together they swept Xia into the air and over the fence before hopping it themselves.

It was an exercise in Magical control, endurance, and teamwork to run on foot while levitating Xia between them.

Running through yards and hopping fences worked to their advantage because they'd practiced it, while the police and guards were only trained in Magical combat. They couldn't drive through yards, and they weren't good at hopping fences or scaling walls. Eventually, they had the bright idea to call for more cars to circle the neighborhood, but it was too late by then. Xia had recovered enough to run, and the three of them were fast and skilled. They escaped into the night, finding their way to the motel with Reggie and Eric and locking themselves in. They were five exhausted fugitives, all drained of their Magic and unlikely to escape if caught again.

They stayed on the move, only stopping to rest for a couple hours at a time. A manhunt was underway. They dared not return to the cottage, and they kept Xia bound so she couldn't escape.

Even when they made it back to Earth, Xia remained under constant watch. Tiz Agathe made sedatives for her food, and she was never allowed to be alone.

Xia spent her first days on Earth in a depressed fog, eating only when forced. She cried frequently, suffered nightmares, and babbled to Sam in her sleep. Twice, she woke in a fit and attacked the person sitting with her. Tiz Agathe added another potion to her food that would dull her Magic for a time.

Work on the fortress continued. Thilo and the other islanders had completed their work and been well-compensated. Altering their memories was a success. The security measures progressed gradually. Lottie and Meg took over aesthetic and comfort improvements, and

Cosmina had no objections. She was more valuable when helping Solara, who remembered a surprising amount from her childhood spent at construction jobs with her father.

Before long, they had storage, several bedrooms with cots, and small bathrooms with indoor plumbing. They built a collection and storage system for fresh rainwater and an easier way to collect it from the river that cut through the island.

Using a bit of Destiny's Magic, they even managed to create a small electricity supply to keep an icebox in their makeshift kitchen.

The group began to feel safe and relatively comfortable in the fortress. The building and maintenance kept them busy. There was always something they could do, and no one was lazy.

They were distracted, though. News of Sam's death had shaken their little group to its core. Xia's breakdown was just as bad. Everyone was afraid.

Xia became the perfect example of why love was impossible for them. In this life, getting too close to someone was asking to have your heart ripped from your chest. Everyone became a little more solitary. Lottie stopped visiting Roman in his cell. Meg avoided Lottie. Nino and Hiroto couldn't work together without fighting. Eric and Reggie hardly spoke. Every relationship, even the friendly ones, felt strained and fragile.

Destiny was desperate to know how things were going on Cantamen and worried sick about Amara being left with no one to monitor her blog and security. She also missed Scorpia. She wasn't sure if she should continue avoiding the woman she loved to protect them both, or savor every moment while they had the chance.

After a week at the fortress, Xia started to lift from her funk. She had not expected to ever care again about anything, but her body's will to survive surprised her. It also annoyed her. She had no right to enjoy the taste of a meal or the feel of her legs stretching in the morning, but she was doing it. She had no business laughing at the jokes she overheard or being amused by gossip about Nix and Cosmina and their relationship. The bubbling in her chest and the tugging upward of her mouth occurred regardless. Even if she recognized and corrected the behavior to something more appropriate, she could feel the will to live and a low baseline of joy returning to her body.

She asked Cosmina to help her build an altar for Sam at the fortress. Cosmina escorted Xia into the jungle and kept a close eye on her as they gathered what they needed. She did not attempt to escape. She even tried a bit of small talk as the hours passed.

As Xia poured her love into the second altar for Sam, with more control and less grief this time, Cosmina maintained a respectful distance. She had to stand guard, but she also recognized a profoundly private moment when she saw one.

Sam came to Xia in a dream that night. When she asked him why, he told her she hadn't been ready before. He told her there was more life in store for her; more joy, more success, and more purpose. He told her his part was over, but she had a bigger role, and he needed her to fulfill it.

"If you waste your life, then you also waste mine."

He faded away then, far sooner than she could ever accept. She sat awake in the dark and cried for hours. The next day, she threw herself into the work of building the fortress.

She poured concrete until her body ached, collected water until her legs gave out. She sanded wood until her hands bled and practiced weaving banana leaf rugs until her shoulders screamed and her vision crossed. No task was too tedious or challenging. If someone lamented emptying the fishing nets, she would complete the job herself. If she wasn't busy, she made herself available to help others. She became more social than she'd ever been before, asking people about themselves and inviting them to discuss their lives before the Council had stolen them.

Most people didn't like to talk about it, but that was fine. She only wanted them to know she was willing to listen if they'd like to share. She thought it was important to keep those memories alive.

Xia's healing inspired Lottie to visit Roman for the first time in a while. Part of her stayed away because she knew people were suspicious, but also Xia's grief terrified her. She realized just how much the other group members meant to her, especially Meg and Roman. And people who meant a great deal to you were people it would hurt to lose. And she'd already lost so much in her young life.

Roman lay on his cot, bouncing a ball off the cell wall. He cut his eyes lazily in her direction, then bolted upright as he recognized her. "Lottie!"

Her heart fluttered in a way she wished it would not. "Hello, Roman."

"I'm happy to see you." He didn't smile, but the set of his shoulders and weight of his gaze confirmed he was very invested in her visit.

"Yes, I'm...sorry I've been away for so long." She sat on the foot of his cot as he pulled his legs beneath his body. He looked good. Pale, but that came with living underground. He looked well-fed and had clearly passed much of his time with exercise.

"Meg said you were going through something. I hope everything is okay," he said, studying her appearance right back, noting how stiffly she held herself and how her brown eyes avoided his.

"A member of our group was captured, and he killed himself before we could rescue him," Lottie said. Roman's eyes widened, then softened.

"I'm sorry to hear that. Was it someone I know?"

"I don't think you ever met him."

"He must've been very committed to make such a sacrifice for all of you."

"He was. We all are."

"Were you close to him?"

"No, but someone else was in love with him, and her grief rattled me." Lottie shrugged. Was there any point in being coy? "I've been struggling with my feelings."

"And so you've been avoiding me."

"Yes."

He continued to study her as she stared at the floor. After a moment, he said, "I've been thinking about another way I can help the group. Something significant I can do to prove I'm on your side and my loyalty no longer lies with the Council."

Lottie lifted her eyes to him. "And have you thought of something?"

"Yes. But I wanted you to be the one to present it to Nix and Cosmina."

"Because you think I'll be more willing to fight for you?"

"Because I think it's going to work, and I want you to get whatever credit may come of it. Because you deserve to be more than a pretty face who gets treated like everyone's caretaker."

Lottie tensed. She'd never admitted those feelings, but maybe they were obvious to anyone who paid attention. "I see. Well, in that case, I'm listening."

"I can help you build a teleporter that would connect this fortress to the cottage on Cantamen."

Lottie blinked several times. "Say again?"

"It won't be easy to do, but I know how to do it. And I will gladly help. But I want to be less of a prisoner. I don't want to live in this cell. I'm willing to be confined to this fortress, but I want to be more like a member than a prisoner. And this is how I'll prove my loyalty. These are my terms."

Lottie allowed his words to settle in her brain. "How do you know how to build a teleporter?"

"I have two degrees. It's the main work I did for the Council. They have teleporters in the bigger facilities' basements, which they use for secret travel, prisoner transport, and emergency escape. I helped design and build them. I can do it *and* find a way to cover up the Magic it uses, at least most of it."

Lottie continued to bob her head like it was only loosely attached to her neck. "I see."

"Will you tell Nix my terms?"

"I will, but I can't promise he'll agree to them."

"He still doesn't trust me."

"He may never. Nix is a suspicious person, and his obligation to protect us makes it worse."

"So long as you ask him. That's the only thing within your control. Will you return and tell me how it went?"

Lottie swallowed. "I'll come back. I won't stay away so long again."

Roman smiled. "I hope you don't."

The next time Roman's cell opened, less than an hour later, Cosmina was on the other side. She ordered him to follow her, and he tripped over his own feet to do so quickly. She led him to the center of the camp, where everyone waited beneath a tarp that stretched between the side of a building and two trees. It covered a fire pit built in the center of a raised wooden platform. His eyes found Lottie, nervously braiding her own hair and avoiding his gaze. He scanned the rest of the faces around the fire. He'd seen most of them in passing, when they'd brought him meals or during transport, but there were a couple he didn't know and one that was conspicuously missing. Because he was negotiating for his freedom, he didn't ask about the sickly-looking witch.

"I want to start by making it clear," Nix said, his voice carrying over the patter of rain against the tarp, "that you are a prisoner here for a good reason, and we are unwilling to grant your freedom."

Cosmina shifted her long legs as she settled on the straw mat next to Lottie. She gave Nix a sharp look. "However."

"However," Nix went on, shooting her a quelling look of his own, "my team makes valid points that you've been helpful. You have nowhere to go. If you're able to help us build a teleporter, then I'm willing to relent a bit."

Roman nodded. "Define 'a bit.'"

"We cannot allow you to return to Cantamen. This fortress would be your permanent home, but you could be free to walk among us here, provided you do not attempt to escape or otherwise betray us."

"Any loyalty I once felt for the Witching Council has been reversed. I've had little more than time to think for weeks, and I've come to the conclusion that helping your group is being on the right side of history." Roman made sure to speak loudly enough for everyone to hear.

Nix pulled his knees to his chest and folded his elbows atop them, half-smiling at Roman. "Everyone here has taken a blood oath. Would you be willing to go so far?"

Roman already knew this, from asking Lottie about the scars he'd seen on everyone's palms, so he was not caught off guard as Nix hoped. "Yes."

"That'll come later. For now, explain how we can create this teleporter."

Roman had practiced this speech a dozen times, but still tripped over the details and got ahead of himself in the actual telling. It was difficult to condense such a topic to the basics. He started with his personal experience. He'd been a lazy, unmotivated youth with no ambition upon graduating. His parents had forced him to get a job, and he took one at a transport center because he thought it would be easy. But he found himself interested in teleporter technology. After a year of working there, he returned to Specialized School and spent the next three years obtaining degrees. He accepted a position with the Council right after graduating, the youngest person ever to hold it. He helped modernize the technology and build multiple secret transporters in basements of high-security government buildings.

Then he explained how Reggie, Eric, and Tiz Agathe could store their teleporting energy for later use, a little at a time. Then they got to the bad news: special containers were required to hold this energy, and building one would be impossible. However, stealing one or two from the Council should be doable.

Building the machine itself would be the easiest part, but to safely teleport between planets, he recommended Council-grade supplies. From building secret transporters, he also knew the spells to mask this energy from the Council's gridlines.

"Fortunately," he said, knowing the word was debatable, "I know a single facility that contains everything we need in a hidden basement. If you can pull it off, you can get everything at once."

"Why do I get the feeling this is where we learn it's too good to be true?" Hiroto muttered.

"It's the Crystalcliff facility," Roman said, both ignoring and answering his question.

Nix inhaled sharply through his nose.

"Does it have to be?" Cosmina asked, leaning forward.

"If you want to do it all at once, then yes."

"Realistically, could we break into multiple smaller facilities instead?" she pressed.

"You could try, but it might not be easier. The only facilities with teleporting equipment will be well-protected regardless. The supplies are guaranteed to be guarded. I think you're better off working as a unified front in a single big raid, as opposed to splitting into multiple smaller attacks and creating more risk.

"More important, though, is that Crystalcliff is where they keep the extra goods, if nothing has changed since my arrest. If you can take what you need without getting caught, it could be years before they realize anything is missing. But if you steal from a smaller facility, they'll know right away you're planning something with teleporters, and start monitoring for that type of Magic."

"Is this really beneficial enough to attempt?" Nino asked.

"How are we supposed to fight from Earth if we can't teleport back and forth?" Solara posited.

"I thought this would be more of a refuge for our rescued prisoners, not a home for us. I thought eventually we'd return to the cottage to work from there." Nino furrowed his brow.

"Who stays and protects the rescues? How do we get them here if we can only carry two people every four days? Without a way to teleport, does this fortress really solve our problems at all?" Solara asked.

Silence settled as everyone pondered this. Finally, Cosmina said, "Okay, a show of hands. Who thinks we have to attempt it?"

Gradually, every single hand around the fire rose into the air. Cosmina looked at Nix.

Nix nodded. "Let's start planning tomorrow morning. Lottie, will you take Roman for a walk around the fortress to thank him for his information, then return him to his cell for the night?"

Several spines straightened in surprise, including Lottie's. "Um, of course." She flushed as she got to her feet. Roman rose and brushed invisible dirt off his knees before following her away from the group.

Nix dismissed them and wandered off on his own to think.

Despite their reservations, no one wanted to waste any time getting started on the teleporter. Roman became a busy man, working all day and only returning to his cell at night. Nix was impressed by the wealth of information the man contained on transporters. He also admitted begrudgingly, to Cosmina only, that he appreciated how Roman had worked the knowledge to his advantage. Some saw it as manipulative, but Nix recognized a strategic mind when he saw one. Maybe there was a place for Roman after all.

Or maybe it should make him more suspicious.

They kept a close eye on Roman, but never did he behave erratically or attempt to escape. He was helpful, worked diligently, and went where he was told. He returned to his cell each night without complaint, ate the food he was given, and did unrelated work when asked. Slowly, he began to win everyone's trust.

They spent weeks studying blueprints and memorizing the facility's layout. They sent a few people back to Cantamen to check on things. Tiz Agathe had returned long ago, and everything seemed undisturbed. If Xia's Magical altar to Sam had alerted the authorities, they'd decided to overlook it.

Destiny and Meg returned next. Tiz Agathe sent Destiny into towns unattacked by Xia, and Destiny spent hours catching up on the news.

Oslo Walden's poor wife had gotten a clear look at Xia and heard Nix use her codename. She was also an excellent artist, so several accurate sketches of Xia in various positions had been released to the public. The Waldens were offering a substantial reward for any information leading to her arrest. Destiny stared at the sketches,

knowing Mrs. Walden and the police did not find their
ferocity as lovely as she did. Nix would want to know
about this right away.

Nix sent a letter to Rinna. She replied quickly, offering
four decent fighters willing to volunteer as guards. She also
requested Nix take three rescued prisoners who were young
and not taking well to survival mode. Tiz Agathe took a
letter to Nix from Destiny and returned three days later
with Reggie, Eric, Cosmina, and Nix in tow. Rinna and her
teleporters brought their seven relocatable members to the
cottage, and Nix explained the requirements for living in
the fortress. Cosmina was pleased to see Conley, now using
the codename Luca, amongst the fighters. In the end, all
seven agreed to go, and plans were made for the trip.

Xia would have to remain on Earth indefinitely. Too
much of her identity had been compromised. Nix had
worried about telling her, but she accepted her
consequences with grace.

"It didn't help, you know," she said as he turned to leave.

He turned back to her, his face unreadable.

"Killing Oslo. Completing Sam's mission. It didn't make
me feel better."

"Maybe not," Nix said, "but you never have to wonder if
it would have."

Xia turned so he couldn't see her tears. "And I can still
have a purpose here."

"A good one." Nix raised his eyebrows. "An essential
one. The rescues we bring here will need protection and
training. If we want our mission to grow, I would argue that
may be the *most* important part of what we do. You won't

be useless just because you're confined to Earth. You'll still be a valued member of this group."

Xia couldn't find the right words for her gratitude, her grief, or her guilt, so she settled for weak ones. "Thank you, Nix."

He nodded and left her alone.

SUMMER

Opportunity of a Lifetime

Flora 318

Cosmina and Destiny were stretching on the floor and discussing the assassinations when a ruckus outside the cottage sent them running.

Lottie and Meg struggled with a strange woman held between them. Her arms were bound behind her back and her mouth was stuffed with a cloth from Lottie's ripped-open shirt, but that did not stop her from fighting.

Eric was doubled over nearby, a hand covering one eye as he vomited by the treeline. Reggie looked between Eric and the women, as bewildered as Cosmina and Destiny.

The strange woman attempted to kick Meg's feet from beneath her, causing her to stumble. Meg swore, and Cosmina and Destiny regained their senses and rushed to help.

"What the hell happened?" Cosmina demanded. She ordered Reggie to bring her sedative powder.

The woman turned and screamed in her face. Cosmina recoiled, momentarily blinded, then grabbed the woman and covered her mouth to end the ear-splitting sound.

"She has fucking supersonic voice!" Lottie shouted over the noise. Cosmina had already figured that out. Reggie arrived a moment later and the rogues held their breath as he dusted the powder in the woman's face. Her eyes rolled back to the whites as she slumped to the ground.

Cosmina winced at the way her body folded. "Who is this?"

Meg stepped over her unconscious body and fished in her pockets until she found a wallet. Removing her identification, she read aloud, "Gracia Hallowstone, Level Four Security Clearance."

"A Crystalcliff *employee?*" Destiny gasped.

"She caught us doing surveillance and was going to rat us out," Lottie explained. "We had to take her." She looked apologetically at Gracia, folded over her own knees on the hard ground. "I think we should move her."

"Get her into Roman's old cell. Leave some snacks and water too, and an ice pack. Make sure she's okay. We don't want to kill her." Cosmina sighed as Lottie and Meg levitated the Councilguard away. She turned to Destiny. "Why can't we ever catch a break?"

Destiny's brown eyes rounded. "I'd say we've been pretty lucky, all things considered."

"What are we going to do with another prisoner? And she's seen where we stay, too."

"Maybe Rinna will lend us Nelson and his memory manipulation. Or Tiz Agathe can work her Magic. We can just alter her memory, put her to sleep, and have Reggie and Eric drop her home."

"Or," Hiroto said, striding from the treeline with his hands folded in the small of his back, "we could use this to our advantage."

"The Council is not going to negotiate one hostage with us," Destiny said. "You know they would let her die, and they'd say it was an honor for her to do it."

"I'm not talking about that. Did you see her face?"

Cosmina and Destiny exchanged a confused look. Eric returned from rinsing his vomit from the clearing and looked at Cosmina. "Yeah, she looks like you." He retrieved Gracia's ID from where Meg had dropped it on the ground and handed it to Destiny.

Destiny squinted at the ID, then laughed and passed it to Cosmina. "They're right. She could be your brunette sister."

Cosmina stared at the ID for a long time. They were more familiar with her face than she was, but she hadn't noticed the woman looking like her. The ID, though, could work. If she put on a brown wig and colored her eyebrows, this could absolutely be a picture of her. Gracia even had the same piercing blue eyes, if a bit darker. And Cosmina still had that brown wig from their very first mission somewhere around the cottage.

"I would have to do this, like...right away." She turned the ID over in her hands a few times, then looked up at Destiny. "Can you pull up the employee schedule and check when her next shift is?"

"I don't feel comfortable with this," Destiny said. "We haven't done enough surveillance, and it sounds like Lottie and Meg caused a scene."

Eric shook his head. "I don't think anyone saw us take her. They may have heard her screaming, but we disappeared so fast they probably thought it was some kids fooling around."

"An employee disappearing during her shift would be out of the ordinary," Destiny objected.

"She was leaving the facility when she found us."

"Will you please just check her schedule?" Cosmina asked. "Then at least we'll know if there's any way to take advantage of this."

Destiny sighed and went into the cottage for her laptop.
"You'll really do it?" Hiroto lifted his eyebrows,
impressed with her nerve.

"If it's practical." Her voice sounded surer than she felt,
and she left to find Nix before anyone could pry further.

Cosmina stood in the parking lot of Tidefall Coastal
Prison with her hands in her pockets. This land was a
frozen tundra at the base of a mountain, making it
impossible for anyone to escape and survive. Snow
blanketed everything in sight almost year-round. She ran
her thumb absently over the Council ID badge they'd stolen
from Gracia. The dejected-looking night shift employees
left their cars and cast long, uninspired looks at the
building. Cosmina had observed employees of other
facilities, and most of them seemed relatively content with
their lives. Even if turnover was high, the staff seemed
happy until they weren't. They organized potlucks, took
their lunch breaks together, and told jokes in the hallways.
Sometimes they lingered by their cars at the end of their
shifts and asked about each other's families. That was not
the case here. It made Cosmina dread whatever awaited her
inside.

This was her last chance to back out. If she did, most of
the group wouldn't even blame her. This was both a once-
in-a-lifetime opportunity and one of the dumbest ideas
they'd ever entertained. Part of her still couldn't believe she
was here.

She took a deep breath and clipped the badge to the
lanyard around her neck. The rest of them were nearby,
even if she couldn't see them. And if they managed to pull

this off, they could gain some headway in shutting down this whole damn Program.

They just had to survive tonight.

She joined the security line, mimicking the attitudes of the other associates. They all avoided eye contact and communicated in nods and noncommittal grunts, so she did the same. She relaxed a little as the machine scanned Gracia's badge and beeped calmly. She dropped her personal bag onto the conveyor belt and stepped into the metal detector.

She was sneaking a few things into the facility, but Roman insisted it would work. A baggie of sleeping powder was concealed beneath a thick layer of padding in her bra. An extra lining sewn into her pocket hid a small plastic vial. She feared her heartbeat would give her away, but a guard handed back her bag and waved her on.

Cosmina was intentionally early. This was Gracia's first scheduled shift at this prison, so she had a good excuse to wander the lobby and look around.

Destiny had done some digging, and Gracia was having a rough couple weeks. After committing some violation that had been redacted in the official reports but must have been serious, she was transferred to Tidefall against her will. Her phone, which they'd confiscated, contained texts with her friends and family detailing the shame she felt and the difficulty she'd had in finding an apartment. She was not happy with the one she ended up renting and hoped something better would pop up soon. And when she encountered Lottie and Meg, she'd just been stopping by the facility to make sure she knew where it was and what the parking situation was like. Just trying to be a responsible employee. Instead, she'd been kidnapped by a gang of criminals.

Cosmina located the bathrooms, her eyes falling on a giant information board posted above the water fountains. To reach it, she had to step around a guy eating spaghetti from a takeout box and a girl lying on her back and reading a book.

Two large, framed photographs with gold-embossed name tags pinned beneath them presented the faces of Directors Joanne Ricket and Reynada Blight. Even their portraits looked self-important. The prison's mission statement was printed below, and the word selection seemed intentional. It focused on societal safety and protecting the good citizens of Cantamen from harm. Most prisons would include a bit about the prisoners and their fundamental rights. Cosmina wanted to explore the implications of this blatant omission, but she had more pressing matters.

As more employees arrived, she joined the fray headed for D Unit, where Gracia was assigned for her first season at Tidefall. The crowd filed into a conference room that didn't have enough chairs, enabling Cosmina to remain on her feet by the exit. At the front of the room, a lanky guy with greasy, disheveled brown hair and a blackening eye leaned against the wall next to a fair-skinned redhead with a perfect ballerina bun and a beaming smile. Cosmina wondered what kind of monster could emanate such joy in an environment this depressing.

As the last employees filed in for the shift meeting, the door closed. The redhead clapped her hands twice, even though no one was speaking and everyone was already looking at her.

"Alright, welcome to work! Thank you for always coming prepared to do an exemplary job and make D-Unit the most efficient team at Tidefall Coastal for the sixth season straight!" She attempted to lead a round of applause, but it was met with only a few pity claps. She gave up, undeterred. "Gunther tells me second shift had a rough evening, so we'll need to be excellent teammates and play catch-up at the start of our shift. But it's nothing day shift hasn't done for us, right?"

Cosmina scanned the room. No one seemed surprised or put out by the news, or even as though they'd heard the words. Was everyone dead inside?

"Your tablets are loaded with your assignments and your shift leaders for the night. If you have any questions or concerns, your team leaders and I are available through the Messaging Portal as always. The last thing on the agenda is to welcome our newest team member, Gracia."

The redhead gestured to Cosmina, who forced a smile and small wave. A few disinterested eyes shifted her way, but mostly they ignored her. This might be easier to pull off than she'd thought.

"And we're dismissed!" The disgustingly cheerful woman clapped her hands again, then strode to the back of the room and handed Cosmina a tablet. "I'm Nell, your shift supervisor. The programming on this should be the same as other facilities, so I trust you know how to work it. Your temporary PIN is just your seven-digit birthday. Be sure to set up a more unique one soon. Taking these home is forbidden, so register for a locker before the end of your shift. And we charge for replacements, so don't lose it."

Cosmina took the tablet, hoping she didn't look as tense as she felt.

"Enjoy your first shift. Don't hesitate to reach out if you need anything."

"I won't, thank you."

Nell smiled. Cosmina followed her into the hall and watched as she walked to a door and slipped inside without sparing anyone else a glance. Cosmina imagined her locking the door, closing the curtains, and sinking into a chair with her face buried in her hands, already drained from a mere hour of her charade.

But maybe she was wrong. Maybe Nell was one of those morally challenged people who loved this job.

It was a good thing she had Gracia's ID in her pocket, because Cosmina couldn't even remember her own birthday anymore. The hall was littered with people, and not a soul was paying attention to her, but she still ducked into a bathroom stall to check Gracia's birthday. She had no doubt her every move was being recorded on hidden cameras around the facility.

Her tablet stated her first task was to report to the third floor, also known as D3, where the last six rooms on the hallway were assigned to her. She was to debrief with someone named Bella.

Bella was an intimidating blonde, poised in the middle of the hallway with her arms folded across her chest. She peered down a couple of inches at Cosmina through half-moon glasses. Cosmina was not accustomed to other women being taller than her. She straightened her spine and lifted her chin to compensate.

"You must be the new kid," Bella said.

"Gracia." Cosmina offered her hand.

"Bella." The woman ignored the gesture and turned to face the door on their right. "These two started a new treatment today and have been making a mess all evening." She approached the metal door and held her badge over a scanner, rendering the door invisible. Cosmina recoiled before she could stop herself, but Bella had her back turned and didn't see it.

The room was small, containing two twin-sized cots in the far corners. In the center of the wall between them were a small toilet and a tinier sink. The walls were gray and bare concrete, but high above the bathroom was a horizontal line of three round windows just wide enough to stick an arm through. They were too high for anyone to actually reach, but Cosmina suspected they opened Magically when ventilation was needed.

A man in a rough green gown attempted to land all of his vomit inside the small toilet. Another man, who looked much grayer and sweatier, was collapsed on a cot, his head and arm hanging over the side. A pile of vomit covered the floor next to him.

Cosmina's stomach turned.

"Orid." Bella moved her badge to hide the scene from view. "I'm leaving that for you. I'm fucking sick of this today."

"No problem," Cosmina said, her voice too high-pitched to sound natural.

Bella moved to the next door. "These two had their dosages increased a couple days ago, and one of the side effects is definitely rage. Get back-up if you need to go in there tonight. One of them got Gunther good earlier."

Cosmina smiled to herself.

Bella left the second her sub-par debrief was finished. Cosmina found the cleaning closet and prepared a mop and bucket. After cleaning the vomit in the first room, she levitated the man on the floor back to his cot and placed buckets by their heads. She took cool washcloths and wiped their faces, arms, and chests, whispering small comforting spells she hoped would provide a little relief.

Then, because her tablet indicated she could reach the shift nurse through the Message Portal, she let the nurse know they were projectile vomiting and unconscious. She wondered if the nurse cared more than Bella. The latter would make appearances in Cosmina's nightmares for a while after her display of astounding callousness.

The first four hours of her shift were busy but uneventful, and emotionally draining. And then, at her first scheduled break, the real work began.

She watched and waited as most of the employees filed through the security line, no one eager to spend a minute more than required in this place. She couldn't blame them.

She found the fourth-floor break room with the window that faced Solara's station and let herself in. One woman sat in the corner eating celery sticks and hummus. She eyed Cosmina wearily.

Cosmina swiped Gracia's ID badge over the vending machine, buying a water bottle and bag of chips, then flopped into a chair far from the other woman. "Do you mind if I dim the lights? I've got one hell of a headache."

The woman shrugged and looked away, chewing her celery. Cosmina rolled her eyes as the lights dimmed to nearly off.

She counted ninety seconds as she sipped her water, then left the room, muttering that she needed a painkilling potion. The lights came on again immediately, but it didn't matter. The signal had been sent.

She hit the stairwell running and pounded them two at a time, never encountering another soul. When she reached the first floor, she glanced in both directions and dashed across the hall, ducking under a rope that marked this hallway "Admin Only." As she ran, she pulled leather gloves from her pocket and put them on. When she reached the end of the hall, she found the innocuous wooden door across from the emergency exit, exactly where Roman said it would be.

Holding her breath, legs poised to run, she grabbed the doorknob and whispered the spell Roman believed would still unlock it.

The door clicked open, and she breathed a sigh of relief.

Pushing the door farther open to ensure it stayed, she turned back to the exit and found herself face-to-face with Nix through the glass. She kicked it open, both of them braced to run should the alarm sound. But Destiny had deactivated everything upon the signal, and the first floor was silent.

Nix held up two fingers, closed his fist, then held up two fingers again. Twenty-two minutes to pull this off. Then he pointed down the hall, back the way she'd come.

Cosmina shook her head. Nix lifted his eyebrows and gave her a small shove in that direction, then waved the rest of the infiltration team through the open basement door ahead of him.

Cosmina relented, knowing it was the right thing to do even if it felt wrong. Part of her mission was to get them inside the facility. But she also needed to protect Gracia, because they planned to return her to her everyday life as soon as the mission was complete. And that meant Cosmina needed to create an alibi for her during this break-in. Which she hated, because it would mean wandering around the facility while her team risked their necks to rob the place.

She went back to the employee entrance and hovered in the foyer, scanning her tablet for any useful information. She didn't dare take the thing outside, but she skimmed the notes for her wards and committed what she could of the shorthand and lingo to memory. She checked to see if the shift nurse had responded to her message; they claimed to have given anti-nausea medication and checked vitals, which were fine.

Cosmina took a breath through her nose. This facility was not dedicated to medical experiments, so the two men in that room may indeed be dangerous criminals. Even so, she couldn't justify medical torture. She wished she knew their names, but Tidefall completely dehumanized their prisoners. They were all referred to by their room and bed numbers.

She hoped D341A and D341B would find peace one day soon. For now, there was nothing more she could do for them.

Eight minutes left. Cosmina marked off her completed tasks plus a couple of harmless ones she hadn't done. Then she sent a message to Nell and her team leader that she'd fallen ill and was going home for the night. She turned off the tablet and placed it in Gracia's locker without waiting for a response, deciding that was a problem for Gracia herself, and headed through the security line.

One of the guards furrowed his brow and checked his watch as she dropped her pack onto the conveyor belt. "You've got five minutes left on your break."

"Yeah, I'll be right back. Forgot my tampons in the car," she said. The guard paled and fell silent, waving her through the detector.

She walked quickly to Gracia's car, wasting no time backing out of the spot. Gracia's badge opened the gate to the premises and she pulled out slowly, arriving at the rendezvous point down the block with a minute to spare.

Cosmina looked weird with brown hair. Nix had thought so during their first mission, but found something truly offensive about it this time.

He was relieved and a little surprised she didn't put up more of a fight about her role. Despite being the key to making the entire thing happen, she felt the part she played was minor compared to everyone else's.

She had no idea what she was talking about. Every minute of her being alone inside this facility had been agony for him. Seeing her face was the first he'd felt able to breathe in hours.

Nix followed Lottie, Meg, Solara, and Hiroto down the concrete stairs to the basement. A small transport machine rose from floor to ceiling in the center, surrounded by a glass wall. According to Roman, it required iris and fingerprint scans and a PIN number to unlock.

Surrounding the glass wall was a wooden one with two guard posts. If Roman was correct, in the back of the room, behind the teleporter, would be a closet where they kept their extra supplies, also behind at least one guard.

The guards were unimpressive. One of them, a middle-aged man with a round stomach and a neatly trimmed goatee, was reclining in a desk chair with his ankles crossed atop the desk, snoring. Another was a girl who looked too young to have such a job and stood at the other guard station, wearing earbuds in both ears and watching a movie on her phone.

Before Nix had finished taking in the scene, Hiroto and Solara had stuffed sleeping powder up the snoring guard's nose. Lottie and Meg placed a rag over the girl's mouth and lowered her unconscious body to the floor silently.

The guard in the back was an old and feeble-looking man, eating a sandwich and working a crossword puzzle.

The area around him was well-lit and open, so they couldn't get close enough to use the powder. Solara took aim and hit him in the arm with a sleeping dart. He was facedown in his plate before he could even yelp.

The presence of this much sleeping powder in the room would make them drowsy even if no one inhaled it directly, so they had to move fast. Hiroto borrowed the old man's badge and hand to unlock the storage door. Lottie and Meg, wearing three backpacks each, started cramming empty containers inside. Hiroto and Solara filled their own packs with as many other supplies as they could fit. Nix stood guard at the bottom of the stairs, listening for any sign they were caught.

His team reappeared with two minutes to spare. Hiroto locked the storage room and positioned the old guard casually at the table. Solara blew a quick antidote around the room as they backed out, Nix leading the way up the concrete stairs.

Noting the hallway clear, they dashed out the emergency exit and into the frigid night air with their stolen goods. No one spoke, terrified of pushing their luck as they kept to the shadows and ducked around the building. The empty canisters clanged together in their backpacks, forcing them to move slower than they wanted.

As they reached the wall they'd climbed to get inside, a commotion broke out behind them. Turning to look, they saw a facility guard wrestling with thin air.

"Nino sure likes those invisibility potions," Meg muttered, pulling the backpack straps from Lottie's shoulders.

They levitated their goods over the wall to Reggie and Eric, who took off in a sprint the moment they had everything. They would run a few blocks, then teleport straight to the cottage when they were a safe distance away.

They took turns levitating one another over the wall, taking far longer than planned. They had to carry Nino, too, when his invisibility wore off and he could no longer sneak out the main entrance as planned. They sprinted for the rendezvous point.

When they reached Cosmina in Gracia's car, she was ready to charge back into the facility after them. They piled in the SUV, Nino laying down inside the trunk before closing it over himself, and Cosmina hit the gas, waiting on no one to buckle.

For a long time, the only sounds were Nino groaning and vomiting as the effects of his invisibility potion settled in. But as they neared the campsite where Reggie and Eric would pick them up in the morning, Cosmina asked, "Did we do it?"

"Yeah," Lottie said when no one else answered. "Yeah, I think...as long as Reggie and Eric got away, I think we did it."

"It's not over yet," Nix said.

Six hours of restless sleep later, Reggie and Eric appeared at the campsite with Nelson. Since this theft benefitted both rogue groups, he'd agreed to help them with Gracia's memory.

"There's vomit in the trunk," Nix told him. "It's Nino's, but Cosmina gave the excuse that she'd fallen ill and needed to go home, so maybe you could make her believe it's her own puke."

Nelson nodded. "Easy. Anything else?"

Cosmina passed him a sheet of paper. "I wrote a few details for you to plant in her mind."

Nelson skimmed the notes. "Nell, bubbly redhead, shift supervisor. Gunther got a black eye from a prisoner. D341 projectile vomited for hours. Locker number 186, passcode and PIN for tablet are still birthday but need to be changed. Got it. I'll take care of it."

Cosmina passed him the keys, and he drove off toward Gracia's house. Reggie, Eric, and Nelson had already left the sedated woman asleep in her bed, guarded by Scorpia and Destiny.

The rest of them stood around and debated who should go first. Reggie and Eric had gotten stronger since they'd been teleporting between planets, but they didn't want to push their luck.

"Cosmina goes back first," Nix said. "She's been the most public since we got here. Nino goes, too. He's sick as hell from the invisibility potion."

Solara and Hiroto volunteered to stay, so Nix sent Lottie and Meg along with Cosmina and Nino. The three of them settled in to wait until Eric returned for them that evening.

Cosmina was already gripping Reggie's arm, so it was easy to catch him when he stumbled upon landing. Lottie and Meg were holding Nino up between them, so there was no one to help Eric, who collapsed to his hands and knees on the hard ground.

"We'll be right back," Cosmina promised him, looping Reggie's arm around her neck and helping him into one of the private bedrooms inside the cottage. Meg got Nino to the couch, where they laid him on his side and placed a bucket by his head even though he hadn't vomited in a couple hours. Lottie hurried to the kitchen while Meg went back for Eric. They forced the teleporters to eat and drink something before letting them sleep.

Lottie cut a chunk of bread off the nearly-stale loaf and toasted it, then smeared some applesauce on top. She found the last anti-nausea potion in the emergency stash and added it to a sleeping ishti, along with some honey and fresh-ground ginger. Nino was resistant to eating, but Lottie insisted. Meg went outside to stand guard, and after Nino and Cosmina fell asleep, Lottie took food and water out to join her.

After six hours, Reggie and Eric drank Magic-boosting ishtis and left. Cosmina woke Nino and forced him to eat more toast and drink some water, then took over guard duty so Lottie and Meg could sleep.

After eating, Nino joined her outside. Cosmina looked up at him. "You don't have to do guard duty. You're ill."

"I need the fresh air." Nino shrugged. "Did we really pull it off?"

"Not until everyone is back. But, yeah, the big stuff is done. Reggie and Eric said the moment they got back here with the supplies, Tiz Agathe took them to Earth. We know the Council can't track her. They won't be getting their stuff back."

"Incredible." Nino winced as a wave of nausea washed over him. "You know, when I agreed to join the proactive group, I was skeptical about whether we could actually accomplish anything. But this...this feels like accomplishing something."

"Rescuing all those people was nothing? Returning all those missing children? Killing those political figures?"

Nino gestured vaguely with one arm. "Drops in a bucket. And unsustainable. But if we can have a teleporter and keep growing our fortress on Earth, imagine the army we could build. The stunts we could pull."

"Stunts. Is that what we're doing?"

Scorpia and Destiny walked out of the treeline, supporting Reggie between them. Cosmina ran to help, despite the dread she felt at seeing Scorpia, who still didn't know what had transpired between her and Nix. Scorpia and Nix had never established a relationship, but Cosmina couldn't pretend there wasn't an element of betrayal to what they'd done.

She had never expected things to get messy this way.

Once Reggie was asleep, Scorpia went to her cot while Destiny filled Cosmina in. Nelson claimed his manipulation of Gracia's memory was successful, but they couldn't wait around to verify. She was still asleep when they'd left and would sleep through the night yet.

Destiny went to bed. Eric appeared in the clearing twenty minutes later with only Hiroto in tow. Cosmina rose to her feet, her chest constricting.

Hiroto explained Eric had not felt he could transport all of them, so Nix and Solara found somewhere to hide for the night.

Cosmina knew she wouldn't be able to rest until Nix was within her sight again. She treated a wound on Hiroto's arm he couldn't remember receiving, gave him food and ishti, then went back outside. Nino sat alone by the fire and stared into the treeline.

The following morning was unpleasant and chaotic. Reggie and Eric doubled up on Magic-boosting ishtis to get Nix and Solara while the team busied themselves preparing for their return. They would be sick for days after this.

Scorpia checked the emergency stash of potions and gasped. "What the hell, guys?"

Cosmina and Lottie, the only other people in the kitchen, continued their chores and said nothing.

"This thing is damn near empty. These are supposed to be for emergencies only."

"We've needed a lot of them in the last few weeks," Lottie said, pausing to glance over her shoulder at Scorpia.

"You've had a lot of emergencies? There are zero anti-nausea left."

"I gave Nino the last one yesterday."

"Okay, well, there should be more. We're not supposed to use these every time we have a minor inconvenience."

"We haven't been," Cosmina said, her voice clipped. Lottie glanced uneasily at her.

"No? Then where are they all?" Scorpia folded her arms and glared at the back of Cosmina's head.

"I'm confused." Cosmina dusted spices off her hands and turned to face the dark-haired woman. Her wide-set black eyes were fixed on Cosmina, her ferretlike face expectant. "Did you think the stash was going to replenish itself while you were hiding out with Rinna?"

Scorpia's snowy-white face flushed. "Hiding? How dare you. What was the plan if I never returned?"

"The plan for potions? Someone else would have made them."

"Someone else? Don't make me laugh."

"Scorpia, you have a damn strong affinity, but potions aren't complicated. Tiz Agathe could certainly train another potion maker for us."

The way Cosmina said Scorpia's name made the hairs on Lottie's arm stand on end. The energy in the kitchen was red-hot and electrified. Lottie could no longer pretend to do anything other than listen.

"Really?" Scorpia's voice rose steadily in pitch. "Then why didn't someone start training, if you need me so little?"

"We've been preoccupied with other things—" Cosmina's thought was cut short by a faint cry from outside that sent all three women running.

Nix and Solara stood between Reggie and Eric in the center of the clearing, dirty but unharmed. Nix's black eyes immediately found Cosmina's blue ones, and she felt the world's turmoil settle. They both smiled.

"Nix!" Scorpia shot like a bullet at him and leaped into his arms. He caught her, his mouth falling open slightly. His eyes never moved from Cosmina's, even as Scorpia's legs wrapped around his waist and her arms around his neck.

Cosmina's smile vanished. She turned away, catching the grimace on Destiny's face as she steered Reggie and Eric inside. Cosmina followed, ready to make them eat something.

"What are you doing?" Nix pried Scorpia off of him and put her down.

She looked up in surprise. "What do you mean? I was worried about you."

"We don't act like this."

"Right, of course." Scorpia rolled her eyes. "Forgive me, I forgot to play pretend for a moment."

"Play pretend?" Only sheer willpower kept Nix from chasing Cosmina inside the cottage, and his voice was tense because of it.

"Yeah. Pretending everyone doesn't already know about us. Pretending anyone would care if we acted like this all the time."

Nix hesitated. "Scorpia, let's talk later."

"Later."

"Yeah. Right now, I need to address the group."

"The group. Of course."

Nix ignored her attempt to goad him. She well knew the group took priority over their relationship, even if she was unaware of how their relationship had changed recently.

The group convened without Reggie and Eric, who were already asleep. They recapped the mission. No one could verify that Gracia was alright or had no recollection of them or their camp. No one could confirm Tiz Agathe had made it to the fortress with the supplies, but they did feel safe assuming. No one knew what had happened at the facility following their escape, but Destiny had been monitoring as much as possible from Gracia's house and had seen nothing to indicate they were aware of a security breach.

The crucial pieces had fallen into place. They had the goods on Earth, presumably, and the entire team was back at the cottage. Roman would begin work immediately, and Tiz Agathe would return in a day or two. They only had to hold down the camp until they could start making trips back to Earth.

Reggie and Eric would not be working for several days. They'd be lucky if their Magic wasn't injured after this mission. Nix ordered everyone to be available to them for whatever they needed.

After they hashed out the rough schedule for the next few days, Nix dismissed them and watched through lowered eyelashes as Cosmina, who had been unusually quiet through the meeting, disappeared into the woods. She had volunteered for the afternoon guard duty. Nix wondered when she'd last slept.

He stood and looked for Scorpia. There was no point in putting it off. She was going to be furious with him sooner or later.

He spied her heading into the woods and followed. He was about to call her name when she perked up and began jogging to Destiny, who was walking with a bucket for gathering wild food. He watched with interest as Scorpia bounded up to the other woman and hugged her. Destiny stood stiffly and did not hug her back.

Nix slipped behind a nearby tree, where he could eavesdrop.

"What's wrong?" Scorpia asked.

"What do you mean?" Destiny did not look at her.

"You seem upset."

"Why would I be upset? The mission went great."

"Then it's something else."

"I'm fine. I just need to restock whatever I can. We've really depleted our stores."

"We still have plenty for several days. Gathering too much before we go to Earth would be wasteful. We haven't spent time together in weeks, why don't we work together on my potions? You can gather whatever you find along the way."

"I don't think you've seen the shed since you got back. I really need to focus on gathering."

Scorpia's eyebrows crept together in the center of her forehead. "You're upset with me. Again."

Destiny turned to face her for the first time. "Well, I'm trying not to be, but you're making it pretty difficult."

"What?" Scorpia's eyes widened. "What did I do?"

"You asked me to choose you, and clearly, that isn't really what you want."

Behind the tree, Nix inclined his head.

"What do you mean? Of course that's what I want. You told me no."

"I did not tell you no. I told you I'm in love with you, but the group will always be first. That doesn't mean we can't be together, but today you made it clear you really want Nix."

Nix stiffened, his blood hot. He'd harbored suspicions about Scorpia's feelings for Destiny, and here was his confirmation. At least he wasn't the only bad guy here.

"That's not true. I just wanted to make Cosmina jealous, and it worked. Did you see her face?"

"Why are you so hellbent on hurting Cosmina?"

"Because she doesn't know her place. She thinks she's special because Nix asked her to lead the group with him, but he only wants to fuck her. She's stupid if she thinks he wants more."

Nix closed his eyes, regretting his decision to eavesdrop but stuck unless he wanted to interrupt.

"Okay." Destiny turned to walk away. Scorpia snatched her wrist so fast the movement was a blur.

"What's your problem? Why are you so defensive of her?"

"Unlike you, she's done nothing to hurt me."

Scorpia released Destiny's wrist like it had electrocuted her. "I never meant to hurt you. I wasn't leaving you. I was leaving this group and its actions. I missed you. I came back for you."

"You came back for the mission. You couldn't resist being part of it."

"I don't understand. Everything was so perfect at Gracia's house—"

"Yeah, and then the second you saw Nix again, you literally threw yourself at him! You asked me to choose you, but you won't even choose me!"

"I told you, I just wanted to remind Cosmina of her place."

"What's her place, Scorpia?"

"Co-leader. Not girlfriend."

"And why do you care if Nix likes Cosmina if you choose me?"

Scorpia fell silent.

"That's what I thought." Destiny stalked away. Scorpia watched her go without protest this time.

Nix stepped from behind the tree. "You'd better go catch her, because I'm here to end whatever this was between us."

"Whatever this was." Scorpia turned to him with deadness in her black eyes. "Being tortured together. Escaping together. Falling in love while on the run together. Working together for years. And you call it 'whatever this was.'"

"It's a trauma bond," Nix said. "And it seems we're both holding on when we've moved past it. I don't see why we should keep doing that."

Scorpia's eyes flashed. "It's Cosmina, isn't it?"

"It wouldn't matter if it was Tiz Agathe. The result would be the same."

"But why did it have to be her?"

"Why is it Destiny for you? Why was it Xia for Sam? Why is it Roman for Lottie? Love has no rhyme or reason, Scorpia, it simply comes, and sometimes it goes. Ours has gone."

"I can't stand it. I can't lose to her."

"This isn't a game to be won or lost. And you love Destiny now. I've suspected for a while."

Scorpia glared up at him for a moment, then hung her head. "She's right. She doesn't deserve to feel like anyone's second choice."

"Is she your second choice?"

"Would it change anything if she was?"

"For you and me, no. For the two of you, yes." Nix shoved his hands in his pockets. "I've often felt you would prefer her to me. I'm not angry. This is a mess, and neither of us is blameless. But I am curious; what happened?"

Scorpia kicked a stone by her foot. They both watched it bounce several feet, then settle to rest by a gnarled tree root.

"Will you tell me your side if I tell you mine?"

"If you'd like. Though, I must say it might hurt you."

"I deserve to be hurt." Scorpia sank against a tree trunk and hugged her knobby knees to her chest. Her sleeves tugged up with the movement, exposing her bony, pale hands and wrists to him. He'd always known her appearance was deceptive and had thought of her as strong and beautiful. She looked fragile to him now, though. Even when they'd been imprisoned together, he'd rarely seen her look so defeated.

He knelt beside her, balancing on the balls of his feet. "You don't have to tell me if it's too hard. It doesn't really matter. I'm only curious."

"No, you deserve to know." Scorpia leaned back on her hands, turning her head away from him. "Des caught my eye as soon as she joined the group. I had never been attracted to a woman before, so I had a weird struggle with my sexuality. Rinna helped me through that, having gone through it herself. You and I were never official, so I decided not to feel guilty about it. And, for a long time, Des was just a good friend I thought was pretty, so there was no point in stirring things up.

"Then we started the proactive group, and Des told me if I was joining, she was too. And I felt bitter about you wanting to lead the group with Cosmina. No matter what excuses you gave me, I felt like you thought she was better than me. She's obviously more beautiful than me, and stronger, and more Magically powerful. And Des is more open and positive than you. She speaks often of my good qualities, my potions, my strength. Being around her felt nice, while being around you made me feel inferior, competitive, and angry.

"And, over time, we fell in love, but we didn't discuss it. I wanted to salvage you and me. I always wanted a future with you. And then I sort of lost it a few weeks ago. She was angry with me, and I asked her if she was different from you. If she would choose me over the group if it came down to it. And she said no. What can I say? I admire ambitious people who live for a higher purpose. But my biggest ambition is to be more important than their higher purpose.

"Anyway, she made me feel like a brat, so I went back to Rinna. I always knew I'd come back. I just didn't imagine you'd move on in that time. And now I've lost both of you because I cannot, in good conscience, go back to Des just because you dumped me."

Nix sat on the ground with her and studied her face. His heart twinged with pain for her complicated emotions. He was familiar with them. "Do you still want to hear mine?"

She nodded, wiping her eyes.

"You know I hated Cosmina for a long time. I didn't trust her, and I was furious with Rinna for being so enamored by her that she'd make stupid decisions. Of course she's beautiful, but I didn't acknowledge it. I wanted to break her. I thought if I was hard enough on her, she'd show her true colors. And I was right, but her true colors were not what I expected. I thought she was just a spoiled, rich brat who never had any real problems in her life. I thought she'd be a burden but protected by Rinna's favoritism. Maybe I was right about her past, but not about her character. She's strong, resilient, and brave. I once overheard an argument between her and Rinna. If she'd been a spoiled brat hiding behind favoritism, she would have agreed with everything the leader said and fawned over her, but she didn't. Cosmina disagreed, and she didn't back down. When Rinna insulted her, she fired right back.

"That fight changed my mind about her. I realized she wanted more from the group, and Rinna's adoration was one-sided. Cosmina held her own beliefs, and no one could change her values out of loyalty alone. I learned I have the utmost respect for that." Nix paused to take a deep breath. "After that, it was like crashing headfirst down a hill, unable to catch my footing. The guilt I felt over you, the anger with myself, my concern for Rinna and her feelings, the contempt I clung to, none of it mattered. I couldn't stop myself from falling for her. I never acted on it until..." His voice trailed off.

Scorpia turned her head to face him. "Until?"

"We went to Earth together."

Scorpia's eyes shifted. He could see her making calculations in her mind. He waited.

"After I returned to Rinna, then."

"Yes."

"And you didn't know if I was coming back."

"No. But it probably wouldn't have mattered."

Scorpia winced. "Do you always have to be so blunt?"

"Yes. I have no interest in pretending to be nobler than I am."

"We both screwed up. We betrayed each other. I don't need to lie to myself either. But I don't know how I'm going to stay here now. Between you and Cosmina and Destiny…"

"You're always welcome here. But if you need to go, there are no hard feelings on my part. I won't pressure you either way. I'll just say this is a great example of why love makes things complicated for us, and I was right all along to avoid it. And if you stay, you have to be civil to everyone, and that includes Cosmina."

Scorpia scoffed. "How could I do anything other than bow to her now? She got you to choose her. I had years, and never managed it." She pushed herself to her feet and brushed off her clothes.

"It won't be like that. I'm only telling you all this because it's the right thing to do. I don't even know that anything will ever happen between Cosmina and I again. I just know it's time for you and me to end, and you deserve the truth."

Scorpia nodded without looking at him. "I'm going to work on my potions now."

Nix watched her go, feeling sorrier than he had before.

Aim to Disarm

Arbora 318

Cosmina and Nix were the first to return to the fortress when Tiz Agathe could take them. Xia, Luca, and Roman had already made substantial progress on the transporter in an underground room beyond the prison cells. Reggie and Eric brought Lottie, Hiroto, and Nino a few days later. Everyone busied themselves layering masking spells around their transporter.

Tiz Agathe made trips between the planets. Reggie and Eric stayed to begin filling the containers with their teleportation energy. It was a tedious task that neither of them could master right away, but Roman was patient. Soon enough, they were able to start storing small doses for later.

The group on Cantamen dwindled to just Destiny, Scorpia, Solara, and Meg. Everyone else was in the fortress building the teleporter, and Solara and Meg were anxious to join them.

Destiny and Scorpia were not. They both preferred the familiar, comfortable life at the cottage to the unknown newness of the fortress.

"You really are the fastest potion maker I've ever met," Destiny remarked, watching Scorpia cap another vial. The emergency stash basket was overflowing again.

"Thanks. It's a gift, I suppose." She'd almost asked Destiny to tell Cosmina what she'd just said, but she was making an effort not to discuss Cosmina or Nix anymore, especially in bitter tones.

"It's a real gift," Destiny agreed. "Sometimes I'm jealous."

"Why? Your affinity for Magical tech is way cooler."

Meg got up and walked away into the treeline.

"I wouldn't say cooler," Destiny said, and then a sharp whistle from the woods brought them both to their feet.

Meg crashed into the clearing, literally surfing the body of a black-clad man twice her size. He landed in the dirt on his back and skidded several feet with Meg balanced atop his chest. She stomped on his face, breaking his nose and sending blood spurting into the air. Her opponent unconscious and choking on blood, she sprang off of him and turned back to the treeline, where more witches were making their appearance. Scorpia pressed a hand to her throat.

The Council had found the cottage.

Destiny flung lightning at their attackers. One of them created a barrier and blocked her attacks from hitting anyone. This was the perfect distraction, because Solara was behind them, and the moment the wall vanished, she lit all their feet on fire.

The witches shouted and stamped out the fires. Scorpia struggled to breathe. She knew she should join in the fight, but she couldn't make her body move. Her heart beat between her ears, and the ground seemed unsteady under her feet.

A female witch used hydrokinesis to extinguish everyone's feet, then whirled to face Solara, who was already throwing more fire. A burst of it caught another woman's ponytail before the barrier-maker could react, and Scorpia screamed with the alighted woman. "Are you trying to kill someone?"

Her allies looked at her, confusion on their faces. A Councilwitch seized the opportunity to throw handcuffs at Destiny. She didn't recover in time to dodge and found herself with her hands bound in front of her with cuffs designed to inhibit Magic use, which usually rendered witches powerless.

Destiny was amazed the Council was still underestimating them. She would have thought they'd be considered a more serious threat by now.

Destiny had a lot on her plate. Between being the only rogue who could hack and manipulate technology, guilt over Sam's death and Xia's exile, and Scorpia's behavior, she was overwhelmed. And this attack, the sneer on this man's face, and Scorpia's useless panic was the tipping point. It enraged her.

Just to show him she could, she somersaulted on her cuffed hands and landed a kick with both feet in his stupid, startled face. Using the distraction to her advantage, Meg launched herself at the barrier-maker and pinned her face-first in the dirt with Meg's foot between her shoulder blades, one arm twisted behind her back. With a swift kick to the head, their primary defense was unconscious.

The hydrokinetic witch had made Solara her personal target, and the two were locked in battle. The other Councilwitches did what they did best and seized on the weakest target: the woman in handcuffs. As they came at Destiny in pairs, Scorpia released a strangled noise. She couldn't be sure if she was breathing or even if her heart was beating.

Meg rushed to Destiny's aid.

Water extinguishes fire, but getting wet does not hurt like being burned. Solara got close enough to the hydrokinetic to grab her by the throat and slam her into a tree trunk, then lifted her knee into the woman's stomach and knocked the air from her lungs.

Meg knocked two Councilwitch heads together.

Scorpia staggered as the world spun.

Meg whipped a dagger from her boot and threw it, neatly slicing the outer thigh of a witch who was sneaking up on Destiny as she fought another. Blood erupted from the wound and hit the dirt with a sickening splattering sound.

Scorpia's vision faded in and out.

Solara dropped from a tree branch onto a man readying a pair of cuffs to throw at Meg. Once he was down, she grabbed him by his ear, lifted his head off the ground, and smashed it down again, knocking him out.

There was only one Councilwitch remaining, and he looked decidedly less confident than he had when they'd arrived. Still, his orders were to capture these witches or die trying, and there was nothing more dishonorable to the Council than disobeying orders.

He advanced on Meg.

From her position behind the man, Destiny wiggled a knife from her own boot. Even with her hands bound, she was a good shot. She took aim at his back.

Scorpia's legs chose that moment to finally move. "NO!" She charged Destiny, tackling her astonished friend to the ground. Scorpia grabbed for the knife, and in the struggle she dragged it across Destiny's arm, opening a cut that made them both cry out.

"What are you doing?" Solara and Meg screamed together. The Councilwitch saw his opening and sent a blast of energy at Meg, knocking her several feet through the air. Solara pummeled the guy with fire, sending him up in flames.

He stumbled around for a minute, shrieking in pain. Then he collapsed to the dirt, silent.

Scorpia screamed and screamed until she dissolved into sobs. Solara ignored her and rushed to check on Meg. Destiny shoved Scorpia off her and sat up, turning incredulous eyes to her friend.

Meg was sore but uninjured. Solara helped her up, then rushed to Destiny. She sped through the usual enchantments the Council cycled for cuffs, sighing with relief when one caused them to click open and fall off her wrists.

Meg limped over, stooping to snatch the cuffs in one hand and Scorpia's wrist in the other. Scorpia tried to resist, but Solara grabbed her other arm and helped Meg wrestle her into the cuffs. Destiny watched wordlessly, rubbing her raw wrists.

"What the hell?" Scorpia leaped to her feet the moment they let her go.

"You attacked a teammate. You can't be trusted," Meg said.

"Des!" Scorpia turned to her friend with wide eyes.

Destiny cut her gaze to Meg's before their eyes could meet. "We have to get out of here. It's only a matter of time before they send more. They may already be on the way."

"Let's pack what we can." Solara extended a hand to help Destiny to her feet. Meg went to the shed. They all left

Scorpia in the clearing with the immobile Councilwitch bodies, her mouth open, trying to make sense of the last ten minutes.

After grabbing several bags and throwing whatever they could into them, they fled the cottage, hoping against hope they could return for the rest of it soon.

They didn't travel far, setting up camp in a spot near the river beneath a rock outcropping. They were surrounded on three sides by an embankment and protected should it rain.

Solara tied a rope around Scorpia's waist and wound it around a tree.

"How am I supposed to flee if we're attacked?" she demanded, fury flashing in her eyes.

"You aren't supposed to flee, you're supposed to fight. If Destiny can do it with her hands cuffed, so can you," Solara said.

Destiny stared at the ground and said nothing as Meg cleaned the cut on her arm. It was mild, but it stung. She wasn't sure how she felt about the rope, but she wasn't inclined to argue for Scorpia at the moment.

Her anger softened when she woke for watch duty in the morning and heard Scorpia sniffling. Scorpia's bony back was to her, but she recognized the shoulder tremble of a person trying to keep their crying to themselves.

Destiny looked away, out over the river. Nix had been right to keep love and relationships at arm's length. When she first agreed to help the rogue group, she never would have dreamed that Scorpia would one day attack her during battle.

"I swear I didn't mean to hurt you, Des," Scorpia whispered. Destiny stiffened, looking over again. Scorpia was sitting up now, facing her. She looked miserable. "I don't know what happened. I couldn't breathe. I froze, and when I saw you were going to kill that man, I snapped. I don't think I can handle any more death."

Destiny blinked. She hadn't been about to kill the man. She always aimed to disarm or wound, never kill.

"I wasn't going to tell you because I didn't want you to think..." Scorpia struggled with what to say, then sniffed and wiped her eyes on her sleeve. "Nix ended things between us. He's fallen in love with Cosmina."

"When?"

Scorpia flinched. She hadn't expected a response. "The day he came back from the mission."

"The day you threw yourself at him."

"Yeah."

A long silence settled over them. Finally, Destiny said, "When Tiz Agathe comes back, I think you should tell her that you need help. You were obviously affected by the assassinations, and you're not coping well."

"I think I should just go back to Rinna. For good this time."

"That won't solve anything." Destiny looked Scorpia in the eyes. "Rinna's group sometimes has to kill too, and what happens when you snap and attack a child or an untrained rescue? You have to address the problem at the root, and that's in your mind."

"You think I'm crazy."

"Don't do this. Get help or don't, but I don't feel sorry for you right now. You've treated me like shit, and I've been more than patient with you."

Scorpia swallowed. "That's fair."

Tiz Agathe had many Magical barriers around her cottage, so when she attempted to return and arrived instead by the river, she knew something was amiss. She walked until she saw Council guards prowling the woods. Then she hid and eavesdropped until she learned the four women had escaped, and the cottage was empty. The Council was looking for them, though.

The attack had occurred the day before. They could not have traveled far. Using her fabled tracking skills, she located their camp within the hour. Solara ran to greet her.

"Oh, Tiz Agathe, thank skies you're safe. We had no idea how to warn you."

"You waste your worry on me. The Council is near. We must depart at once."

"Can you take all of us?" Meg asked skeptically.

"Yes, and your things, so pack quickly."

The young women obeyed, though they all wondered how safe this was.

Tiz Agathe observed Solara untether Scorpia from a tree, then check cuffs around her wrists for security. She did not ask.

Within an hour of their arrival on Earth, Cosmina locked Scorpia in the underground prison. There were four rooms down there. She picked the one caddy-corner from Roman's so they wouldn't be able to communicate much. Roman only slept down there nowadays anyway.

Scorpia was non-combative, resigned to her fate.

Tiz Agathe was ill for a couple days, too much so to teleport between planets, but she went to the nearest city with a transport center the moment she recovered enough strength. She wanted to return to Cantamen and sort out the mess with her house. Unlike the others, Tiz Agathe was a citizen with rights. She could use the transport centers as she wished.

The teleporter beneath the fortress was nearly complete. Soon, the only thing left to do would be building its sister on Cantamen. They used to think this would be the easy part; now, they weren't so sure. Even if Tiz Agathe managed to get her cottage back from the Council's seizure, it might not be a safe hideout anymore. Witches had fought them there, injuring several government officials and killing two. Regardless of what else they knew, they had enough suspicion to keep an eye on that clearing forever.

Nix suggested maybe Tiz Agathe shouldn't try to get it back. Claiming it as her house would only associate her with the rogue group. Even if they found no proof, the Council would always suspect she was aiding them. The old witch chuckled and said the Council had been suspicious of her for a century and had yet to muster the competence to catch her.

"I will die a free woman," she said. "You waste your worry on me."

"We're lucky that witch is on our side," Cosmina muttered the moment she was out of earshot.

The fortress itself was growing, too. Already it was surrounded on three and a half sides by six-foot walls that would later be eight feet tall, and then perhaps ten. Nino had built an underground shelter that was furnished and stocked with food if an extended stay was required. They had started building upward, placing a narrow hallway in the middle of a few rooms on either side. Eventually they hoped to have three, maybe even four, floors.

Hiroto had found a flat expanse of land near the fortress center and declared it the training area. A ceiling had been built on posts, leaving the site open but covered. Wooden containers were constructed for weapons storage and enchanted to unlock only for the group members. They would not unlock for Roman or Scorpia, since neither of them had ever been to the fortress without being a prisoner.

They also planned a mazelike series of hallways into the inner fortress, so anyone unfamiliar with the layout would get lost inside. Layers of protective enchantments were added every day, both at the fortress and all across the island. A heavy glamour, created and maintained by Lottie, disguised the growing building as the ruins of an old military fort with a small, abandoned camp in the center.

It was all coming together, and everyone felt their heart swell with pride when they stood back and looked at it. The cumulation of all their ambition and hard work, rising to life before their eyes.

Eric brought Destiny back to Cantamen after a few days. There was plenty of work to do on the fortress, but Destiny was most helpful on the witching planet.

Scorpia's spunk returned. People began to report to Cosmina and Nix that she refused to eat and accused them of poisoning her. She would hurl her old food when they entered with fresh food and shout obscenities and insults until they left.

After two days of these reports, Cosmina announced she would handle it. Nix was not sure about this but did not object. He didn't think it was a good idea for him to see Scorpia, so he let Cosmina try first.

"Be nice," he said as she prepared Scorpia's dinner.

"I'm always nice," Cosmina said mildly, without looking at him.

"No, you aren't. Will you promise to at least be civil?"

"I'm always civil. But I'm not going to coddle her."

"Destiny thinks she has PTSD or something from the assassinations."

Cosmina did turn to face him then, her pale brows furrowed. "Really. From the enormous part she played in the assassinations, she developed PTSD?"

"An event doesn't have to be huge to cause trauma."

"She survived medical experiments in a lab and lived on the run for years."

"Yes, but everyone has a breaking point. Including you, though I hope we never find it. Will you try to be understanding?"

Cosmina huffed. "I don't plan on hurting her, Nix."

"Thank you."

Cosmina carried the plate down to the prison cells. The moment she opened the door, the obscenities and food-flinging began. She stopped with the door open only a crack, protecting her from the onslaught, and took a deep breath. After a moment, things went quiet.

"Are you done?"

She heard a sharp intake of breath, and then, "What the fuck are you doing here?"

"I'm bringing your food. Are you done throwing the old stuff?"

"I'll find something else to throw at you, don't worry. Why don't you stop hiding behind the door and face me?"

"See, I would, but I just washed my hair, and I won't be able to again for a couple days." She used a bit of Magic to see through the door and walls, confirming Scorpia was out of weaponry in her cell. She was also dirty and pathetic-looking, even with fury contorting her features. Her black eyes were narrowed, but they were dull and had dark circles under them. Her lips were pursed, but also pale and chapped. Her thin black hair was greasy and stringy, and she had dirt caked on her delicate hands and smeared across her pale face and arms.

Cosmina stepped through the door. Scorpia looked her up and down. "Surely you don't think I'm stupid enough to eat anything you bring me."

"See, that's the thing. We don't have a surplus of resources here. If you're just going to waste the food, we're going to stop bringing it. Someone else can eat it."

"That's a good way to treat your teammates. Starving them to death. I suppose it would solve all your problems."

Cosmina laughed out loud. "What? Which problems of mine would be solved by your death?"

"The one where Nix is in love with me." Cosmina's smile faded. Scorpia's widened. "It must be hard to see how distant he's been."

Cosmina inclined her head. Maybe this woman didn't have PTSD. Maybe she was insane.

"You must be feeling pretty rough since spreading your legs didn't work out for you."

Now Cosmina was really surprised. Nix told her he'd talked to Scorpia and ended things. He'd said nothing about telling her what happened between them.

Scorpia relished the look on Cosmina's face. "You didn't know why we broke up? I'll bet he's been different since then, hasn't he? It's because he doesn't really want you. You may be beautiful, but he still hates your guts. And now his own, because he gave up the best thing that ever happened to him for a moment of cheap fun."

Well, it had been quite a bit more than a moment. And also more than once. And Nix had seemed the same as always to her.

"The difference between you and Nix is you like to pretend you're a blameless victim. You try to convince everyone that people are just so mean to you for no reason." Cosmina made her voice extra-whiny to show Scorpia how she felt about that. "But Nix owns his mistakes. He doesn't act high-and-mighty or pretend he doesn't mess up. That's why I find his version of things more believable than yours." She slid the tray under Scorpia's cell door, so roughly much of the food bounced or rolled onto the floor. "Eat it or don't, I couldn't care less. But until you start eating, we'll only be bringing you two meals per day. We're not going to waste food for you to throw at us like some sort of baboon."

"It'll always be in the back of your mind that I had him first!" Scorpia called after her as she went to leave.

"Nix is a *person*, Scorpia!" Cosmina erupted, whirling to face the skinny, ferret-faced woman with fists clenched. "I don't own him. Not his body, not his past, not his future. I don't care who he's loved or touched or fucked." There was more she wanted to say, but she'd already lost too much of her composure. She turned and left, ignoring whatever Scorpia said next.

Scorpia was partially correct. Cosmina didn't care that Nix had prior lovers; she did too. It didn't even bother her that one of his previous lovers was in their group. People hooked up sometimes. As long as nobody got pregnant and everyone could behave like adults, it was a non-issue. It would be stupid to start a relationship with anyone and expect they hadn't slept with someone else.

Cosmina's biggest worry was that when the rumors spread, as she knew they would, others would feel she had wronged Scorpia. They might respect her less for it. This group was her family, and she couldn't bear the thought of them hating her.

And if people respected Nix less, how could they lead the group? Everything could fall apart since Scorpia knew of their indiscretion.

"How did it go?" Nix leaned over the kitchen counter to stretch his back and shoulders. Cosmina noted the shift of his shirt and ripple of his bicep absently.

"You told her about us. I didn't know that."

Nix stood abruptly. "I thought I told you."

"You said you talked to her and ended things. You said you were clear, and there was no way she didn't understand."

"I said I was honest and told her about you."

"Yes, but…" Cosmina's voice trailed off. She took a shaky breath. "I didn't realize you told her *everything*."

"What did she say to you?" Nix took a step toward her that felt protective, and maybe a little angry. Cosmina lifted her eyes to him. It was the first time he'd ever indicated he might defend her against something.

"She said I must be insanely jealous because spreading my legs didn't work out for me. Or some such nonsense." Cosmina shrugged, but the gesture was sad. "Don't you think she's going to tell everyone, and then they'll think we're shitty people?"

Nix cleared the distance between them and wrapped her in his arms. "Not particularly. I think she could have, but she's done herself a disservice by being so awful lately. After refusing to defend the cottage and attacking Destiny to save the life of a Councilwitch, most people think we should kick her out. Someone or other asks me every day why we're keeping her around."

"Well, we can't just throw her out on the street." Cosmina attempted to pull back and look at his face, but he tightened his hold on her and rested his chin atop her head.

"Exactly. See? You get it." His voice softened, and he closed his eyes. "I'm sorry, Cos."

"For what?" she asked, her voice muffled against his shirt.

"The drama I've brought you into. How mean she is."

"Please. She's a nuisance at best."

Nix chuckled. "And I think most of them have already guessed about us, if I'm honest."

Cosmina opened her mouth to ask why he thought that, but a popping sound next to them sent them shouting and scuttling away from each other. Destiny and Eric appeared in the kitchen with their backs to them. They spun quickly at the commotion, in time to see Cosmina bang her shin on a cooler and Nix slam his hip against the counter in their hurry to separate.

Eric struggled to suppress a smirk. Destiny looked between them in shock for a moment, then cleared her throat. "Sorry to startle you."

"It's fine," Cosmina gasped, sinking onto the cooler and rubbing her shin.

Nix winced but pretended he was unhurt. "You're back a day early."

"I got everything I needed, so we decided it was safer to return than spend another needless night on Cantamen."

"That was wise of you," Nix said. "Should we call a meeting to discuss what you've learned?"

Destiny started to nod, but Cosmina stood quickly. "Do you need anything first? Food? Rest? Water? A shower?"

Destiny smiled. "Thank you, but no. We spent the day in a motel, so we're fine. And we'll eat with everyone else."

Cosmina exhaled through her nose as the throbbing in her knee began to ease. "Then we'll round everyone up, if the two of you want to go ahead to the meeting room."

The meeting room was one of their largest, with a long rectangular table in the center and enough chairs for all of them and several more people. Nix and Cosmina always sat at opposite ends, with everyone else filling in between them wherever they wished. Roman had been a fixture at the meetings for weeks now. The only people not in attendance were Scorpia and Tiz Agathe. Destiny noticed but said nothing. She would inquire later, privately, about Scorpia's well-being and any news of the old witch.

For now, she opened her backpack and removed the articles she'd printed and the newspapers she'd stolen. She handed them first to Nix, trusting him to skim and pass them along.

"First, Amara's blog was discovered by a late-night television talk show host, and he featured it on his show. It reached hundreds of thousands of new viewers overnight, and people are talking."

"Is she safe?" Cosmina asked.

"We went to check on her. She and her family are safe. I checked her protections, and they're all still intact. I added a few more now that the Council will have even more reason to identify and stop her."

Cosmina nodded, but her fingernails found their way between her teeth.

"News reporters are asking politicians and Councilwitches about the children we returned, and families with missing children are pressuring officials to put priority on their cases again. There have already been two protests held outside prisons, led by young radicals and attended by dozens of people. That newspaper has three opinion pieces stating that every government facility must be independently investigated, and that's from one city alone."

"That's exactly what we hoped would happen," Solara said breathily.

"It also raises the stakes," Lottie said. "The Council will be quick to switch gears, and they'll put more effort into stopping us."

Meg nodded. "We aren't just a minor nuisance anymore."

"Then we'll have to be just as quick," Luca spoke up.

The rest of the room turned to him. He'd proven to be a good fighter, hard worker, quick learner, and willing helper of any task, no matter how menial. But he still rarely spoke.

"Well, we can't lose momentum. The world will get bored and stop talking about this sooner than they should. We have to keep stirring up trouble, so they keep asking questions."

"Luca's right," Nix said, drawing the attention back to him, "and Lottie is also right. Our previous methods may not serve us anymore. We always knew we'd eventually lose the element of surprise, and we may have reached that point now. We should all focus on training our Magic and learning everything we can about the Council and its programs." His eyes fell on Roman.

Roman flexed his hand to feel the tug at his brand-new, scabbed-over palm wound. "I'm at your service, as always."

"Thank you. We'll focus on that for the time being, but I'd like to start planning some sort of real mission soon. A raid may be too risky, but...something. If anyone has ideas, I'd love to hear them."

The room stayed silent for several moments.

"Well, we have some time to think about it."

Later, after filling Destiny in on Scorpia and the lack of news from Tiz Agathe, Nix found Cosmina and asked her to take a walk with him in the jungle.

"It's nearly dark," Cosmina said, her mind traveling to wild cats and apes who might consider them prey.

Nix grinned. "We'll return before nightfall. Besides, we can handle a predator or two."

"Can we?" Cosmina asked skeptically, but she followed him through the gap in the unfinished fortress wall into the jungle beyond.

They walked in silence until they could no longer see the fortress behind them, and then Nix grabbed a branch above his head and pulled himself into the tree. Once he'd moved to a different limb, Cosmina followed.

They climbed until they were a couple dozen feet off the ground. Cosmina was startled to find a wooden platform above her head. It was circular and surrounded the tree, wide enough for one or two people to sit comfortably or even lie down.

Nix poked his head over the side. "Are you coming?"

She found the ladder and pulled herself onto the platform. Peering into the jungle, she could see more of them built around other trees. They all looked sturdy and new, not damaged by years of pelting rain.

"Who put these here?"

"I've been building them," Nix said. "They'll be good for setting traps and keeping watch. Also hunting. And hiding, if we ever need to escape the fortress."

"You are really brilliant," Cosmina said, turning to face him.

Nix shrugged. "I have to show you something, and I need your opinion."

"Okay."

He reached into the pocket of his rain jacket and produced a tiny wooden box, delicate inscriptions crawling over every inch of it.

Cosmina sucked in a breath. "That's an *excieo* box."

Nix nodded solemnly. "We could use it to gain another advantage over the Council. One they won't suspect until we hit them with it. It may even help us with scouting, and guarding the fortress, and overall morale."

"Where did you find that?" Cosmina's icy blue eyes were wide.

"Thilo sold it to me. He said his father insisted I should have it."

"The father who believes you'll bring sacred Magic back to this island."

"The same, yes."

Cosmina shook her head in disbelief. "Nix, this is...this is huge."

"Do you think we should do it?"

Cosmina tried to think. On one hand, it would mean needing more resources for the group. More work. More emotional attachments. More to lose.

On the other hand, if she said no and anyone ever found out she kept them from this, they would never forgive her. And it really could help their group; in the aforementioned ways, and unexpected ones too.

"Yeah," Cosmina said. "We should absolutely summon our familiars."

Nix grinned.

Note from the Author

Thank you so much for reading! I hope you loved the first part of Cosmina's story. I would appreciate it so much if you could leave a review or share my work! This is the best way to support an author, especially a self-published one like me.

If you'd like to connect with me or stay updated on the series, you can visit CalistaGraylock.com or find me on Instagram @calistagraylock

THE STORY CONTINUES IN…

Cantamen

The night before leaving Earth, Abby sat alone in her bedroom and stared out the window. She felt the same as she always had. A part of her still thought this might be a big prank. She had the same nagging doubt she'd had the last two years she'd "believed" in Santa.

Sure, Mom, Santa brought those gifts.

Sure, Mom, there's another planet where witches live.

Of course there are elves at the North Pole, making toys all year.

Of course I can do Magic and hear people's thoughts. I really, definitely believe that.

At least she would find out soon enough.

The three of them would spend the next few days at her father's house on Cantamen. After dropping Abby off at Karin Svensdotter's, Paloma and Beatriz would return to Earth. They'd visit Cantamen to see Abby during break weeks.

Abby looked around her room. Her mom had promised to keep it the same for her, but how much would she change in the next four years? Maybe she'd come back an entirely different person, one who hated these royal purple walls and black curtains and gold picture frames. Maybe Graciela, who would be seventeen then, would hate her for never leaving "college" to visit. Maybe Donovan would forget all about her, and she'd never know if he finished his novel.

Maybe she wouldn't come back at all.

Morning came, and Abby put herself on autopilot. After the last of her belongings were in the car, she took a few minutes to wander from room to room and let nostalgia make her sad. Paloma had purchased this home after her divorce. When Rhiannon's family moved to Havenbrook a few months later, they stayed here while house-hunting. Abby had thought for sure Rhiannon would stop being her friend once she got to school and realized Abby was a loser who got bullied, but Rhiannon had been loyal. She made people be nice to Abby, or suffer. There was no one quite as skilled in the art of social hierarchy and public humiliation as Rhiannon.

Two years later, when Abby's grandfather died, Beatriz moved in with them. Her uncle Antonio stood in the kitchen and argued with Paloma that they were slighting his family; Beatriz should have been moving in with him. Abby remembered peeking around the corner and watching her mother as they argued. She looked strong, and held her ground. He'd thrown a glass at the wall, and Paloma had ordered him out. When he'd resisted, she said, "You know I can make you." And Antonio had left immediately. Abby had been amazed because Antonio scared her very much. He also refused to say her name correctly, always calling her Gabriella. She had wanted to be as strong and brave as her mother one day.

She did not feel strong today. She wedged herself into the cramped backseat and waved goodbye to Lydia and Graciela, who had come to see her off. Graciela looked more stricken than Abby had expected, and Lydia held her daughter as the car pulled away.

The drive was long and quiet. Abby stared out the window and thought about everything she was leaving behind. Her dreams of going to Brown, forcibly replaced. Donovan, who could have been a really great boyfriend. Graciela, who would no longer have Abby as the family scapegoat and would be put in that position herself, as the only other girl.

The transport center was a dilapidated old building in the middle of nowhere, at the end of a long dirt road. There were no houses around, just open fields and the occasional cow. A few cars sat willy-nilly around the building, which lacked a proper parking lot.

Two men came to greet them, both wearing black suits and looking like FBI agents without the sunglasses. They even had earpieces, with tiny microphones attached to their ties. Paloma opened the trunk, and the men moved their suitcases onto a rolling cart.

With the skinnier of the men pushing the luggage behind them, the muscular one led the way down a long, dim hallway with a dirty tile floor and closed doors lining both walls. It looked like an abandoned school. Abby wished she could see behind the doors.

At the end of the hall was a black double door. Muscles placed a palm against the spot where the two doors met and mumbled a word Abby didn't catch. They swung open to a brightly-lit, modern hallway nothing like the one they'd just crossed. Abby followed her elders, gawking. Past the doors, it looked like a fancy government building, though a small one. It smelled overwhelmingly of disinfectant. The few people they passed were dressed professionally and greeted them briefly.

Muscles led them to a counter where a tall woman with a brown bob sat typing at a computer. "We've got one for ya, Anne."

Anne surveyed their group, smiling when her eyes reached Abby. "Starting school?"

Abby nodded nervously.

"Don't worry." Anne walked around the desk and offered Abby a quartz wand. "All you have to do is hold the other end while I work my Magic."

"What does it do?" Abby looked at her mom.

Anne looked surprised. "Well, you don't think everyone on Cantamen speaks English, do you?"

Abby had never wondered what people spoke on Cantamen. If she had, she would've assumed it was like Earth, with regions that spoke various languages.

"Cantamen has a universal language," Paloma explained. "Anne is omnilingual, and the spell she'll perform will transfer her knowledge of Cantaminian to you."

"This is what we do for all of our Earthers," Anne added, beaming.

Earthers. As she gripped the end of the quartz, Abby wondered if that was an insult.

She felt no different after the spell, until everyone switched to a new language, and she felt the words translate in her mind the same way Spanish did. She responded in kind, and they moved on, pleased. Abby walked in a haze. She hadn't expected to become trilingual today.

Another set of double doors also required Magic to unlock, but these slid sideways into the wall when they opened. Behind them was an empty, round room with a metal railing running the length of it. Muscles stepped aside and gestured for them to enter. Beatriz and Paloma thanked him, and Abby hurried after, afraid of being separated.

Scrawny pushed their belongings inside and gave Abby a little wink before stepping back through the doors, which promptly slid shut. Abby's knees were trembling, so she grabbed the railing for support.

She felt like she was being tilted to the left, and then it was over. The doors opened again, no more than six seconds after closing, and a new man in a black suit entered and grabbed their luggage cart.

Another employee positioned outside the teleporter extended his arms to either side in a welcoming gesture. "Welcome to Cantamen! What brings you, folks?"

"My daughter is going to Karin Svensdotter's!" Paloma announced.

Abby smiled weakly as the man beamed down at her.

"Congratulations! That's wonderful news. Good luck with your studies, young lady."

"Thanks, I will," Abby said, realizing a second too late that made no sense. No one acknowledged her slip-up, but her cheeks burned as the man led them through the receiving center. This one was larger and more crowded than the one on Earth.

The other big difference was all the Magic.

An employee stationed at the entrance closed her eyes and touched each luggage cart before motioning for travelers to move on. The barista behind the coffee counter floated four drinks in the air. A man entering the building with his family held their luggage cart effortlessly over his head with one arm so another family could pass them. And, perhaps most shocking of all, dozens of people acted as though all of this was perfectly normal.

Abby was startled when they emerged from the building into a gray and gloomy parking lot. A misting rain fell on her bare shoulders and legs. She rubbed her arms to smooth her sudden goosebumps. "What happened to the sun?"

Paloma smiled and handed Abby a jacket she'd brought.

The transport center employees parked their cart by an impossibly shiny black SUV. They saluted in their general direction before returning to the building.

"It's early fall in the part of the world where your father lives," Paloma explained. They climbed into the car, and her mother turned on the heat.

"What about at Karin Svensdotter's?" Abby asked. She'd be more prepared when she arrived at her new school.

"It's not too far from North Ashdown, where we are currently, so the seasons are similar. But the campus is farther north, so it tends to be colder, with more snow in the winter."

Abby's eyes widened. "I have zero snow clothes." It rarely snowed in Georgia. Even when it did, it accumulated to nothing.

"We'll get you some," Beatriz promised.

"Speaking of seasons, the calendar is different, too. Instead of months, Cantaminians use seasons of the Zodiac. There are twelve, each twenty-eight days long. Today is the third day of Canis, the first season of the new year."

"What?" This felt like a very important detail to have missed in all her reading.

"We'll get you a calendar, too," Beatriz decided.

"Okay." Abby looked around at the black leather seats as Paloma backed the car out of the space. "And why are there cars? Can't we just teleport everywhere?"

"Teleporting takes Magic, and a lot of it," Beatriz answered. "They figured out how to store the energy for later, but it's still a limited resource, so some of our travel has to be done the old-fashioned way."

"I see."

They stopped for lunch at a little restaurant a mile from the transport center. Abby tried not to ogle the Magic going on around her, but it was a losing battle. Their server floated a pitcher over to refill her water while taking another table's order. When Paloma's coffee went cold, the manager came over and warmed it by gripping the mug in both hands for a moment. Beatriz and Paloma regarded her with amusement, as did other patrons who noticed her awe.

The restaurant was a ten-minute drive from her father's home. It was a nice house, nicer than any single man who was always at work needed to have. Then again, so was Donovan's dad's house. Maybe workaholic men just felt compelled to have something to show for their long hours.

Jackson was not home, but had left them a passcode to get inside. Paloma showed Abby to the room that would be hers for the next four years. She explained that Jackson would return in a day or two. He hadn't wanted to overwhelm Abby too much, so he was giving her some space before entering the picture himself.

Well. At least he was thoughtful.

Abby didn't bother to unpack since she was leaving again in three days. She dropped her belongings on the sand-colored carpet and cast a disinterested glance around the room. It was all neutral colors, with creme-colored walls and navy blue curtains and taupe bedding. A large

canvas painting of a beach hung above the bed. There were
a couple of seashells on the nightstand next to a framed
photograph of...

She stopped short.

Her gaze shifted back to the painting. She recognized it
now, after the photo provided some context. The footprints
in the sand. The tiny pair of shoes kicked off too close to
the water. How lopsided the whole painting looked. This
was a replica of a photo she'd snapped on a disposable
camera when she was seven, the summer before her
parents' divorce. The last trip she'd ever taken with her
father.

She looked back at the nightstand. The seashells were
from that trip, too. And the photo of her: tiny, with black
hair flying out of her father's attempt at a ponytail,
sunscreen smeared in her too-long bangs, wearing a yellow
swimsuit and grinning from ear to ear with her little hands
on the wheel of a boat. Jackson sat behind her, holding the
wheel steady and staring ahead at the sea. Paloma would've
been behind the camera. Abby thought she could remember
her mother in a light blue bikini and sunglasses, black hair
whipping in the wind, laughing as it got stuck in her mouth.
But maybe she was making that up.

How sad that he'd had to go so far back in her life to
find a memory they shared.

Then again, she hadn't expected him to do something
like this at all. Maybe he did care.

She went back downstairs, where Beatriz and Paloma
were having a hushed conversation that ended abruptly
when they saw her. She decided not to care what they'd
been saying. "What are your unique abilities?"

Paloma inclined her head, surprised this conversation
had gotten lost in the hubbub of the summer. "Deflection. I

can create barriers that protect against physical objects and Magic energy. And blood boiling."

"Blood boiling? Holy shit," Abby could not stop herself from saying. Why would anyone need that ability? Especially her mother, who wouldn't even kill spiders? She suddenly understood what Paloma had meant when she'd said she could make Antonio leave her house if he didn't go willingly. She swallowed.

"Yes," Paloma said, smiling sadly, "sometimes abilities are sort of pointless."

Abby turned to Beatriz, desperate to change the subject. "What about you, Grandma?"

"I'm a healer. That's the only ability I ever developed, but, like most witches who only develop one, I'm especially adept at it."

"That explains why you were a nurse."

Beatriz grinned. "I was more effective than the doctors."

"What about Dad?"

Paloma pulled her feet onto the sofa next to her and grabbed a throw blanket off the back. "He has astral projection and agility."

"Astral projection? Sending his consciousness somewhere outside his body?"

Paloma nodded, watching Abby closely.

"Can other people see him when he's astral projecting?"

"His body, yes. His consciousness, no."

"Is he a spy for the Council?"

"Sometimes. It isn't technically his job anymore, but astral projection is somewhat of a rare ability, so he helps out as needed, as I understand it."

"But he was a spy for the Council." Abby's eyes widened. "That's kind of cool."

"I suppose so."

Abby found her way back upstairs when she grew weary of asking questions. Instead of going to her own room, she stood in the hallway and looked at the other doors. The guest bathroom was open. It was small and dull, with a glass shower that didn't even double as a bathtub and no decorations beyond a gray bath mat. The rest of the doors were closed.

She picked one at random. Her arm felt heavy as she reached for the knob. Should she be snooping? She'd only just gotten here.

She expected it to be locked, but it opened with ease. The room beyond was a private study. A large map of Cantamen hung on the creme-colored wall above a simple wooden desk. Brown curtains covered the windows. A leather recliner sat in a corner, next to a bookshelf lined with just the right amount of books. The carpet was beige and recently vacuumed.

Abby kept her footsteps as light as possible as she entered the room. She went to the map. She looked for names she recognized, finding North Ashdown and placing her finger on it.

"You are here," she whispered.

Far to the East, she found a region called Bien, where Merga Bien's campus was located. She touched it too. "That's where everything changed." She found Karin Svensdotter's, northeast of Ashdown. The campus was smaller than Merga Bien's. She raised her eyebrows and touched her finger to it as well. "And that is where it will truly begin."

She turned to the shelf. Most of the books were non-fiction, intended for research and education. Some were in foreign languages. She wondered if Jackson was multilingual or if translation was somehow easier for witches. Surely he'd picked up some Spanish in his years married to Paloma. Did he remember any of it now?

She considered exploring the other rooms, but one of them would be her father's bedroom, and she didn't want to know that much about him. She returned to her own room. Days on Cantamen were thirty hours long, and she had no way to fill them beyond talking to her mom and grandma.

She decided she might as well take a nap.

CPSIA information can be obtained
at www.ICGtesting.com
Printed in the USA
LVHW110803170821
695469LV00008B/885